T0279113

Even If
It Breaks
Your Heart

Even If It Breaks Your Heart

ERIN HAHN

W

WEDNESDAY BOOKS
NEW YORK

First published in the United States by Wednesday Books, an imprint of St. Martin's Publishing Group

EVEN IF IT BREAKS YOUR HEART. Copyright © 2024 by Erin Hahn. All rights reserved. Printed in the United States of America. For information, address St. Martin's Publishing Group, 120 Broadway, New York, NY 10271.

www.wednesdaybooks.com

Library of Congress Cataloging-in-Publication Data

Names: Hahn, Erin, author.
Title: Even if it breaks your heart / Erin Hahn.
Description: First edition. | New York : Wednesday Books, 2024.
Identifiers: LCCN 2023036235 | ISBN 9781250761279 (hardcover) |
    ISBN 9781250761262 (ebook)
Subjects: CYAC: Love—Fiction. | Rodeo—Fiction. | Grief—Fiction. |
    Family life—Fiction. | LCGFT: Romance fiction. | Novels.
Classification: LCC PZ7.1.H238 Ev 2024 | DDC [Fic]—dc23
LC record available at https://lccn.loc.gov/2023036235

Our books may be purchased in bulk for promotional, educational, or business use. Please contact your local bookseller or the Macmillan Corporate and Premium Sales Department at 1-800-221-7945, extension 5442, or by email at MacmillanSpecialMarkets@macmillan.com.

First Edition: 2024

10 9 8 7 6 5 4 3 2 1

For Jonah and Alice. There.
I used your real names this time. Happy?
Love, Mom

—

For GH. You should be here to read this dedication.
Not the book, obviously, but the dedication.
You'd have loved that.
How I feel because you aren't, is pressed
between the pages of this story.

PROLOGUE

I was never gonna live forever, but I thought I'd make it to eighteen. I'd hoped, anyway. But hopes these days are kind of like this hospital room—dim, but never dark enough to block out all the bullshit. It's impossible to achieve full darkness in a hospital. It's all blinking monitors and a bright yellow glow slanting under doorways or from behind drawn curtains. I'm actually looking forward to the time when everyone gives up on me, if only because then I get to go home where I can get some fucking sleep.

I don't mean that.

I reach for the book next to me and pull out a folded piece of paper. My eyes flicker to the closed door. Case is here somewhere. His coat is draped over the chair next to my bed. He's probably next door with that kid Ryder. Hell, the little dude's only twelve. He needs Case more than I do. Suddenly, dying at seventeen doesn't seem that bad.

I unfurl the paper and skim the contents with a pang of regret. I swallow it back immediately, choosing not to go there. Not tonight.

I didn't start this list for my best friend. I started it for myself. But things change, and it turns out dying makes me a sad sap. I grasp a pen in my stiff fingers and scratch a few words at the bottom.

I don't know what made me think of her. All I know is lying here, I have no time and also too much time. To think. To remember. To feel. It's too much feeling. A lifetime of fucking feeling and no outlet. What I wouldn't give for a bull right now. The meanest motherfucker they could find me. I'd hold on forever.

I write her name down because it's no longer for me. It's for him, and he has all the time in the world, so he'd better not waste it.

One

CASE

I'll be honest, man, this is a lot higher than I'd thought it would be."

Walker doesn't say anything, but the word *wuss* hangs in the crisp night air between us, hovering amid the clouded breath repeatedly pulled from my chest. Fuck, I hate heights. Always have. I fight the urge to look down, down, down, past my dusty boots dangling too many feet above the earth.

"Corn silo," I mutter before turning to him. "You said *corn silo*, right?" Wrapping a single arm around the cold metal frame, I accidentally clink the glass bottle grasped in my freezing fingers against it. I lift an ass cheek and dig with the other hand in my back pocket. I pull out a worn piece of paper and use my teeth to unfold it, squinting and lifting it to the pale glow of moonlight overhead.

"Right here. *Jump off a corn silo*," I read aloud. I throw my head back with a groan. "Fuck, we're so stupid." I glare at my best friend pointedly as I start to shiver. I didn't bring a coat up here. "Grain bin." I gesture to the wide metal bins approximately thirty feet below me. "You meant *jump off a grain silo*. I can't jump off this—I'll die."

The last words strangle in my throat, and I take another long pull from one of the Dr Peppers I've lugged up here with me. Walker shakes his head full of dirty-blond hair, his smirk knowing, his lean frame balanced precariously on the bin's edge. I can barely make out the lettering across his chest, but I recognize his favorite shirt and know it reads GIVE 'EM HELL. Whether he's shaking his head to say, *Don't die!* or *What's the big deal?* or *You're the dumbass who climbed up here!* I'm not sure. I look at the paper again, holding it up.

"Your handwriting is barely legible," I say. He rolls his eyes. It's an old argument. As a kid, Walker spent so much time with medical tubes stuck in his hands, he learned to write on a tablet.

"Well, I'm not fucking jumping off a corn silo. What other death traps are on this list?"

A cloud passes over the moon, and I crush the paper in my fist. Not like I can read it up here, anyway. "Unbelievable," I mutter. Suddenly, the bottle slips in my fingers, and I jerk to grip it, throwing my center off-balance. For a heart-thudding moment, I fight to remain safely seated on the narrow ledge of the silo, and the paper drops from my grasp. My gasp is carried away on the breeze, and dark spots blur my vision as Walker's crumpled list floats lazily toward the earth. A beat later, the bottle I'm holding follows with a faint, tinkling shatter on the near-frozen ground.

I wrap my entire arm around the bar, resting my forehead against the icy metal. "Now what?"

My limbs go from trembling to all-out shaking from the cold. Or the previously consumed booze, uncomfortably sloshing around in my gut. Or the suffocating guilty feeling from what went down at the party tonight. Or, more likely, *fear* because I'm *over fifty feet* above the ground in the middle of the night without another living soul awake for miles.

"You don't have your phone on you, by chance?" I joke to Walker, who I swear snorts in response. In my head, Walker's always doing that half-snort, half-breathless laugh of his.

My throat narrows, and pain rears sharp behind my eyes. I swallow it back and inhale the night into my lungs, filling them to near bursting.

I can practically hear my best friend's wheezing scoff in return. *Show-off.*

"The least you can do is get me some help. Isn't that what ghosts are for?"

I imagine Walker staring at me plaintively, his expression clear.

"I know. You're not a ghost. You're not really here. You're in heaven or whatever, perving with Taylor in your awesome not-sick bodies. I get it. But for *one fucking minute*, could you just, like, help me? Your best friend? Stuck on a fucking corn silo in the middle of the fucking Texas Panhandle?"

Red and blue lights glitter out of the corner of my eye, speeding toward me with the *blurp! blurp!* of a siren.

"Seriously?" I shoot a glare at Walker, but he's gone. Of course he is.

"Give Taylor my best," I mutter, squinting my eyes against the rapidly approaching lights below. My boots are still dangling over the narrow rungs of the mile-long ladder. Part of me is tempted to hustle down on my own just so I can be like, "Oh, hey, Officer. What's up? Nice night. Just checking on this corn, here."

But the swoop in my gut churns, and the ground swerves up at me dangerously.

I might ride bulls for fun, but even I have my limits.

"Good evening, Officer!" I shout down. They probably don't even hear me.

A voice booms from a bullhorn. "Case Benton Michaels? Is that you?"

"No!" Under my breath, I mumble, "S'my granddad." Fool ranchers naming three generations the same damn thing. I attempt to scoot out of the beam of light, and my stomach swoops all over again as I slip backward. Grasping on to the rusted frame, I yank myself upright.

"Just wait there. Nice and easy," a male voice drawls over the bullhorn speaker.

"Where the hell else am I supposed to go?" I rest my head against the cold metal and let my eyes slip closed. I'm so tired. Like I've lived a thousand years in the last two hours. An eternity in the last six months.

"Stay right there, Case. Hold on tight. A fire truck is on the way."

My eyes snap open. Sure enough, I can see the flashing lights of a fire truck in the distance, closing in. Then the front doors of the farmhouse open, and the backlit forms of several people rush out into the chilly night.

"Great." I reach for another bottle out of the cardboard holder. Don't want it to go to waste. Dr Pepper was our thing. Two kids on the rodeo circuit trying to be cool and look older than we were. Glass bottles that could clink like the real thing. Ironically, intoxicated me, the one who ran out of his own house party an hour ago and decided tonight was the night to cross something wild off Walker's list, was the one who chose the soda.

Had to do the thing properly.

This venture was screwed from the start is what I am saying.

A familiar snort echoes into the silent night. Walker's back.

"That was fast." I raise an eyebrow, and the idiot manages to look smug. He should. Heaven had better be one massive sexcapade for him or I'm canceling religion. "This seems a bit overkill. Police *and* fire trucks?" I gesture wildly to the commotion below with my free arm. A frigid gust whistles through, nearly knocking off my worn Dallas Cowboys hat. I tighten my hold, looping both arms on either side of the ladder.

"Keep as still as you can, Case!" the officer shouts. "Help is on the way. We're all here for you. I've called your dad."

I groan at Walker, who's kicking his boots out over the edge, pleased as fuck. "You realize they think I'm suicidal. Dick," I add. I tend to cuss more at Ghost Walker than I did at Living Walker.

His dark brows arch in a silent question.

I take a deep breath and shake my head. "No," I say. "Definitely not. I don't want to live like this anymore, but I don't want to die. I just . . . fuck, man. *You're* the one who made the list." And he's the one who got too sick before he could accomplish anything on it. So he left it to me.

"Case! We're coming up. Just hold on until someone can secure you."

"Okay!" I yell. I accidentally drop the Dr Pepper I've been holding. It sails down and lands with a muffled clatter. Another one bites the dust. "Oops. Sorry!" I think I hear the echo of Walker's airy laugh, but when I look, he's gone again and I'm alone.

Always alone.

A firefighter is climbing the ladder toward me, and I swallow hard. I hope he doesn't fall. That would suck. But within moments, I'm secured with a clip, and both the firefighter and I are descending toward the ground. I try to hop down the last two rungs, but my boot slips on an icy patch and I fall straight on my ass.

Fucking *ow*.

"Christ, are you drunk?" comes a voice from the crowd.

"Dad?" I croak. Great. Just great.

Case Benton Michaels Jr. rocks on booted heels, his hands casually slung in the pockets of his sport coat like he's assessing the going rate for grass-fed longhorns and not his only son's life. Likely pulled from some business mixer or other, where "the whiskey is expensive, and talk is cheap."

Kerry, our live-in housekeeper, is a few steps behind him and still in her robe. I'm warmed by the fact she, at least, was in a hurry. She surges forward, but once she's assured I'm in one piece, any concern that might've been on her face melts into something that looks a lot like disappointment.

"I think I broke my ass?" I offer with a wince, almost like an apology. Like, *I know I was stupid and climbed a corn silo, but on the bright side, I hurt my tailbone so . . . look! Consequences.*

"What the hell are you thinking, Case? You could have died," my dad grumbles.

"I think that was the point," the officer murmurs under his breath.

"No! No," I repeat, irritated. "That was *not* the point." The firefighter helps me up, removing the clip, and I rub at my rear with a grimace.

"What was the point, then?" Kerry asks, her tone slightly strangled. It slices me to the quick, adding to the hundreds of guilt–paper cuts gouging my skin. I swallow back my sigh.

"Walker, the dipshit, always said he wanted to jump off a

silo—" I cut off, tilting unsteadily and searching the ground amid the flashing police car lights. "Hold on. I dropped the list. It's here somewhere. . . . There!" My limbs are stiff and achy with cold, and it takes me two tries to pick up the piece of crumpled paper covered in my dead best friend's scribble. I smooth it out and refold it, tucking it securely into my back pocket. "As I was saying, Walker apparently never learned the difference between corn silos and grain silos, because if he thought his weak-ass lungs were going to climb that ladder, he had another thing coming. I mean—" I laugh to myself. "Okay, maybe in peak condition, but even I—"

My dad interrupts me, his voice heavy with resignation. "Were you drinking?"

I bite down on my tongue. This coming from the man who has practically shoved the contents of his liquor cabinet at me every bump in the road since the night of Walker's funeral? *Nothing a stiff drink can't fix, Case.*

Unaware of the staring contest between Case Jr. and me, the helpful officer flashes his light to the pile of broken glass shattered on the hard earth.

I tear my gaze away and gesture to the bottles. "Three for me, three for Walker. Dr Pepper, I swear."

Kerry whimpers.

"Okay," I cave, ignoring their pained expressions. "Six for me, but I accidentally dropped the sixth. And the one before it. Slippery fuckers." I take a deep breath and meet Kerry's eyes. "I promise I wasn't trying to die."

She starts to nod, but changes course halfway and shakes her head as if catching up. "But you almost did, anyway."

I look askance, my palms infused with sweat, because a few hours ago, I may have lost my shit in the middle of my own house party and shouted at Kerry—a.k.a. the sweetest woman in existence, a.k.a. the woman who practically raised me—to "get these assholes off my property." But that was Intoxicated Case. He makes dick decisions.

Sober Case makes sad ones.

"We'll talk about it later. At home. Where's the Navigator?" my dad asks. Case Jr. always refers to my car by its full name like he's making sure everyone knows we're richer than they are. I don't remember how I got here, but I doubt it's a good idea to say that right now, so instead, I shrug. There. That's ambiguous.

His sigh is the longest-suffering, and he wilts several inches before looking to the officer.

The officer plants his hands on his belt. "I'll put an APB out for it. We'll call when it's found. In the meantime, the Richardsons don't want to press any charges." He turns to me. "They're big fans of yours, Case. They want you to know they're rooting for you."

I press my lips together to keep from saying something snarky about the Richardsons' son, Pax, who's probably still drinking beer in my living room as we speak. I'm not in the mood to rat him out.

The fact is, everyone used to root for the *both* of us, Walker and me. Two North Texas boys battling it out in the rodeo arena and trading belt buckles. But that was before Walker got too sick to compete.

Now there's only me, and I'm not exactly collecting accolades these days. Who am I to cast aspersions or whatever?

My dad loads me into his Benz ("Okay, Case, get in the Benz so I can take you home"), and I tilt my head against the glass, watching as my breaths fog and disappear over and over and over.

I look to my left, where Walker's ghost is sitting across from me, silent, no breaths to fog his window. Which is the problem, isn't it? He wouldn't be wasting away like this. He wouldn't throw away this chance. If I had died, Walker wouldn't be drinking Dr Pepper with my ghost on a corn silo. He'd be in the arena. He'd be riding bulls and catching glory. Walker is the fearless one, grabbing life by the horns and wrestling it into submission, wringing out every last drop.

He *was* the fearless one.

I'll never be.

Two
CASE

'm no longer drunk by the time I wake up, but I almost wish I were when I descend the long, lushly carpeted staircase, walk past the great room, and enter into a too-gleaming kitchen. That's where I encounter Kerry's sigh. I'm used to failing my dad. Expect it, even.

But Kerry's pursed lips and compulsive swiping of the spotless granite countertop say, "I'm not mad, I'm disappointed," *loud and clear*. I've been called a lot of things—entitled, arrogant, cocky, thick-skulled, to name just a few—but I'm not *rude*.

"Forgive me, Kerry," I beg our housekeeper right away, stilling her assault on the counter and loudly pecking a contrite kiss to her soft cheek. "I was an asshole."

She pretends to tsk my cussing but doesn't disagree. Instead, she shuffles over to the Nespresso and passes me a coffee, black. Confused, I accept it. "Thank you?"

"Drink up," she says in a gruff tone I've always thought sounded like water rushing over boulders. Raspy after decades of smoking in her youth, but smooth and soothing all the same.

"You're gonna need it. You were expected in the stables fifteen minutes ago."

I suck a blistering sip between my lips and grimace. Coffee drinking starts early on a ranch, but I've never gotten into drinking it black. My dad, obviously, drinks his coffee black enough to *put hair on your chest*, and so did his dad before him. I come from a long line of hairy-chested men. It's not only our names and accrued wealth we pass down in this family. We also inherit a mindless adherence to toxic masculinity. I'm pretty sure it's in the will.

My mom died of an aneurysm when I was a baby, and I have zero memories of her. I suspect my dad loved her as much as he's capable of loving anyone or anything outside of our ranch, but he's never liked to talk about her. Kerry raised me, and any shred of goodness I might possess is because of her and Walker.

Top of the list of Kerry's Life Lessons is *Don't be a little asshole*. It's a short list, and I like to think I'm accomplishing at least that much in my eighteen, nearly nineteen years, but yesterday would prove otherwise. I have a lot of ground to make up today.

"Better refill me, then," I say.

Kerry pulls out a sleek silver thermos, topping it off with the remainder of the pot, and trades me the still-steaming cup in my hand.

"Thanks. And, uh," I clear my throat awkwardly, "thank you for clearing out my, um, *friends* last night. I hope they didn't give you any trouble?"

Kerry shakes her head, her pinned, rust-shaded curls bobbing near her ears. She's picked up her rag and is back to aggressively polishing the granite once more. "No trouble at all, but that's cuz I didn't clear 'em all out. There're a few stragglers in the guest room."

My stomach sinks. "Stragglers?"

She tucks a smirk into her cheek, but it sneaks out her eyes. "They insisted they were too intoxicated to get home."

I look to the ceiling with an annoyed grunt. "Uber makes it out here just fine."

Kerry lifts a shoulder, undeterred. "Better hurry them along before your dad shows up looking for you."

My stomach squirms guiltily. I grab a banana from the stocked fruit bowl on the island before reconsidering and grabbing two more, making my way back up the stairs toward the guest wing. Without knocking, I swing open the door and flip on the bright lights.

"Rise and shine, interlopers!"

In the guest bed, Pax Richardson and his girlfriend, Madi Wallen, are a tangle of (thankfully clothed) limbs and sour booze breath.

"Fucking A, Michaels," Pax groans. "Turn off the light."

"I can't. You aren't supposed to be here, and I'm due in the stables."

Pax pries himself from Madi's grasp and rolls to his side, planting his bare feet on the floor. He's wearing his swim trunks, which is puzzling, since our pool is winterized, but I decide not to get into that now.

I chuck the banana at his head, and he doesn't bother ducking—just picks it up and peels it deftly, cracking the stem with a flick and taking a bite of the flesh.

Leaning against an armoire that was probably new before the Alamo, I ask, "Why're you here? Kerry kicked everyone out."

Pax smooths his overgrown sandy hair and swallows a mouthful of banana. "*You* kicked everyone out, actually. Aggressively, I might add."

"Okay, I kicked Brynn and *whatsherface* out. And I wasn't aggressive about it. I was *firm*."

Madi mutters from a sea of down, and I raise my brows at Pax.

"Darcy," he translates.

"Who?"

Pax shakes his head. "Man, you're a dick."

"We prefer the term *rodeo fuckboy*," Madi says, opening her eyes blearily.

I scratch at the back of my neck, feeling uncomfortably hot. "Darcy and Brynn. Right. I remember now. Darcy's the tall one. In my defense," I say, swallowing a surge of bile that's only partially from my hangover, "I told them I only do one-night stands. Before anything happened. I was very clear. No repeats, no feelings. It's not my fault if they got to thinking they're different."

Pax pushes out a breath, exasperated, and gropes around for his shirt. I find it on the floor and hand it to him.

"I won't apologize for it," I force out, defiant.

Madi scowls, scrambling out of the bed. "You're disgusting, Case."

The guilt rises again, but I shrug. There are probably healthier ways of escaping grief, but until last night, sex at least didn't have major consequences.

"Look, Madi, think what you want, but you're hungover from *my* beer and waking up in *my* house. You're giving me a headache, and I have work to do. Kindly collect your things and leave."

She glares at me and begins to pull on her jeans.

Pax clears his throat. "Look, I know I'm not Walker. No one could replace that guy. He was literally the best human to have ever existed. But I've known you since we were in diapers and watched you do a lot of stupid, reckless shit on the backs of fifteen-hundred-pound beasts *for fun*. Hook up with whoever you want . . ." His girlfriend growls, and he shoots her a look. "Easy. I'm not the one fucking around, and truthfully, they're old enough to make their own choices." He turns back to me. "I was . . . *concerned* when you ran out of here after shit hit the fan with the girls. It was like you had a death wish. You were running off half-cocked, saying something about a corn silo and some list Walker made for you."

My eyes slide shut, and I sink to the bed. "*You* called the police."

Of course he did. Of course it wasn't Walker. *Walker's dead. He's not your fucking guardian angel, Case.*

Pax butts into my self-flagellation. "You didn't get charged for anything, did you?"

"Nah. I think I pled 'angst.' I figure it's a onetime get-out-of-jail-free kind of thing. Plus your parents love me too much to charge."

"Christ, you really went to my house?" He whistles low. "Lucky guess on my part."

"Yeah. Closest farm for miles. I might've been feeling reckless, but I didn't feel like traveling far."

Pax squints one eye, considering. "He meant *grain bin*, didn't he?"

I nod.

He chuckles. "For a rodeo kid, Walker didn't know shit about livestock."

That makes me snort. I used to say Walker was the most citified rider on the circuit. He broke in his boots at my ranch. "No kidding. I probably should have thought of that before I climbed up the thing."

Pax nods slowly, clearly not knowing what to say. Eventually, he settles on, "We'll get out of your hair."

I pass him the thermos and soften my voice. "Thanks for caring, man. And for calling the cops. I was kind of stuck up there."

He clears his throat, and I try not to think about how things were never this stilted with Walker. I'm relieved when Pax twists open the lid and inhales deeply. "Mm-hmm. Kerry's coffee." He takes a sip and grins as if we weren't just tiptoeing around death and misery and my dumbass late-night mistakes. Like he's already shaken it all off.

I bite back a sigh. Must be nice.

"Now get out of my house before my dad comes back and finds you two and I'm stuck mucking stalls until I'm thirty."

—

By the time I refill my coffee (adding a generous pour of the special oat milk Kerry hides in the back of the fridge for me, toxic masculinity be damned) and steal four pieces of bacon from the stove top, I miss my dad doing his morning rounds by a good forty-five minutes. I didn't plan it that way, but I ain't mad about it.

It's been years since I've gone down to the stables this early. Even during my heaviest rodeo training periods, I'm more likely to be in the arena late and nowhere near the actual livestock. Mucking stalls is one of the few punishments Junior has in his arsenal. Essentially, go clean up horse shit and think about what you've done. It probably has something to do with how he and my uncle were raised to work hard and get their hands dirty, and because they did that *so well*, I haven't had to follow in their footsteps.

Well, joke's on him. I was fixing to come down here regardless.

Not to shovel horse shit and think about my life choices, but that's as good an excuse as any.

I'm comfortable on horseback and this is a working ranch, but it's different from how it used to be. Cowboys ride four-wheelers, and our horses are mostly relegated to adventure trail rides. Wealthy weekender tourists come in from Dallas and Austin and want the real "ranch experience," so they get a lesson in roping sawhorses, climbing the rocky trail at sunset, and overpriced Swiss chocolate s'mores paired with even more overpriced Hill Country wines. Every now and again, I'll get asked to jump on a mechanical bull when an avid rodeo fan comes to stay, but I've made myself pretty scarce in the year since Walker fell sick.

This ranch has been in our family for generations, but my dad and his brother, my uncle John, were the ones who brought it into the twenty-first century and made it the tourism empire it is today. As Uncle John likes to say, "Cattle come and cattle go, but 'Home, Home on the Range' will last forever." And, look, I appreciate that everything I have—which is a substantial amount—is because of this place.

It doesn't mean I want to spend the rest of my life working for Case Jr.

The sun is a late-winter watercolor version of itself, still low in the sky. I relish in the crunch of the grass under my work boots as I cross the yard toward the stables, and inhale a deep, cleansing breath of crisp March air. It's tinged with the aroma of manure and leather polish. This isn't all bad. Honestly, I should do this more often. Not the chores or whatever, but it wouldn't hurt to get up with the sun and maybe get some training in. My sometimes-coach Brody wouldn't know what to do if I pitched a switch to early-morning workouts. Might be worth it just to watch his expression while he seesawed between shock and dubiousness.

I stroll down the paved center aisle of the stables, greeting the horses as I pass, regretting I'm empty-handed. Next time, I need to remember to ask Kerry to slice apples or carrots for me to share.

"Hello, beautiful," I murmur, approaching an imperious Apaloosa mare. I glimpse at the chalkboard name placard. "You new around here? Queen Mab? Haven't seen you before." I hold out a hand toward her nose in offering. She shakes her head, shifting backward and letting out a snuffling snort—obviously unimpressed with my lack of gifts.

A clear, melodic drawl behind me warns, "I wouldn't if I were you. Mab'll bite off your fingers and then kick ya for not saying thank-you quick enough."

I spin to face the owner of the voice. It belongs to a pretty, dark-haired girl about my age wearing dusty jeans, work boots, and a too-big barn jacket. She looks familiar, but I'm struggling to place how.

"I ain't afraid."

The girl rolls her dark brown eyes. Her lashes are thick and inky, and I must be tireder than I'd thought because I lose myself tracking their flutter. She interrupts my preoccupation and flashes a bright smile. "I bet not." Her front teeth have the smallest gap between them that braces could've probably fixed. I'm glad they didn't. "Still," she muses, tapping her chin with a gloved finger, "it's hard to hold on for eight seconds when you can't grip the rope cuz you've lost your fingers to a cranky mare."

My shoulders straighten. A rodeo fangirl, then. Cue swagger.

I shift my weight, casually, crossing one boot over the other. "I can hold on for *far longer* than eight seconds, when needed."

She winces and holds up a hand. "Oof. Let me just stop you right there. When needed? Ew. I'm Winnie and—"

Unperturbed, I hold my hand out. "Case Michaels."

She glares at my outstretched limb as if she'd like to bite it off as much as the horse does. I tuck it in my pocket as she narrows her eyes.

"I'm Winnie," she repeats more slowly. "And I'm supposed to be putting you to work this morning since you turned up"—she checks the worn plastic watch on her wrist—"nearly an hour late."

"*You're* putting me to work?"

"I know." She makes a face. "I don't love it either, but boss's orders. So, there's the rake"—she gestures to the wall—"and the wheelbarrow"—I bite back a groan—"and the piles and piles of horse shit." *For fuck's sake, I'm not an idiot. This is my ranch.* "I suggest you leave Mab alone. I'll be back to exercise her in a few, and you can sneak into her stall then."

I open my mouth, and she whips around, her sleek ponytail swinging in my face, her maddening hand dismissing me. "Don't care, Case Michaels. It was annoying to meet you. Have a nice life."

Three
WINNIE

There are two types of people in this world: the ones that think "barn" is the best smell ever invented, and those who are wrong. Joanna Gaines could bottle this up, combine it with beeswax, drop it in a refurbished tin can, and make the Target crowd go spare. It's *that* good. And it doesn't change! English style, western style, north or south, mountains or plains, a stable is a stable is a stable, and it always smells like coming home. Getting your shit together. Finding your center.

As I said, two types. Some people aren't horse people. They don't get it. Couldn't possibly. They've never experienced the feeling of strolling down the center aisle just after sunrise. The soft nickering of horses, the swish-flick of their tails against solid wood, the creak as they shift, their soft noses pressing their greeting. The air is heavy and wet with the scent of freshly mown grasses, worn leather, rich manure, and decades of dust, swirling and settling in the beams of dawn. The clinking of bridles dancing in the powerful breeze of a massive fan. The scuff of work boots on packed dirt and concrete. The warm and weirdly gooey feel of slobbery lips lapping up carrots and sugar cubes.

I digress. It's just . . . it's my favorite place.

Which is why I wasn't thrilled to hear *he'll* be here today, invading my sanctuary. Sure, he's the boss's kid and has every right. One might even argue it's his duty to be here cleaning stalls and leading trail rides and exercising the stock, except in the eighteen months I've been working here, I've only ever seen Case Benton Michaels *the Third* in the stables twice. First, when he was looking for the specific medicine ball he prefers to use for his balance training. Second, on the day of Walker Gibson's funeral.

Neither time did he notice me. Which was perfectly fine. I have enough on my plate. I don't need to add "babysitting the arrogant rich kid" to the stack.

That is, until approximately twenty minutes ago when I was sucker punched with the realization of why the famous Case Michaels is being forced to slum it today.

He's . . . not doing great. According to the rumors, he climbed up on the Richardsons' corn silo drunk last night. He could have died. Sure, Case rides bulls, which is about as reckless as you can get, but despite his many, *many* faults, Case is known around the rodeo circuit for his measured brand of reckless. His singular focus on riding is one of the things that makes him stand out. In the chute, he's all business.

He and Walker Gibson were like two sides of the same champion-worthy coin. They balanced each other perfectly. Walker was hilarious and easy and up for anything, while Case was earthbound. He kept Walker grounded and as safe as he could.

More than once, I saw Walker step up to the chute without

his vest or his helmet or, *ew*, his mouth guard while Case ran after him. I wonder if it had to do something with the fact Walker was terminal and Case was in denial.

People like Case Michaels and Walker Gibson were born for rodeo. Grit in their bones, bravery oozing from their pores.

People like *me*, too. Not that I would ever say that out loud and not that I could ever in a million years act on the impulse. But deep down inside, I know it's true. Queen Mab confirms it. Camilla, my mentor and the stable manager here at the ranch, only purchased Mab six months ago, rescuing her from an auction where she was sickly thin and dull-coated. Camilla said she saw a special fire in Mab's eyes that begged and pleaded for wide-open spaces.

It's what Camilla said she saw in my eyes the first time we met.

And when Mab and I gallop out of the stables, we find our freedom together. No responsibilities, expectations, or restrictions. Just endless blue skies. The Michaels ranch spans thousands of rolling acres, and Mab and I have covered them all.

Regardless of my earlier slip of sympathy toward the boss's kid, it's not until I'm bringing Queen Mab back from her (our) workout that I remember the rodeo boy is even around. Still cleaning stalls from the look of it.

In my defense, riding Queen Mab is akin to a religious experience and often has the promising effect of completely emptying my brain of any and all bullshit.

Mab hesitates at the entry to the stables where the ground transitions from a fine gravel to concrete. It's one of her weird quirks. She can take it at a bit of a trot, but when it comes to a slow stroll after a hard workout, she does this little stutter step, and I need to coax her through with a click of my tongue and a gentle hand to her shoulder.

I have no idea why she is the way she is, but it doesn't bother me much. Mab runs like the wind, has the most stunning form of any horse I've ever laid eyes on, can turn on a dime, and seemed plenty put off by Case Michaels.

That makes two of us.

I recall the way he leaned in, all slick, holding out his hand to introduce himself as if I didn't already know his name. Even now, I flare my nostrils and lead Mab past him to her stall (which I note is spotless, but seriously, that's the least the idiot could do; I'm not about to give the dude props for *doing his job*).

"Does the Queen approve of her quarters?" Case croons over the wall that separates Mab's stall from a tall, dark, and handsome Thoroughbred named Jose Swervo. I wipe the scowl from my face as he pops his through the bars.

He is *not cute*. Not even with flushed cheeks setting his blue eyes to sparkling. Not even with straw dust in his hair making him look like a little kid.

Mab, the traitor, nuzzles him through the iron bars. He chuckles low, and I ignore the way it makes the little hairs on my arms stand straight.

"Okay, okay, I thought you might be into Honeycrisp. You minx." He pulls a handful of apple slices from his shirt pocket and holds them out in his flat palm.

Mab gobbles them up, giving his fingers a couple of licks for good measure, then allows Case to stroke her soft nose. She looks every inch the royal. He laughs again, and his dimple pops. Damn.

"Apologies, Your Majesty. I came unprepared earlier."

Mab shifts her weight, and I realize I've been standing behind her inside the stall like this is the first time I've ever been around a horse in my life and I'm hoping to get kicked in the gut. I shake myself and ease out the door, sliding it shut behind me with a quiet thud. The Michaels ranch has been around for generations, but the newly renovated stables are straight out of a Pinterest fever dream. Dark hardwood, clean matte-black hardware, skylights brightening the center aisle. No expense spared. Room and board is at a premium, which translates into me working my ass off so none of the clientele question the exorbitant fees.

But it's an incredible opportunity to work and train under Camilla Gutiérrez. Worth putting up with a world of grief, which is why I studiously ignore the ongoing lovefest between Mab and Case and instead reach for a pair of quarter horse siblings, Reba and Dolly, waiting in the next stalls for their scheduled trail ride in less than an hour. I make a mental note to grab Jose Swervo from the corral. I'm not leading this one, but Camilla had a dentist appointment in Amarillo this morning, so I told her I'd get everything arranged ahead of time. And leading trail rides is usually part of my job—a part I love, even—but I need to pick up my sister, Garrett, at her "kid geniuses who build robots" workshop soon.

(Because smart kids don't just like to learn Monday through Friday; they want to go to school all the days to do all the learning all the time for all the money.)

I've picked up an extra ride tomorrow to make up the difference, which'll suck because it's Sunday and that's my only day off, but oh, well. It's an investment. Garrett can buy me a nice car when she's working for NASA someday, or when she figures out a cure for climate change.

"You wrappin' up already?"

I crane my neck over the sway in Dolly's back where I've just tightened the cinch to sturdy her saddle.

"Not that it's any of your business, but I've been here since before sunrise. So 'already' is a bit of a stretch."

He's undeterred by my sass. "I was thinking maybe if you're about to be off the clock, we could take a ride around. I'll show you some of the ranch."

Hidden behind Dolly, I mouth *What the . . . ?* to myself, because this guy cannot be serious.

Unbelievably, he's still going. "I'm sure you've seen some of it, but we own pretty much everything your eyes can see, looking in every direction."

I bite back a snort and arch my eyebrows. "Is that right, Simba? Everything the light touches is your kingdom?"

Case blinks but recovers quickly, his full lips quirking despite the pink creeping up his ears. "Ha. Okay, hakuna matata, very funny."

Not cute, not cute, *not cute.*

I wrap myself in sarcasm, tugging it up around my ears and over my heart. "As much as I'd love to see pride lands à la Michaels, I have plans. I'd take a rain check, but we both know that won't happen."

His expression falters. "Did I do something to offend you? Is it because I was late this morning? I'm sorry if—"

If only. Basically everything about this guy and his money and his career and his attractive-despite-being-hungover appearance offends me. But even I can concede that's not his fault. Not all of it, anyway.

I slide a bridle over Dolly's long nose, coaxing the cold metal bit between her teeth and securing the buckle. "Listen. I have real obligations after work and also, I'm just not interested. So thanks, but no thanks." I busy myself with the reins, and eventually, I hear his steps walk away. Pressing my lips together so

I don't call after him and apologize for being so blunt, I grab Reba's saddle and repeat the familiar steps to get her ready for her rider.

The truth is, I'm pretty sure before today, Case didn't even know I existed. And while I don't care about that, I'm also not a masochist. There's no frigging way I'm gonna join him for some dreamy horseback tour of his land. That offer reeks of rich-boy playbook.

Not that I could, anyway. I have shit to do. Real-life shit like making sure there's food in the fridge and the electric bill is paid on time. Things I doubt Case Michaels has considered even once in his life. I bet his fridge is perpetually stocked with his favorite snacks. And ice cream. The expensive kind. Like those little pints of Ben and Jerry's.

"All set, Winnie?" I'm startled out of my daydreaming by Camilla. She's in her customary trail riding gear: black felt cowboy hat, heavy pueblo jacket over jeans, and worn boots. She holds out a steaming cardboard cup.

I accept the drink and inhale the hot cocoa scent into my lungs. "Yum. Thank you. I needed this."

"Rough day already? I was hoping a nice long ride on Mab might've done the trick."

"Good point. Almost forgot. Mab was glorious this morning. Hold on." I raise a calloused finger and close my eyes. "Let me just go back to that for a sec." I nod, a smile spreading across my lips. "There it is. All better."

Camilla narrows her artfully lined blue eyes but decides not to question further. Wouldn't be anything new, anyway. Mab is a gift, but some things are just hard to shake loose, and abject poverty is one of those things.

I sip my cocoa gratefully, then duck into the tack room for

my backpack and keys. On my way out, I raise my cup in a salute. "Thanks again, Camilla. I need to dash. Last time, Garrett was waiting out front, tapping her foot all dramatically."

What I don't say is last time I got a flat tire on my way to pick up my little sister. I was forced to change it out myself before limping along on the spare for an entire nerve-racking week until I could afford the patch. Why is it when you don't have a lot of money, everything costs *more* money?

I make a loop around my car like I have every time since then, checking for nails or miscellaneous ranch debris. Once I'm sure it's clear, I toss my backpack in the passenger seat and am on my way with a roar of my muffler. I check my rearview mirror and think I catch Case's gaze following me out. But it's probably just the dust cloud.

Four

WINNIE

"Can we get chocolate shakes and fries?" my ten-year-old sister, Garrett, asks, shoving my bag to the floor and dropping into the passenger seat before slamming the car door shut. She stares straight ahead, tossing her long, auburn french braid over her shoulder without bothering to wave goodbye to any of the other kids waiting for their rides.

"Hello to you, too."

She grins, her freckles scrunching together. "I *mean*," she says, "hello, Win. How was your morning?"

I smirk at her redirect, easing away from the curb. "Eventful. Mab was in rare form."

"Fun," is Garrett's polite response, though she couldn't care less about horses. If I didn't remember the day she was born, I might question our relation. "Can we get fries and shakes from McDonald's?"

I slip my sunglasses down over my eyes and do the mental math. My dad was paid this week and I immediately took care of the mortgage, so that took most of that. I don't get paid until next Thursday, but I budgeted for groceries. I can't afford the snack on top of a trip to the Piggly Wiggly, but if we use it in place of an early dinner, I could probably make it work, then meal plan starting tomorrow for breakfast.

Except I have work tomorrow.

I could get up super early. Walmart is twenty-four hours.

"Make it linner," I say, using our word for *lunch* and *dinner* combined, "and you're on."

"Can I still get a small shake?"

"On two conditions." I hold up two fingers and drop one. "You have to eat your chicken nuggets first. A six—make it a ten-pack. *Linner*," I repeat. It's late afternoon, and I want to make sure she's eaten enough to last the day. I think I might have some mealy apples left over. I could cut them up and make cinnamon-sugar apples later tonight for dessert.

"Deal," she agrees easily.

"And you can't rub it in Jesse's face," I warn, talking about our fourteen-year-old brother. "I have to get him two Big Macs these days, he's growing so fast."

"You got it!" She reaches forward and turns up the radio volume on some song I've only ever heard in sound bites on TikTok and starts dancing in her seat.

After getting my dad's text with his order, I pull through the drive-through, double-checking the screen and grabbing my debit card as the cashier confirms my total.

I hand my card through the window and eventually pass the chocolate shake to my sister. She frowns, taking it.

"What? You said chocolate, right?"

"I did," she insists. "But you didn't order anything for you!"

I press my lips together and reach for the bags the cashier is passing to me, tucking them on the floor near Garrett's tiny feet. Her shoes look nearly worn through. I want to say something like, "We can't all eat chocolate shakes and two Big Macs apiece," but that's not helpful, and it's not Garrett's fault we're broke.

Instead, I shrug lightly and gesture to my empty hot cocoa cup between us. "Camilla bought me lunch. I'm full."

Which isn't a total lie. Anxiety can be very filling.

—

I climb the cinder block steps of our front porch and swing open the door. "Linner is served!"

Garrett flicks on the lights, and I drop the deliciously greasy bags of food onto the clean Formica table that triples as our office, kitchen, and dining room. A minute later, my dad comes out of the bathroom, rubbing his damp, receding hair with a worn towel.

He smiles at us tiredly. "You two are a sight for sore eyes."

"Hi, Daddy," Garrett chirps.

"Where's Jesse?" I ask, emptying the bags and setting the table.

My dad sighs, and I tug out my cracked iPhone 6 to text my brother.

I BROUGHT HOME DINNER. WHERE R U?

Thirty seconds later, he writes back: FREDDIE'S. PUT IT IN THE FRIDGE, I'LL EAT IT LATER.

I bite back a frustrated growl and slap my phone down on the table with a little more force than necessary.

"He comin' home to eat?" my dad asks.

"Apparently not. He's at Freddie's. He wants me to throw it in the fridge for him."

My dad whistles low between a gap in his teeth that matches

mine. "I remember when I was fourteen with my head up my ass."

"Anyone else want his burgers? Have at them. They won't be any good cold, and the microwave is on the fritz."

"I keep meaning to have someone look at that . . ." My dad trails off. We both know he doesn't mean it, though.

"I'm good," Garrett says, and I notice she's watching me with that wrinkle between her brows again. It's easy to see my little sister and assume she's just like every other ten-year-old, but she's not even close. She's like ten going on Einstein, Freud, and Marie Curie rolled into one precocious package.

I hold the sack out to my dad. He shakes his head.

"You should eat it, Win," Garrett presses.

I take out one of the burgers because she's right, and then I stuff the other in the fridge before slamming it shut.

I slump down in a chair and try not to notice the empty one across from me. Jesse's been MIA more and more lately—staying out late with his group of friends, exploring all the new freedom that comes with being in high school. It would be helpful if he'd get a job, but with my dad working third shift and me needing my car to get to both the ranch and Garrett, I can't be driving Jesse to a minimum-wage job, too. Plus, he's only a freshman. He *should* be focusing on his grades. And being a kid. Just because I got a job at his age doesn't mean he should have to.

But it would be nice if he were around *some*. If he could take on a little responsibility for Garrett. Or clean up around the trailer. Or be the one to shake my dad awake for work every day at four when he leaves his phone on silent.

As usual, I can't tell if I'm angry at Jesse for being irresponsible or if I'm just jealous.

I graduated from high school early, over a year ago, and the idea of me leaving town for college was never even considered. It's always been a foregone conclusion I would stick around. I turned eighteen, and no one aside from Garrett even acknowledged it.

That's not to say I don't love my dad and brother. I do. I get things are hard. My mom ran out after Garrett was born and never looked back. That's some real baggage-building shit right there. Jesse has gobs of resentment toward everyone: At me, for trying to mother him so damn much. At my dad, for being absent 95 percent of the time. At Garrett, for being the golden child accepted into the gifted programs of her choice on a full scholarship. The hard truth is Garrett's special without even trying, and there's no way she's gonna end up stuck in a trailer park for the rest of her life.

The rest of us can't claim the same.

Well. That's not entirely true. Camilla offered me a place to rent on the ranch. Bless her heart, she even phrased it as if I'd be doing her a favor being on-site. But even as reasonable as it is (and it was a *steal*), I can't afford the rent when every penny I make goes toward robotics camps for Garrett and a smartphone for Jesse so he can call home and let us know where he is. Plus, who would take care of these guys? All the day-to-day stuff that needs doing?

I mean, Garrett's ten, so what are we talking here? Eight more years? I'll be twenty-seven by then. That's not too old for college and a career, right? Lots of adults go to college later.

Like *single moms and dads*, but still. And here I am, never even had a real boyfriend. A few quick hookups this last summer with tourists on solo trail rides. But making out with a guy you were hired to hang out with isn't exactly worth bragging about to your friends.

If I had friends. All the friends I might've had in high school left for college last fall, leaving me behind.

My forehead drops forward on the table with a groan. I'm pathetic. Worse than pathetic.

I need a friend. And a boyfriend. Unbidden, a smooth, full-lipped smile, bracketed on one side by a deep dimple, intrudes into my thoughts, and I whimper.

Not cute. Not cute. *Not. Cute.*

"You okay, Win?"

I raise my head and crack open one eye. My dad's gone, but Garrett is still sitting at the table, her remaining nuggets lined up in a neat row in front of her.

"I'm good, kiddo. Just thinking of someone."

"Someone?"

My breath catches. "I meant some*thing*."

Her expression twinkles. "I don't think you did. *Whoooo* were you thinking about?"

I sigh, casting a glance at our dad's bedroom. The low buzz of a college basketball game filters under the door. I guess I should be grateful he hasn't left us for the VFW yet, but it's still early. Monday through Friday nights, my dad works at the tire plant. Saturdays and Sundays, he sleeps most of the day to remain on his third-shift schedule. And after, he belongs to the Church of Stale VFW Hall and Darts.

"I met Case Michaels today."

Her eyes widen. "The bull rider?"

Garrett might not care about horses, but she knows her rodeo. Some of the events, anyway. She's intrigued by the mechanics of bull riding. Or is it the physics? I don't know.

"Yeah, I think he was in trouble or something and his dad made him do chores."

My sister's eyes are little half-moons of humor. "Did he have to clean up the manure?"

This makes me laugh, and it feels nice. "As a matter of fact, he did."

"Did he hate it? I would hate it."

I think back to this morning. I wasn't around him long, but it didn't seem like he was bothered by the stalls. "I don't think he hated it. He doesn't seem to like early mornings much, but he worked hard to charm Queen Mab with some apple slices."

And maybe it charmed me a little, too. Unfortunately. I stuff down the feeling.

"Is he a horse boy?" Garrett asks, her tone singsong.

"Maybe," I offer, refusing to take the bait. "Or more likely, he just likes the adrenaline rush. Mab'll bite your hand off."

"Did she bite him?"

"Not today," I say in a tone that implies, *But there's always next time!*

I take a bite of my burger, and Garrett watches me with that thoughtful expression on her face.

"Hmm."

I raise a single brow at her. She shakes her head. "Do you have to go to the grocery store tonight?"

I sigh. "I should. It's either tonight or early tomorrow before work."

"I'll come with and help if you'll let me braid your hair and watch *Downton Abbey* with me after."

I pretend to consider this. I don't need the help and don't love *Downton Abbey*, but I can see the offer for what it is—a chance for sisterly bonding—and accept it.

"Finish your nuggets," I tell her, "and I'll grab my coupons."

"Can I add the totals in my head as we go?"

"Can I have the last sip of your chocolate shake?"

"You have a deal."

"And you're easy to love, kid."

Five

CASE

I never tried to be popular in high school. It always just happened that way. I've never had any misconceptions about my appeal; it's absolutely rooted in my family's wealth and grown out of rodeo celebrity. I'm not saying I didn't use it to my benefit, but I didn't actively seek it out. Another thing Walker used to give me endless shit about.

What we couldn't know, or at least what I never imagined, is being the best friend of the dead kid is a whole new level of notoriety. The ladies love a sad boy. And a sad boy who drunkenly climbed a corn silo in the middle of the night is especially interesting, if the multitudes of texts lighting up my phone are any indication. (One very persnickety stable hand notwithstanding.)

I don't know how to react to the recent influx of attention for something so humiliating and stupid, so when Pax waves me into his hot, overcrowded kitchen and whispers that he stocked the lesser-known downstairs fridge with a six-pack of Lone Star beer, I waste no time. The door to the basement is familiar after a thousand games of hide-and-seek when we were kids, and I don't bother to let my eyes adjust to the darkness before scrambling down the stairs. The change is glaring. Down here, it's cool, quiet, and musty. It smells like uncomplicated memories, and I'm mightily tempted to stay down here and drink my beers alone. Suddenly, my reasons for coming tonight feel hollow: the dangling carrot of an uncomplicated hookup and another item from Walker's list (jumping into a pool, at a party, naked—yeah, I know). Even if I'm starting to wonder if he made this stuff up to fuck with me. Like one day I'll get to heaven and he'll be like, "Oh shit, man, I thought you knew I was kidding!"

It's not like we talked about this stuff when he was alive. He was always sick, but not. Chronic, but living with it, you know? Until he wasn't. When the entire world went to hell, it was as if there was this cosmic fuckup with management and Walker's papers were misfiled. If he'd gotten sick two years earlier, or maybe a year later, he'd have gotten his transplant and his uneventful hospital stay, and it would have been okay. He could have lived the rest of his life like everyone else.

Instead, his lungs decided they'd had enough, right in the midst of a fucking pandemic. He didn't have a chance in hell.

I tug open the downstairs fridge with a clatter of bottles and pull one out, twisting off the cap and downing half in a gulp. The sooner I get this party over with, the sooner I can go home.

Maybe I should just go home. Walker's list isn't going anywhere, and I haven't been able to shake off the guilt from Madi calling me a "rodeo fuckboy," even if I have been open with the girls I've been hooking up with. I'm still able to drive, and Pax's basement is a walk-out. I could sneak out the back and no one would be the wiser. They might not even remember I was here, which is equal parts depressing and a relief.

Just when I'm about to leave, I hear multiple voices over loud footsteps tromping down the stairs. One of the voices is instantly familiar, and I bite back a curse. Christine.

"Case!" she startles as she flips on a light, her manicured hand pressed to her chest. She's trailed by three guys around our age. "You scared the shit out of me. Are you sitting here alone in the dark?"

I bristle at the pity implied in her tone, even if that's exactly what I'm doing.

"Not me."

She narrows her eyes, her false lashes tangling in a way I used to find attractive, before she pulls open the fridge door.

"Oh! Jackpot, boys. We've got Lone Stars down here. Want one?" Her question is directed to a tall, vaguely familiar guy who might be rodeo-affiliated or might just be Texan. He seems to know who I am, and we exchange nods before I turn back to Christine.

"Those are mine."

She looks dubious. "All of them?"

I shrug and grab a second before she huffs and picks something else, closing the fridge with a bump of her curvy, denim-clad hip.

"We're gonna sit out on the patio. Pax said there's one of those classy little propane fireplaces out there. Wanna join us, or are you going to stay drinking in the dark?"

I don't even want this second beer. I just didn't want her to give it to her friends. Christine and I hooked up early on in my personal crusade to sleep away my misery. She's beautiful, sweet, and flirty on one hand, while also jealous and more than a little shallow on the other.

I'm plenty shallow enough already. Or at least I used to be.

Even if I hadn't made the one-time-only rule, I don't need to date a carbon copy of myself. Christine has seen it as a sort of challenge ever since.

I'm not an idiot. I know it's nothing to do with me so much as she likes the competition, but I'm too tired for games. It's why I made the rule in the first place.

Ghost Walker gives a grunt of assessment in my brain, though I'm pretty sure in real life, he'd hate my fucking around. He'd say something about how it "wasn't me" and "just because you can doesn't mean you should." But what is me, then? How do I know this isn't me? I have no fucking clue who I am anymore.

I follow Christine and her posse of guys through the sliding door and out to the patio. By the time they have the gas pit lit, someone has already fetched me a third drink. I accept it gratefully, but don't drink yet. I still haven't decided if I want to stick around.

"The silo looks real pretty from here. What d'ya think, Case?" Christine asks, her smile wicked in the firelight.

My lips curve in a fake grin. "It's a little cold for me, thanks."

"Did you really try to jump off?" one of the guys asks. The one who nodded his greeting. Now that I think about it, his name might be Copper. Or Cooper. He definitely used to do rodeo with Walker and me in junior high. I don't know the other two, but they perk up at his bold question.

One tries unsuccessfully to hide his snicker. "I heard you were too wasted to get down on your own."

I glare.

Christine idly swirls her bottle in the dancing light. "My theory is it was a bid for attention."

"I don't need cheap stunts to get attention," I say and take a long draw from my beer. This third beer sloshes with the last two, and I realize I'm trapped here. I can't drive like this, and staying here makes me want another drink to drown out everyone else.

"So you *were* suicidal, then?" I barely hear the third guy's question.

A louder group comes toward us from the edge of the yard, thankfully interrupting the conversation. They look pretty drunk even though it's still early, and as they get closer, I realize they're young. High school young. Maybe fifteen years old, tops.

"Who's that?"

Christine sneers at the display as if she didn't just graduate last spring. "Oh, that's Pax's little sister, Chelsea, and her friends. I hear she's dating the Sutton brat."

That gets my attention. "Sutton?"

Christine flicks her curled hair and shakes it out, sending the scent of expensive-smelling shampoo in my direction. "Yeah, you remember his sister? She was in our class? I think she graduated early or maybe got pregnant and dropped out. Winnie or something embarrassing like that?"

I feel even more annoyed at myself for not recognizing Winnie Sutton straight off. Even Christine, who barely notices anyone outside of her circle, knew Winnie back in school. "I didn't realize she had siblings."

Christine narrows her eyes, noting my interest. "Two, maybe? That dark-haired fool over there is Jesse Sutton. He's the one dating Chelsea, who apparently has *no problem* picking through trailer trash."

Ghost Walker and I suck in twin breaths. "What the hell is

that supposed to mean?" I ask Christine. She slow blinks at me, like she's confused at my outburst. To be honest, I'm a little taken aback myself. But, for real, has Christine always been this mean?

"It doesn't mean anything," she drawls. "I just don't care for fleas in my bed." The guys snicker.

"The kid can't be more than a freshman, and his sister probably graduated early because she was smarter than the rest of us. Where they live has absolutely nothing to do with it."

Christine raises a brow. "Okay, who even are you right now? Like, you're the guy always flaunting your money around, asking your housekeeper to deliver your lunch every day at school, driving your brand-new Navigator around town."

I inwardly wince. She's not wrong. "I'm an asshole, true. Walker said it every day. I'm only saying being rich might've made *me* trash, but that's got nothing to do with money and everything to do with me. Stop being such a snob."

"Christ, Michaels. When'd you get so deep?" Copper-Cooper, *whoever*, says.

"You know, you haven't been much fun since Walker died," Christine adds.

Ghost Walker groans, shaking his head as he settles down on the concrete bench next to me. *Not worth it, Case.*

The fuck it's not. "Yeah, well, I guess my perspective has changed. Death will do that."

"Okay, like no offense, Case, but Walker was sick a long time."

(For the record, never has the phrase *no offense* been uttered when the person didn't absolutely mean offense.)

Christine is still talking, and Ghost Walker is shaking his head all the more fervently now. Walker hated confrontation. No time like a good time and all. I also used to hate it, before he got sick. But Christine is still running her mouth off about things she has no earthly idea about. "He was never going to live to be old. It's okay to be sad, but you had to know he wasn't going to be around forever."

For a half second, Walker's voice echoes in my brain: *Leave it. Go jump in the pool and go home.* But I'm a little buzzed and a lot angry, so I don't.

"He could have been old. Or at least, he could have died from something else years and years from now."

Walker's joke was always, *You're more likely to get hit by a bus.* As if no one really gets hit by a bus, but he hoped he might have a shot at it.

Christine sighs patiently, and it's close to making me snap because here she is being all reasonable. "Walker was terminal. Always."

God, I hate that word. "Technically, every one of us is terminal. No one survives life. But sure, if it makes you feel better, then yes. Walker's lungs were shit. He was never going to live long with them. He packed as much life as he could into eighteen years and had excellent odds of getting a new pair of lungs. At least until the rest of the world couldn't be inconvenienced by thinking of others over themselves. Until they decided 1.78 percent of the population was weak and therefore expendable."

"Dude, Case," one of the guys cuts in, but Christine quiets him with a look. It's *that* look that sets me off. The *let it go, he's a sad fucker* look.

I get to my feet, pointing with the bottle in my hand. "No. It's fine. Let him talk, Christine. I want to hear this. *Really.* Please convince me I'm wrong."

She rolls her eyes, and the guy holds up his hands in surrender, backing down. "Never mind."

"Never the fuck mind is right. Because I'm not wrong. And you know what's the worst part? Walker understood it. He was on your side. He used to say to me, 'Why should it matter to them if a sick kid dies? It's natural selection, ain't it?' He'd say he could just as easily die being stomped on by a bull. Or jumping off a corn silo. But that never flew with me, because he deserved a chance. But you fuckers didn't care."

I smash my bottle to the ground, and it shatters in a hundred pieces, making Christine shriek. I stalk back to the basement and pull another cold beer from the fridge. I don't think about it. Instead, I crack the cap off with a flick and gulp it down. This is not at all how I expected tonight to go. I was supposed to show up, have a few beers to get loose, jump in a pool to fulfill Walker's dumb list, and then find a willing distraction to finish off the night. A few hours to pretend I'm the new and improved Case. The one who's still the life of the party. The one who does casual sex. The one who's moved on since his best friend died and is fine on his own. Instead, I'm drunk, sad, and empty as fuck.

I grab the last two Lone Stars, tucking one under my arm, and stomp up the stairs, wincing in the harsh light of the kitchen as I fling open the basement door. The number of people has multiplied. Loud hip-hop thumps from the speakers while a group of kids plays flippy cups on the island. A quick glance shows that Pax has wandered off, possibly with Madi. I waver on my feet, rocking slightly in indecision. There're two girls by the sink, laughing at who knows what. One of them gives me a bold look up and down. She seems vaguely familiar, and I think maybe she's a year or two older. A college student home on break or something.

Someone shouts by the flippy cups, and I see Jesse Sutton with his skinny arm slung around Pax's little sister, Chelsea. From what I can tell, they aren't drinking anymore, and anyway, it's not like Pax, Walker, and I didn't sneak beers at their age. But I still feel weirdly protective of Winnie's younger brother. Or something. Seeing her brother reminds me of the way she brushed me off the other morning, and it makes me feel . . .

Well, I don't like it. Don't want it. Not here and not now. I walk up to Jesse and hold out my last beer. "Here, man. Your hands are empty."

His eyes widen in surprise, but he takes it.

I look to Chelsea. "Hey, Chels, where's your bro?"

"Outside by the pool, I think."

"Fucking perfect." I down the rest of my beer, slamming the glass on the counter with a grimace, and pull off my shirt. I turn for the sliding glass door that leads out the back. Along the way, I yank away my belt, toe off my socks and Jordans, drop my jeans, and slip out into the night. I'm followed by catcalls and cheers. It's cold. Real cold. So I don't stop, and cannonball right into the pool. For a beat, I consider staying under the water forever. It's quiet, surprisingly warm and calm when the rest of me feels anything but.

Then more bodies jump in the pool alongside me. One after another after another. The pool is suddenly filled with half-drunk, half-dressed teenagers.

My lungs begin to burn, and I surge to the surface, shaking my head and making everyone scream and laugh. How fucked up is it that no one can even tell I'm crying? *You're right, Walker,* I think wryly. *This was a great idea.*

A hand reaches out, and I grasp it, using it to pull myself out of the pool and into the freezing air. Pax's gaze is grim. "You're wild, man. You'd better crash here tonight. Remember where my brother's room is? He's at a college visit this weekend." He helps me to my feet and passes me one of the towels hanging on a lounger. "You can use his room."

CASE

I wake early to Pax's silent house. I tap the lamp on the night-stand, and the dim light illuminates a bunch of retro *Baywatch* posters on the walls. I groan under my breath.

My mouth tastes like death, my head is fuzzy as all get-out, and it's way too early in the morning for this much vintage David Hasselhoff.

I drop my bare feet to the carpeted floor with a groan. A quick glance at the alarm clock tells me its barely 5:30 a.m. Which makes sense. I was probably asleep by 10:00 p.m. The new Case Michaels, everyone: party like a firework—flare hot and fizzle fast.

It's too early to bother Pax, but I don't feel like sitting in this room, staring at the walls until everyone wakes up to nurse their hangovers. And I'm definitely not interested in answering for my actions last night.

There's a chance I might be losing my shit.

My temper surges all over again, only this time, Walker's ghost is nowhere to be seen. I'm sure being sober has something to do with Walker's absence, and I'm doubly sure I don't want to investigate beyond that. Not before sunrise, anyway.

I get dressed, leaving the sleep shorts I borrowed folded on the bed. I can't remember where Pax's laundry room is, and besides, I don't know how to do laundry.

I sneak down the stairs and out the door and find my car parked on the drive but mercifully not blocked in. It unlocks with a muted bleep, and then I let out a hiss at the chill of the leather on my clammy skin. I turn on the heated seats, and everything warms up quickly, including my heated steering wheel. I got this car when I turned sixteen and never much thought twice about it. Yeah, of course it's nice—nicer than what my classmates drove. But I've always had nicer things than my classmates. I never thought it made me better than anyone else. My dad did. But not me. Or did I?

Fucking Christine. It's just a car.

I drive the ten minutes home and pull up the long and winding gravel drive right as someone else is turning off their headlights. It's 6:00 a.m. and someone is already here to open up the stables? I don't think I realized Camilla worked such long days.

But as I get closer and turn off the engine, I realize it's not Camilla. And I notice the other car is . . . rough. A true junker. Like, even in the dim, shadowy light of dawn, I can see this rusty Ford Taurus is held together with duct tape and prayers.

Of course it's Winnie Sutton's car. Of course she's coming in to work at the same time I'm stumbling home from a night of drinking and diving naked into a pool full of shrieky girls.

I want to crawl out of my skin as I sink into the earth and also evaporate into the ether.

I hear Walker's chuckle in the back of my mind. Must be some residual Lone Star swirling around in my bloodstream. Nice of him to stick around for this.

I open my door and wave as naturally as possible. I wish I had stopped for coffee or something so at least I could look like I was awake intentionally. Like, "Hey, I was just up checking my stocks and bonds and needed to get my caffeine fix because getting up early on purpose is totally a thing I do." I clear my throat, but it's still gravelly. "Good morning."

Winnie tugs a chunky knit hat over her long dark waves, taking in my wrinkled appearance. "Good morning?" She seems less sure. "Rough night?"

I immediately notice she doesn't even consider I woke up early and I can't help but be pissed at her presumption, correct though it may be.

"Not as rough as I would have liked," I quip back with a leer that feels wrong on my face. Winnie's expression shutters immediately. I should backtrack, but instead, because I'm an idiot, I double down. "Maybe you should try it sometime. Instead of acting like a boring middle-aged mom."

I don't even know what I'm talking about. Winnie Sutton, so tiny in her oversize work coat, with her brilliant, flashing eyes and pink cheeks, is the furthest thing from boring.

"Better to act like an *adult* who is trying to make something of her life than to act like a petulant child who had something bad happen for the very first time ever in his life and can't cope."

"What do you know about anything? I'm coping fine! And it was more than just bad."

Her eyes soften a fraction before they harden all over again.

"You smell like stale beer, look like shit, and are stumbling home at a time when the rest of the world is getting ready for their day. If that's what coping looks like . . ." She trails off, derision thick in the air between us.

My heart is pounding in my chest and maybe a little in my skull. I step closer to her, near enough to smell coffee and laundry soap and leather and barn, and I work at not pressing closer to get more of it, because I'm spitting mad—

But I also feel fucking *alive right now.* "So I went out to a party. I was invited to a party because people *like* having me around. They seek me out. Weird how I didn't see you last night. . . . Or any night." I somehow keep from mentioning how I didn't know who she was, because, even in my fury, I'm aware that says more about my shortcomings than hers. I cross my arms over my chest; she does the same. "But guess who I did see last night?" I pause for dramatic effect.

She rolls her eyes and drops her hands. "Please, don't tell me. I don't care. I have to get to work."

"Your brother," I cut in. "I met Jesse." An exaggeration, but I'm not about to tell her I gave him my last beer. She freezes in place, and her face drains of color so fast I'm glad I kept the last part to myself.

"Was he okay?"

I shrug, feeling off-balance. Did she really not know where he was? "He was plenty occupied with Chelsea Richardson when I last saw him. Seemed to be doing fine." By the end, I'm no longer throwing it in her face. Instead, I'm throwing her a bone.

Winnie deflates, looking relieved. Then her mouth twists. "I didn't realize he was dating Chelsea. That explains a lot, actually."

Fucking A. "You were worried."

Her eyes dart away, and she tries to come off nonchalant, but it's too late.

"He's fourteen, and he didn't come home at all yesterday or last night. He wasn't in his bed this morning."

"Lucky him," I joke. It doesn't suit me to care about a kid I never met or a girl whose default setting appears to be "let down." "Am I sensing jealousy?"

Winnie narrows her eyes. "Hardly. But if he's not careful, he's gonna get the princess pregnant, and then I'll have more shit to deal with."

I don't think that's all of it, but my headache is getting worse and I don't feel up to matching wits anymore. "Right. That's it, I'm sure. Anyway, shouldn't you be at work?"

She inhales sharply, and I instantly regret my snark, but before I can think of an apology, she spins on her heel and marches toward the barn.

I release a long breath and slam the car door behind me. I reach into my greasy hair, tugging on the ends. Fucking hell, I fucked that up. *Again.*

Walking up to the house, I grumble a hello to Kerry and continue to my bedroom without sticking around for what would assuredly be another "why Case is a disappointment" speech. Thankfully, I dodge my dad as well. Within moments, I'm dropping my day-old clothes on the floor of my giant bedroom and crawling under my down comforter. I close my eyes, but here, in the silence and the dark, my headache feels worse. I pull my pillow down over my face, but the pressure isn't enough. I exhale deeply, trying to release the tension from my shoulders and neck, and unclench my jaw until my sour breath becomes too much to bear. I should brush my teeth. And take a Motrin or five. Maybe a hot shower would help?

With a muttered cuss, I fling off my covers and stalk to the window, shutting the blinds against the dawning sunrise. That's the first step. My eyes drop to the piece of paper sitting on the top of my desk. Walker's list, looking worse for the wear after these last eventful weeks.

I pick up a rogue, half-sharpened pencil and strike a bold line through *Jump into a pool naked (at a party)*.

I rub a hand down my face, eyes skimming over the rest.

Jump off a corn silo into a pile of hay / snow

Drive backward down a dirt road in the middle of the night going over 60 mph

Eat oysters

Sing karaoke at one of Case's dad's fancy fundraisers (Naturally, I sang "Friends in Low Places" and the crowd went wild. Too easy.)

Learn a language other than English

Road trip somewhere

Walk the Fareway Freight train trestle

Conquer a bull OUTSIDE the arena

Do something illegal

I draw a line through that one, too, figuring underage drinking and also helping a fourteen-year-old underage drink is likely illegal enough to count.

Befriend Winnie Sutton

The paper crumples in my hand before I smooth it out and slump into my desk chair. Well, Case, you've screwed that one up. Walker thought the "horse girl" always hanging around the stables and leading trail rides, the girl who turned out to be Winnie Sutton, was cute but lonely. If it weren't for the fact he was madly in love with Taylor, I would have thought he had a crush on her. But he genuinely seemed intrigued. And frustrated with me for not knowing more. "You live here and see her all the time," he'd say. "Christ's sake, man, she goes to our school. It's embarrassing how out of touch you can be."

He was right, obviously. Even if I barely go to the stables, I could've still gotten to know her. I always thought he was pulling one over on me, saying she needed a friend, but maybe he was right about that, too. After this morning, it seems like he was. And instead of being a friend, I was a total dick and made fun of her for caring about her brother. Literally nothing she said about me was an exaggeration. Even if it stung, where was the lie? I really am a self-absorbed asshole who for the first time in his life is facing something hard (very hard, but still) and can't cope with it.

I've never been the kind of person who cared about having lots of friends. I've only ever cared about having one: Walker. And he was more like a brother. Being popular and having friends are not the same thing—I've lost my one friend, and now I'm alone.

Not for the first time, I consider this list and wonder if Walker maybe made it for me and not him. Maybe this wasn't a "things I want to do before I die" so much as a "things Case should do when he has to live." The last years of my life have been so tied up in the end of Walker's. Days spent trying to pretend everything was normal. Like I wasn't afraid of the way his skin seemed to hang on his lanky frame or the way his lungs would rattle after something as easy as walking up steps. Like I didn't even notice it. Because he needed one person to act normal. But now he's gone, and I don't have to pretend everything is normal anymore.

Except I don't know how to stop. I don't know how to do

any of this anymore. Making a friend should be easy, but I've forgotten how.

I put the list in a drawer and slam it shut, heading for the shower. I've changed my mind about getting back into bed. I'm done sleeping.

Seven

WINNIE

Two days later, I'm still annoyed with Case Benton and the stupid, ignorant words that came out of his stupid, attractive mouth hole.

(Outside my POS-hand-me-down sedan and his gleaming, top-of-the-line SUV. If ever there was an apt metaphor for the difference between us, that would be it.)

So while I know I have every right to be as frustrated as I am with Jesse, I can't help but think at least some of my ire is because of the dickwad who called me a "middle-aged mom."

Seriously. A mom?

Let's be clear, he isn't necessarily wrong. I feel old. Way older than nineteen. It's as though I went from age nine to *grown* after my mom left us. It's like one of those online quizzes. My *real age*, according to the level of trauma and bullshit I've survived, has got to be at least seventy by now. Seventy-five after my dumbass little brother decided to sneak out after dinner and not answer my texts.

I should throw his drool-stained pillow on the stoop and

lock the door until morning. Or maybe call our dad and tattle on him for having a girlfriend. Or, like, I don't know, wait till he falls asleep, put his fingers in a cup of hot water till he wets himself, and then put the video on Instagram.

If I had an Instagram, that is.

And if he were home.

Instead, I'm sitting up, pacing the kitchen. I gave up trying to read the smutty werewolf romance novel Camilla lent me. Our Netflix subscription stopped three months ago when my dad forgot to leave enough money in our account to cover the withdrawal. I could renew it now or I could look online for a pair of shoes for Garrett. I pick up my phone and sit down at the table, scrolling Facebook Marketplace for a bit, unsuccessfully.

Damn.

I'm about to close out when I see a beautiful pair of women's cowboy boots for sale. Gently used but in excellent condition. I groan to myself. Gorgeous dark brown leather inlaid with turquoise.

I would wear the hell out of those.

They're only a hundred dollars, but that's already a hundred dollars more than I have to spend on anything for myself. Garrett needs shoes. I don't. Maybe I can pick up a couple of extra rides and stow away a little extra cash for myself. Of course, these boots will be gone, but there might be more.

Yeah, right. I bookmark the seller and open YouTube instead, looking through clips of barrel racing. I find a batch uploaded from the National Finals Rodeo three months prior. I already know the results, but don't mind watching the ten-day series again. I lean back in my chair with a creak and pull my heels up to the seat, resting my phone against my knee. I run my jagged thumbnail back and forth on my bottom lip, soaking up every detail I can from the tiny images on the screen. All the riders have their own style of doing things. Some press their bodies forward in the straightaway. Some use their reins as a sort of replacement crop to spur their horses on. Some give the barrels a wider berth, losing seconds but saving points.

I catalog the differences, committing them to memory and visualizing how to implement them into my own training with Queen Mab. If we can't *both* race, at least one of us should. Eventually, I close out the app with a sigh just as the front door finally opens to reveal my younger brother trying—and failing—to be stealthy.

"SHIT, FUCK, WIN!"

"Shh." I hold a finger up to my lips. "Garrett is sleeping, dummy."

"What the hell are you doing sitting in the dark?"

"You know the light keeps her awake. I was online shopping."

He's not fooled. He walks over to the stove top and flips on the small light. "Yeah, right. You're definitely waiting up."

"I shouldn't need to. It's nearly midnight and you have school in the morning. You should've been home hours ago."

He shakes his head. "I don't have curfew. And anyway, why do you care? You're not my mom."

I press my fingers to my temples, massaging away the intruding headache. The same one I get every time we argue. I'm gonna start calling it *Jesse*. "You're right, I'm not. I'm the *oldest*. I'm the one who works full time, pays all the bills, buys all the groceries, picks Garrett up from school, buys your clothes, cooks your meals, makes sure you get to your doctors' appointments and to the dentist, and apparently is the one who waits up and worries over you because you never come home or, worse, you sneak out as if I can't fucking tell!" By the end, I'm whisper-shouting. My composure is nearing a breaking point. I take a deep breath. The last thing I need is Garrett awake and getting involved.

"You're absolutely correct, though. I'm not your mom. I didn't ask for any of this, but it turns out no one else is gonna do it, so if I don't, I'll be abandoning you. And that *is exactly like our mom.*"

Jesse's nostrils flare, and his lips press together. I know he wants to yell back, but there's nothing he can say. Because he knows—*he fucking knows*—I'm right.

So instead, I walk over to the stove light and switch it off. My eyes adjust to the dark and I can still see his outline illuminated, so I step closer, placing my hand on his shoulder, noticing not for the first time, how tall and broad he's getting.

"I love you, kid. Okay? You know I do. Please go to bed."

—

The next day is Friday, my favorite day of the week. Not because it's the start of the weekend but because after finishing mucking out all the stalls and leading my usual morning trail ride, I get to spend my afternoon drilling Mab on the classic clover barrel-racing formation.

It's real hard to remember all the garbage life chucks at you when you're clinging to a thousand pounds of pure freedom by the skin of your knees.

I walk Mab through the formation, leading her close to the barrels but not enough to touch. Not that she'd dare. Turns out, her weird quirk with transitions makes her perfect for avoiding barrels. She hates the idea of rubbing against the strange texture, and I'm not about to teach her otherwise. Because of this, I'm not planning to give her a wide berth when we're running the barrels. I suspect she'll avoid them at any cost. It's a risk, but it'll shave off time, and in a sport where every tenth of a second counts, it's a risk worth taking.

We repeat the steps until the loops become second nature and I can feel Mab getting antsy underneath me. She's impatient to run, and I don't blame her. "Easy, girl. There's a method to my madness."

I nudge her into a trot, and she shakes her head back and forth a few times within the reins to show her annoyance. She follows my cues perfectly, anyway.

Just because I'm doing it, doesn't mean I have to like it is written all over her twitching fetters.

"I know," I soothe under my breath. We trot the formation until I feel my focus drifting and spot Camilla leaning against the arena sideboards. We canter over, and my boss shakes her head, grinning ear to ear.

"You ladies look like a match made in heaven out there."

I press forward in my borrowed saddle and give Mab a scratch in the soft space behind her ears she favors. "Mab's in a mood because I won't let her run willy-nilly. You ready for us?"

Camilla pulls out her well-loved stopwatch. "Whenever you are."

This is when things always get really interesting.

I kick Mab off with a "Yah!" and she shoots out of the entrance like a bullet train, even though the ranch arena doesn't have a whole lot of alleyway to get up to speed the same way a larger venue might. We go zero to sixty here, and we like it that way, hitting the first loop so quickly, my butt barely touches the saddle. We lean together into the curve, and I hold her reins tightly in my right hand as much for balance as to keep her in line. She darts off to the second barrel, my kicking keeping me in time and in the saddle, which is more important than pushing her to go faster. She doesn't need the reminder. This is her favorite part. My inside knee brushes the barrel, but my inside hand is already there when it wobbles, darting out to set it right. Then we're off to the next. This time, I place Mab a little farther out, and she follows my direction without question. We clear the barrel easily.

And then it's the moment we let go. Inside of my brain, everything gets really still. Silent. Crystal clear. Empty. Nothing but fly. Fly, fly, fly.

Mab's hooves barely graze the sand; my rear barely grazes the saddle. My hat flies off my head, and my hair streams wildly behind me, breath catching in my throat.

We rocket past Camilla, and I tug the reins, slowing Mab to a trot and then a walk, both of us panting, adrenaline zipping through my bloodstream.

Camilla is jotting down our time in a little notebook she carries around to track our progress. I don't bother to stop and check our split. I already know it's the fastest Mab and I have ever done. She's gonna make someone one hell of a rodeo horse someday, but today, she's all mine.

"Don't think I didn't see that wobble, Winifred." Camilla's voice is singsong.

"Then I bet you saw those unbelievable reflexes when I fixed it, Ca-mil-la," I shoot back.

As I line us up at the start, I lean forward, whispering in Mab's ear.

"Again."

—

Case finds me brushing Mab and cooling her down after our workout. I'm trapped between a thousand pounds of exhausted horseflesh and a literal wall, but I'm also pretty wrung out and maybe even feeling a little high off my stellar afternoon. So I don't immediately lash out, even if the barest glimpse of his handsome features annoys me.

He clears his throat. "You looked amazing out there."

I bristle, focusing all my attention on Mab's hindquarters. "Thanks. I didn't know you were watching."

"No worries." He shrugs, and I look up at him, incredulous, repeating my words in my head, trying to understand where he got the apology from. "You were a little busy. Do you have any idea how fast you two were going?"

I blink. "Camilla times us, so yeah."

"Are you aware, then, your practice numbers are right up there with the competition? Like, actual NFR leaderboard times? In a practice arena with zero coaching." Apparently, Case Michaels is a bit of a barrel-racing nerd. Which would be interesting to note if it weren't *him* and also if this conversation weren't completely irrelevant.

I brush in long vertical pulls, soothing Mab's muscles and cooling her coat. "Camilla is all the coach we need. Mab's learning plenty, and she's a natural."

I look up to see his answering grin is a mile wide, and his eyes are like, legit sparkling. Oh god. "She's not the only one. What are you doing working in this place cleaning horse manure and leading tourists on rides? You could be on tour winning buckles at every stop."

I don't even know where to start with this idiot. I really don't.

I walk over to a bucket and drop the brush in, letting it clang nice and loud. I slap my hands against my pant legs to get the dust off them and shake them out. Then, I pour oats into Mab's feed bin outside her stall before walking her in and sliding the gate closed behind her. Once I get her settled, I turn to Case, still working to organize my response. In all honesty, I know he means well. He's wrong. On multiple levels. But I'm not so far gone in my own problems I can't see his pep talk for what it is: a compliment. However, one can't live off compliments and good feelings.

I release a slow breath. "First of all, Mab's not my horse. She's Camilla's. I don't own a horse of my own. So trail rides and exercising the boarders is all the riding time I get. I'm happy to do it. Some of the boarders are visited by their owners once every couple of *months*." I jab my thumb at my chest. "I'm the one who gets to be with them day in and day out, and I feel very lucky.

"Secondly, as I'm sure you know, entering rodeos costs entry fees, and a trailer to transport the horse. And a truck to transport the trailer to transport the horse. I can't even afford a saddle to put on my hypothetical horse.

"So while traveling the country winning belt buckles sounds really dreamy"—there's an ache in my chest at the truth of this—"it's not in the cards for me. It might be for Queen Mab, though. And *that* is why I work her so hard." I inhale through my nose, swallowing against the encroaching tightness in my throat. "Someday, a barrel racer is gonna show up here and fall in love with her, and I want her to be ready for her chance."

Case's eyes are stormy. He runs a frustrated hand through his hair, making it stand on end, which, just so we're clear, is *not* attractive *in the slightest*. "But *you* are a barrel racer, Winnie. That's what I am trying to say. You're better than anyone I've seen, and I've seen plenty."

I bite back a frustrated scream and shake my head, my patience running thin. Compliment or no, this needs to be nipped in the bud. "I'm not being stubborn or obtuse here, Michaels. I know my worth, and just because you call someone something doesn't make it so."

"I'm not sure you're hearing me—"

That's it. I'm gonna punch him. And then I'll punch my little brother and then come back and punch Case one more time for good measure. What is with all these boys trying to mansplain my own life to me?

"I understand perfectly. I think you're the one getting too high off the fumes of your SUV and keto lunches. *I'm perfectly aware of how fast Mab and I are.* We're a great team here at the ranch, but this is where that ends, because rodeo isn't in my future. Not everyone can chase their dreams in the daytime." I swallow hard again, my indignation turning to dust and clogging my throat. "Some of us only live them out in our sleep." Just then, the alarm buzzes from my cell phone at my hip, and I sigh. Time to pick up Garrett. "I've got to go."

Case looks like he wants to argue, but wisely steps back.

His expression seems confused, and I wonder if it's because no one has turned him down before. Maybe he's used to everyone always being grateful for the attention. He seems *so* out of sorts I almost feel bad for all the truth-giving I've dumped on his expensive boots. I try to soften my demeanor a little as I pull my jacket off the hook by the door and slide it over my shoulders. "Listen, Michaels. I appreciate the nice things you said and even your enthusiasm. Misguided as you might be, it's nice to hear someone thinks I can be more than I am."

"I'm not wrong," he insists in a low voice.

"And I'm not either. Let's call it a draw. And if you see my little brother out this weekend, kick his ass for me, okay? I'm tired of pretending not to notice when he sneaks out."

—

Garrett is in full-blown tears when I pull up to her school a few minutes later.

"What happened?" I ask, immediately double-checking I'm not late on the car dashboard clock.

She hiccups. "Just drive, please."

I stare at her before glancing at the small group of kids standing in the pickup line, talking in a huddle and casting loaded glances at my little sister. Silently, I pull away from the curb and drive us out of the school parking lot. My sister sniffles but says nothing. Eventually, I pull off the road a few miles from home and park in a Dollar General lot.

"Out with it. What happened?"

Garrett shakes her head quickly, and I can tell she's holding her breath to keep the tears in. She finally releases a shaky exhale. "It's so stupid, I don't even want to talk about it."

"I had one of those days, too. How about you tell me yours and I'll tell you mine?"

She takes a minute to consider, but I'm patient. I know her curiosity will win out. It always does.

"Can I use a cuss?"

I press my lips together, working to keep my face serious. We have a deal in our house. Until age thirteen, only one cuss per year. It's reupped on your birthday.

"If you're sure it's worth it. You have four months to go."

"Oh, it's worth it," she mutters. "Callie fucking Foster told everyone I got my new shoes from a trash bin outside the Goodwill."

I suck in sharply. "Fuck," I echo.

Garrett nods. "I tried to tell everyone I got them brand-new, but Callie is like the president, and everyone listens to her about everything. So all day, everyone was making faces when they walked near me, pretending I stink like a dumpster."

Ugh. When will kids get a new line? I remember them doing the exact same thing to me when I was her age.

I lean forward and sniff. "Nope. Only the same old sweet-smelling Garrett."

She leans over and does the same to me with a wrinkled nose.

"Oh, ha ha," I say. "Yes, I am well aware I smell like a horse."

Garrett's lips curl in a half grin. "You smell like Winnie. I like it."

"I don't know if that's a good thing, but since I like you best of all, I'll accept it."

"I like you best of all, too."

"I'm sorry I couldn't afford different shoes."

Garrett sighs and looks down at her brand-new white knockoff Skechers. "The shoes are fine. I like them! I don't need different shoes. This is all very character building for my Pulitzer-winning memoirs one day."

"That's the spirit. Put that in your pipe and smoke it, Callie fucking Foster."

Garrett giggles, looking happier. "What about your day? You said you'd tell me."

I groan. "Case fucking Michaels saw me barrel racing Queen Mab and has decided to appoint himself my life coach."

"You do ride like the wind," Garrett says, her tone proud. She might not care about horses, but she likes to watch *me*.

"I do," I say without modesty. "But rodeos are a money suck."

"Don't people win a lot of money in rodeos?"

"If they're good, sure. The leading barrel racers can make three hundred thousand a season in winnings. But they also have sponsorships and teams and, like, oh, I don't know, horses. Multiple horses, even."

"Ah," Garrett says. "Three hundred K, though. That's . . . a lot."

"A windfall like that would ruin your memoir."

"Not very character building at all," she admits brightly. "So why does the famous Case Michaels want to be your life coach?"

I exhale. "He thinks Mab and I could make it big. Which"—I shrug, again, not being modest—"he's not wrong. From the numbers, with practice, it's not a stretch. But the obstacles are enormous, and I have responsibilities. I live in the real world, not the rodeo world."

"It's nice he thinks it, though."

"It was," I agree. "Well. Mostly annoying, if I'm being honest, but sort of nice, too."

"Maybe he doesn't want to see you waste your dreams on Dad and Jesse and me."

My expression melts, and I pull her close and kiss the top of her head. "I'm not wasting my dreams on you, Garre. I'm pinning my hopes on you and your beautiful brain. It's an investment."

She quirks another smile and hugs me close. "Then maybe I'll keep trying to think of an idea to make both our dreams work."

I settle back in my seat and turn over the ignition and grin at the intense look of concentration suddenly painting my little sister's face. "If anyone can do it, it would be you. Now pass me my phone. I think today calls for Taylor Swift."

Garrett passes me the phone, and I scroll to "You Need to Calm Down," cranking it as loud as the speakers will go before heading the rest of the way home.

Eight

CASE

Last Year

*T*oday, I'm earlier than usual. I had an argument with Case Jr. about the amount of time I've been "wasting" at the hospital instead of training, but my sleep schedule's all fucked up, and anyway, Brody hasn't been much for training these days either.

Everyone waves me through, from the lobby to the front desk to the nurses' station. They all recognize me by now. Sometimes I'll stop to chat, but not today. Today, I drop off some cookies for the nurses, freshly baked from Kerry, then poke my head into Ryder's room and see if he's awake. I'd brought him the latest Rick Riordan book. It released this morning, and I know he's a massive fan. I promise to check back in later tonight and give his mom another Tupperware of Kerry's cookies.

From there, I make my way down the hall to Walker's room. I figure at this point, room 104 will forever be imprinted on my consciousness. As usual, I stop to brace myself, clearing my face of the argument with my dad, and stiffen up my shoulders. All bullshit gets left at the door. Before I can even raise my hand to knock, however, the door flies open and Walker's brother, Brody, rushes past me, his mom right behind him.

What the—?

Walker's dad approaches the door next, an apologetic look on his face, his hands clenched in the pockets of his beige jacket. He's aged at least a decade over the past month. I wonder what's happened this time? He raises his hand as if to place it on my shoulder, but his face breaks before he manages it, and instead, he brushes past.

Then I hear my best friend's voice. "I understand. You don't have to say anything else. Please go."

I hear more murmuring. The doctor, maybe? A nurse also files out.

"I got it, all right. I'm fucked! I want to be alone!"

Walker's primary physician, Dr. Syed, reluctantly leaves next. He closes the door behind him, distracted, before stopping short at the sight of me.

"He wishes to be alone."

"So that's it?" I ask. "He's done for?"

I know I'm not technically family. Dr. Syed can't really say anything to me. But he manages a nod, anyway, running a hand through his hair as he leaves.

Any other time, I'd have felt bad for the guy. But he'd just told my best friend he's going to die, so I'm not feeling very generous.

I hesitate at the door, calculating the outcomes, running scenarios. I could go in there, acknowledge the news, and let him scream at me to get out like everyone else. Or I could . . . not do that.

I decide I'm not gonna fucking do that. Instead, I take a deep breath, steeling myself. I'm no longer worried about shaking off my fight with my dad. Fuck my dad. This is more. I turn around and weave through the maze of corridors until I find a vending machine. Pulling out my wallet, I feed it a few dollars until it releases two bottles of Dr Pepper (plastic—beggars can't be choosers). Then I slip back into Walker's unit. I get to his door and fluff up my hair, making it look windswept and breezy in a way I know annoys him, and take off my coat, tossing it on a chair outside the room. With a final breath, I paste a shit-eating smirk on my face and shove through the door.

"Hey, man, you'll never believe what I just heard. Remember that douche Steadman? Blaze or Blake or Bobcat or whatever?"

I studiously ignore the tear tracks on Walker's face, passing him a Dr Pepper and cracking open my own. Moving to the windows, I rip open the curtains, pausing to collect myself against the clench in my gut. Get a grip on it, Michaels.

"Benson?" he offers hoarsely after a minute.

I pretend to scoff. "That's not it. Is it? Benson Steadman?" I tilt my head, taking a swig of my soda. "Christ, that's worse than I'd thought." I look over to see Walker sitting still, his expression shell-shocked from the shitty news. Or maybe it's from my barging in and rambling like an idiot. "Sorry, the tubes. I forgot." I take the bottle from hands full of uncomfortable IVs and flick open the cap before passing it back.

He considers it, taking a small sip. "What's the occasion?"

I hold up my bottle and tap his. "To your health, man."

His lips twitch, and his tone's as dry as a salt block. "Apparently, I'm dying."

I don't flinch. At least not on the outside. "Not today, you ain't."

Walker's jaundice-yellow eyes meet mine, full of fire. It's the same look he'd give a bull before jumping in the chute. "Not today," he agrees.

We each take a swig and sit in silence before he goes, "What was that about Steadman?"

"Fucking qualified for the NFR in Vegas. No way he would have if you were there."

"If you were there, too."

I take another sip.

"Do me a favor, man?"

I swallow, recognizing the change in his tone. Walker's throat works, and his eyes fill. I clench my jaw to keep my composure from slipping into a puddle on the floor.

"Depends on what it is," I say coolly. "Don't think you can just pull the 'I'm dying' card."

He gives a wet chuckle. "Fuck," he mutters under his breath, rubbing at his face. "You're a dick, you know that?"

I smirk, and he shakes his head, because we both know I would walk through fire for him.

"Get that fucking NFR buckle next year. For the both of us. I can't stand the thought of Steadman or anyone else getting it. I can barely stand the thought of you getting it, but if it can't be me, it has to be you."

My face screws up, and I turn my head to keep him from seeing it. I inhale a deep breath and clear my throat. "Is that all? Shit. I thought you'd think of something hard."

He chuckles again, sniffling, and we sit in silence, drinking our sodas and ignoring the beeping of the machines and smell of antiseptic.

"I'm so fucking angry, you know?" he says finally.

"Yeah."

"And I know it's not your fault, but I hate you right now."

I press my lips together. "I know."

He sighs. "I don't really."

"I know that, too."

"You have to win that buckle, man. For me. Promise."

I meet his gaze head-on and ignore the sinking feeling in my gut, reminding me I'll never care about anything as much as Walker. He should be making this promise, not me. "I swear. It's yours."

"Ours."

My chest clenches in on itself, cracking in two. "Ours."

—

The first time I rode a bull, I was ten. I was little, the bull was little, and I'm not sure either of us wanted to be there. I vividly remember being in the chute with my dad and my uncle on either side of me, counting me off, and thinking, *Why am I doing this?* It's not that I was scared, which would be a normal reaction for anyone, kid or adult. Mostly, I didn't get it. I had gotten a dirt bike for Christmas, and that thing was fast and smooth and didn't try to buck me off. Why couldn't I ride that thing around instead?

But that was also the day I met Walker. He was behind me in line and super stoked to be there. The kid had nerves of steel. His cowboy hat was brand-new, and his boots were barely creased. Like me, it was his first time ever in the chute, and he was practically vibrating with excitement. Walker was underweight and scrawny, even for ten, and I was sure he'd be thrown the second his denim touched the hide, but he wasn't. He held on against all odds. Scored something like six seconds on his first try. I knew immediately that while I didn't care much about bull riding, I needed to be friends with Walker Gibson.

After that, it was all rodeo all the time for the two of us. Walker somehow made riding bulls less idiotic. To him, it was a great adventure—a way to literally take life by the horns. That we were both pretty good at it felt unimportant. We would have gone week after week even if we'd sucked, but always staying at the top of the leaderboard kept sponsors showing up. For years, we'd dreamed of joining the PBR, the professional bull-riding circuit. For me, it was a competition against Walker—a puzzle to be solved and some bullshit back-and-forth between brothers. But for Walker, it was a fight for his life. I didn't know it at the time, but now I do. He'd talk about the PBR, and I went along with it because what the hell else did I have to do? I had my entire life ahead of me.

I'm starting to wonder if maybe I never really wanted that dream. Maybe I only wanted whatever Walker wanted because, deep down, I knew his dreams were keeping the fight in him alive.

And what I dreamed was for him to live forever.

—

I sent a text to Brody after Pax's party and the subsequent vocal ass-kicking I got from Winnie, asking to meet at 7:00 a.m. for training. Brody used to be Walker's and my coach. He's four years older and rode bulls in the PBR for a rookie season before Walker got sick and he stepped back to be closer to home. We never had a conversation about Brody continuing to coach me after Walker was gone, but I promised Walker I'd get us that gold NFR buckle in Vegas, and despite my recent detour into fuckery, I'm determined to see it through.

Without thinking too hard about it, I've decided to make some changes. Small ones. Intentional ones. Maybe Walker's list really is just him kicking my ass from heaven. Wouldn't be the first time, but it's definitely the last, so I need to make it count. To start, for the first time since kindergarten, I'm not in school. Last fall, my entire world and schedule revolved around Walker's illness. His parents brought in hospice when he was sent home, but we all took shifts staying with him so he always woke to a familiar face. I took the middle of the night so his parents could sleep.

And because that was the hardest time for Walker—when he was the most irritable. Something about lying around, nothing to do but die, makes the silence and darkness of the middle of the night feel extra shitty.

Once he was gone, it felt weird going back to daytime. Like too bright or something. Too loud. But it's been months, and I need to join the living, both figuratively and literally. I also need to channel my energy into something worthwhile, or I might lose my fucking mind.

I might as well focus on the promise I made him the day he learned he was going to die. One more gold buckle, for the both of us, but mostly for him.

So here I am.

—

Brody is short and stocky and everything you imagine a tough-as-nails bull rider to be, except for one thing: the bubble gum.

Lots of riders chew tobacco, but growing up around Walker was enough reason for none of us to want to mess with that. Instead, Brody has always carried around a pack of Big League Chew. The sugary scent precedes him into the barn where I do my training, and I grin, tugging out my AirPods to greet him.

We get right to work on balance. Bull riding takes a lot of guts and strength and conditioning, but the real secret is in the balance. I saw a documentary about J. B. Mauney once, where he talked about balancing on a medicine ball in his cowboy boots for an hour a day, so I've decided to make my goal ninety minutes.

I look ridiculous, but do you know how many muscles you engage to balance on a tiny medicine ball? All of them. The answer is all of them.

I'm finishing up on the ball, sweating my ass off and feeling more than a little shaky, when Winnie and a little girl who could be her pint-size twin pull open the heavy barn door and poke their heads in.

"Oh gosh, I'm sorry," Winnie says, turning an attractive shade of pink. "I didn't realize—We'll just—"

"No!" I stop her, wobbling precariously on the ball and whirring my long arms around. I finally get myself back under control and reach toward her. "It's fine. You can come in."

Winnie scrunches her nose. "Are you sure? It'll only be a few minutes. I need a warm spot out of the wind and out of my hair for Garrett to do some schoolwork."

Brody walks over and tugs the sliding barn door farther open with a rumble. "Come on in. Case's almost done, and there's plenty of room." He holds out a hand. "Brody Gibson. I think I've seen you around. You do trail rides, right?" I inwardly groan. Even Brody knows Winnie? I'm the worst.

"Winnie Sutton." She shakes his hand briefly. "That's me. And this is my baby sister, Garrett. She had to tag along this morning since there's no school because of Saint Patrick's Day or something."

Garrett pushes through, flipping her hair. "It's a teachers' in-service, actually. Whoa!" She freezes, spotting me, dancing on a ball like a bear in the circus. "What're you doin'?"

I wobble slightly and correct again. "Balance work."

She approaches slowly, as though she could knock me over with her attention. I don't bother to tell her my legs have essentially gone numb by this point. "For bull riding, right?"

I flush under her frank stare, trying not to notice too much how closely she resembles her sister. "Right."

"Basic physics. An object in rest stays at rest, and an object in motion stays in motion with the same speed and in the same direction unless acted upon by an unbalanced force."

I release a soft laugh under my breath, careful not to shake up my core. "Exactly. I'm the object, the bull is the unbalanced force."

"Wow. That's brilliant."

"It is, isn't it?" I give her a wink, and her eyes glitter.

"I don't know, Win. I think you could do worse than Case Michaels for a life coach. He seems to know his stuff."

And just like that, the ball flies out from under my boots and my ass hits the ground *hard* and my breath whooshes out with an *oof*. Winnie surges across the room to my side. "Oh my god, are you okay?"

I roll to my feet, rubbing my rear, and feel my face flame. "Oh yeah, I'm just fu—" I remember Garrett and change direction. "Dandy."

"Are you sure?" she asks, clearly too worried to notice my sarcasm. "You hit hard."

"I'm fine, *Win*." I emphasize her nickname. "A little sore is all. And feeling like an ass, but that's not all that different than usual these days."

"Eighty-four. So close," Brody says, making a piss-poor attempt at hiding his laughter. It warms me a little to hear it. He looks ten years younger when he's razzing me like the old days.

Winnie sucks in a breath next to me. "Eighty-four *minutes*? Seriously?"

"Was going for ninety. That's the closest I've been. I usually crap out around seventy-five."

"Ninety," she repeats faintly. "Hell, Case. Now I sorta feel bad."

I hold up a hand. "Don't. Well . . ." I consider a moment, finding my own teasing grin. "Maybe if you feel bad, you can explain to me the whole life coach thing?"

Brody clears his voice. "This is where I bow out. I have to get to work, anyway. Same time tomorrow?"

I nod.

"Registration is all set for Friday night. You're back in it, kid."

"Ready or not," I mutter, ignoring the fact that even though I'm weeks shy of nineteen, he's still calling me "kid." Brody hears me but doesn't comment, instead going through the sliding doors and closing them behind him. I fidget, brushing off my legs, holding back a groan.

"There's an old workbench over here that'll do the trick. Let me clean it off for you." I direct Garrett to the corner and grab for a rag.

"You have a desk? Did you do homework in here?"

I shake my head, swiping at the layers of dust and dirt. "Not often. But this is where my best friend, Walker, and I used to train, and we'd sometimes come right from school, so while one of us was working with Brody, the other would catch up on school stuff."

"That's awesome. I've heard of Walker Gibson, too. You guys were one and two at the National High School Rodeo Association championships."

I glance up at Winnie, who shrugs softly. "She's a rodeo fangirl."

"Just her?" I ask, teasing.

Winnie shakes her head, not taking the bait. "I'd have to sit through the bull riding to get to the barrel racing."

"Of course." I think about pressing the life coach thing but decide to drop it. After all, Walker wanted us to befriend Winnie Sutton, and so far, I've done nothing but mess things up with this girl. I get an idea and lean over the cleared-off bench where Garrett is already pulling out thick books with complicated numbers I recognize from my AP math classes. "You know, I have my first rodeo this Friday night at the county fairgrounds. It's a local event, but I'm rusty as fu—*dge*. Maybe you girls could come and watch?"

Garrett looks at her sister, her dark eyes wide and pleading. "Can we?"

Winnie doesn't look at me, only her sister. Her expression is softer than I've ever seen. Something clicks into place in my brain, watching them.

"Maybe," she concedes. "It might be fun to watch as long as neither of you get any ideas."

Ah. So I'm not the only one pushing Winnie to race.

I press my hand over my heart. "I swear, as your unofficial life coach, to get zero ideas."

Winnie's full lips twitch, and it's the closest thing I've seen to a smile on this girl yet. Baby steps.

Walker's voice nudges in the back of my mind. *Quit while you're ahead, Case. This is enough for now.*

—

I've been in the arena for an hour, sitting on my tailgate, riding bag at my feet, fighting nerves. Walker's ghost legs dangle next to mine as I take a small sip from my water bottle, wishing I had something a little stronger, even if what I got is already roiling in my gut.

Everything feels wrong. The noises are too loud and sharp, the lights too bright and harsh. My smiles are fake, my handshakes are weak, and I can't stop my legs from shaking. I am literally shaking in my fucking boots. Not because I'm afraid of the bull. I've pulled a geezer named Midnight I've ridden at least twice before.

I'm trembling from head to toe because I've never done this alone.

I inhale a deep gulp of air, trying to force myself to calm down. Ghost Walker shakes his head.

"Listen, asshole," I say, "I've never claimed to be brave, and you know it's nothing to do with the ride."

My throat tightens, and hot tears threaten in the backs of my eyes. For god's sake, there's no crying in rodeo. I take another swig of icy water to clear my throat.

I'm not supposed to be this fucked up still. When I promised Walker I would chase the buckle all the way to the NFR in Vegas, I figured I would be ready. Willing. Filled with fire in my gut. I thought I'd be more like Walker and one hundred percent less like me. This was different than the PBR. The PBR was professional. It was a career.

The National Finals Rodeo is one time. One buckle. *The* buckle. All I have to do is keep my shit together long enough to qualify.

If it can't be me, it has to be you.

Turns out, I'm just a wreck.

"Ready, kid?" Brody walks up, all swagger. He looks right at home here. He and Walker always fit in. I thought I did, too, but today, the rodeo feels mismatched and awkward. My stomach churns, and my mouth waters with the telltale acid of bile. Oh no.

"Your girl's in the stands. Just saw her and her sister." He laughs. "That Garrett is hilarious. Reminds me of Walker when he was younger—"

My stomach gives a mighty clench, and then I heave all over the ground at our feet, splattering water and my lunch on my bag.

"Shit!" Brody jumps back. "You okay?"

I moan, swallowing convulsively against another round.

"Shit," Brody repeats, looking closer at me. He grabs my shoulder with his hand and shakes it a little. I gag, and he jumps back, but I hold it in.

"Are you drunk?" he whisper-shouts. "Are you fucking kidding me?"

I drop my head into my hands and consider telling him the truth. I'm not drunk. Outside of parties, I rarely drink. I'm just . . . fucking sad and scared out of my mind to face this alone.

It has to be you.

But what if I can't do this?

Brody thinking I'm a fuckup seems easier to take. "I'm sorry. I thought I could do it, but—"

"You thought? What's holding you back? I've been sitting by letting it all settle, you know? Letting you do your thing because I know it's hard." I look up, and Brody has his hands on his hips. He lowers his voice, but his tone is dark and irritated. "*I know it's hard.* But this needs to stop. The drinking and partying and girls . . . climbing silos and jumping in pools naked and showing up to ride drunk. . . . Do you know what Walker would have given—" He stops, shaking his head. "I shouldn't have said that. Maybe I shouldn't have said any of it. I'm . . . I'm sorry, okay? I get it. I do." His hand reaches for my shoulder, and he squeezes it once before releasing his grip and ripping off his hat. "I have to remove you from the lineup. Don't go anywhere."

I want to tell him, "Don't worry, I won't," but he's already gone. Within minutes, I hear my name and the words *turn out* spoken over the loudspeaker to a round of disappointed boos from the stands. I feel like shit. Garbage. Lower than dirt. I've let everyone down. Especially Brody. Walker was his actual brother, and he's not fucking around making stupid decisions and moping.

Jesus. I've let Walker down.

The secret only Walker's ghost knows is that when I hear my name over the loudspeaker, being taken off the roster, I also feel a little relieved.

Nine

WINNIE

Color me shocked when Case is present, accounted for, and apparently sober bright and early the next morning.

I make a show of looking around and affect a generic cowboy stance (hip jutted out, one thumb hooked in my belt loop, another jerking east). "You know this here is the stables, right? You usually sleep in the big house down yonder."

His face flushes, and he picks a pitchfork off a hook. "Very funny."

"Seriously. What are you doing here? The sun is barely up." If Mr. Michaels is gonna start using the stables as a punishment for his attractive-yet-wayward son on the regular, I'm gonna need to have some words with Camilla. There's not enough work for the both of us.

"And yet, you're here," he points out, a slight edge of annoyance creeping in his tone. Probably because he's hungover. I consider for a hot second giving him shit. He's more than earned it. Garrett was properly devastated to miss seeing him ride, and we paid twenty dollars to get past the gate.

There's something in his eyes, however, that prevents me. Or maybe it's that I still feel bad for last week, when I implied he wasn't able to deal because he's never had something bad happen to him.

Because while that may be true, it's not only "something bad," it's grief. I've never had someone I love die, but I imagine it's the worst thing you can ever experience. I might be broke, but grace costs nothing.

"I'm paid to be here. That pitchfork even has my name on it."

He swings the pitchfork up, squinting in the dimness. I flip a switch in the tack room, and it glows yellow into the aisle. Then I walk over and use my pointer finger to trace the spot where I'd carved my initials into the wooden stake.

I hold my hand out. "I hate the other one. The handle is plastic, and it chafes."

His eyes widen. "You've seriously claimed a pitchfork?"

I sigh, flexing my hand again. He slaps the handle into it, and I beam.

"I don't have a lot in this world, Case Benton Michaels *the Third*, but I do have infinite dibs on the pitchfork with the wooden handle. It's smooth as an eight ball after generations of mucking stalls and molds perfectly to my hands." I lower my voice conspiratorially. "I've earned it."

He shakes his head and reaches for the other fork, but a smirk teases the corners of his mouth. The sight of it eases something inside of me. Like a balance being restored.

"Can I trust you to take that half of the stalls without puking your guts out?"

He heads over without complaint and throws himself into work while I start from the opposite end of the aisle. The only sound is the quiet rush of our breathing, the grating scrape of pitchforks, and the sliding of stall doors. After a while, I start to feel twitchy. I never work in complete silence.

"Do you mind if I put on a podcast?"

He pauses his lifting and wraps an arm around his pitchfork. His breath puffs out in the chilly morning, drawing my attention to his mouth. "Is that what you usually listen to?"

I shrug, pulling out my phone and walking over to the dusty community Bluetooth speaker. "I've tried music, but it makes some of the elderlies antsy."

"Not Her Royal Highness?" he asks.

"Nah. She's cool with tunes, but her tastes are honestly a little embarrassing."

"Let me guess? Olivia Rodrigo?"

My jaw drops. "Wow. What, you pick the one young, successful female singer you could think of to make some snarky remark about?"

He winces and raises a hand in surrender. "Dang, girl. I was only kiddin'."

"For the record, Mab's tastes run to nineties country. Alan Jackson. Travis Tritt. Garth Brooks."

His expression clears. "You're right, that *is* embarrassing."

I pretend to sniff. "Like I said."

He clears his throat and tries again. "So, what do *you* listen to, podcast-wise?"

"Do you know any?"

He shakes his head. "Not really, no."

I smile big and scroll for the most recent episode of my and Mab's favorite. "Excellent."

To his credit, Case makes it about two and a half minutes before he shoves open a stall door and comes to stand in the middle of the aisle, his hands on his trim hips.

I press my lips together. "Can I help you?"

"What the hell is this?"

"Oh, right. I thought you knew. This is called a *podcast*."

"About serial killers."

I lift a shoulder. "Mab likes it."

His eyebrow quirks in amusement. "Mab is into some dark shit."

I fight a smile.

"You're really gonna stand there, holding a spiky metal weapon in your hands, acting like I'm not listening to a recording of an actual autopsy report?"

I open my eyes wide, as innocent as I can manage. "The murderer is still at large, Case. We might be able to help find him before it's too late."

"'We' as in . . . ?" He circles his hands between us.

I'd die before admitting this out loud, but his exasperation is *adorable*. His eyes are puffy with exhaustion, he's got this cowlick sticking straight up in the back, and I have to imagine this is exactly what he looked like as a toddler after naptime. "*Obviously*, you and I. Mab is a horse. She can't understand the autopsy; she enjoys the cadence of the narrator's voice. Finds it soothing."

"Winnie Sutton listens to true crime podcasts."

"Clearly."

"What else?"

"Do I listen to?"

He nods, leaning on his fork.

"A little of this and a little of that." Something has me feeling honest. "Some nineties country if the mood strikes."

His expression brightens like he's been given a gift. "I thought that was Mab's vice."

"I already said it was embarrassing, Case. We don't need to harp on it."

He grins, and I notice how nice his teeth are. White and straight and even. I catch myself running my tongue along the gap in my own front teeth.

"So you like the classics," he offers, easily. "If it's any consolation, I went through a phase in middle school when I thought I wanted to be a pirate like Kenny Chesney when I grew up. Walker was merciless about it."

I snicker. "I love that you thought Kenny Chesney was a real pirate."

"I had this whole plan worked out that after we graduated high school, Walker and I would travel to the Keys and learn how to sail."

I tilt my head, leaning on my own fork. "Not the PBR?"

His expression slips, and his eyes shift someplace in the distance. "That was all Walker. He lived and breathed rodeo."

"I didn't know that. I assumed . . ."

"Yeah. Everyone does. It's okay."

"So about last night," I hedge. "Is that why . . . ?" Because, okay, I *was* pissed when I heard Case's name over the speakers, pulling from the competition. I would give anything to have half his resources and opportunities, and he's just throwing them away.

He considers me for a long moment. "Yes and no. I know what everyone thinks, and maybe . . . I let them think it."

Aforementioned grace or no, I'm dubious. "So you didn't puke your guts out?"

He grimaces. "Oh, no, I definitely did. All over the ground. It was disgusting, but it wasn't alcohol-related. Regretfully, I was sober."

I frown. "So you pretended to be drunk? Because I spoke to Brody after, and he was pretty pissed."

He wavers. "Yeah. He was." Case rubs at the back of his neck. "I didn't fake it. It was more like I would rather let Brody think I was drunk than the reality." He hesitates for a beat before exhaling in a gust and continuing, "The reality being it was my first time in the arena without Walker, and I couldn't face it."

My stomach drops at his confession. It feels like a punch. "Oh."

He frowns. "Yeah. Which, now that I admit it out loud, seems just as pathetic as it would have been if I'd actually been drunk."

I quickly shake my head. "No! Definitely not. Don't think that. You're sad." I rush to reassure him. "That's normal. Human," I offer, as if I know what the hell I'm talking about. My voice is barely above a whisper in the stillness, because suddenly, this feels like a secret. I guess because, technically, it is. "So what are you going to do?"

He scuffs at the concrete with his work boot, tucking his free hand into his coat pocket. "No idea."

"Do you want to do rodeo at all?"

He doesn't answer right away. I watch his face as he truly seems to consider his future, and I work hard to repress the jealousy that he's even given the choice. Clearly, after what he's confessed, now isn't the time for pettiness. "I'm not sure. I thought I did, but I'm starting to wonder how much of that was wanting to support Walker. If he were alive and well, we'd be touring with the PBR right now, and I know he wouldn't regret it one bit. But me?" His hand comes out of his pocket and tugs his hat off his head. He exhales. "I *like* rodeo. I love to ride. But . . . I've never been as fearless as he was. Walker did not give a single fuck, and I've never been able to pull it off the same way. I'm not sure I want to." He fidgets with his hat again. "I've never admitted that before."

"Not even to Walker?"

He chuckles humorlessly. "*Especially* to Walker. I couldn't. I knew I had my whole life ahead of me, and deep down, he always knew he didn't."

At once, I'm struck by how decent Case Michaels is. Sure, he's a rich dope who doesn't seem to have a clue about the real world and how stupid-fortunate he is, but he was a good friend to Walker Gibson.

It warms me toward Case a little. Like a teeny-tiny bit. But there *is* a thaw happening. Walker was a special kind of human. Not because he was terminal—I didn't even know until the very end. He never seemed sick to me, though I'm pretty familiar with the lengths we go to keep people from seeing our vulnerabilities. I'm fluent in the concept of denial, that maybe if we keep those scary parts of us hidden, we won't ever have to face them.

But, eventually, Walker could no longer keep his hidden.

Case picks up his pitchfork and turns to the next stall, conversation apparently over. Which is okay. I turn off the podcast and scroll to find some Kenny Chesney, turning it on low enough so the old ladies in stalls 8 and 9 won't get all worked up. At the first strums of Kenny's guitar, Case sticks his head out and beams, damned dimple popping in his cheek. It's one that says "Thank you," I think. I roll my eyes and wave him off in a way that hopefully translates to "Shut up. It's not for you."

As I shovel, I remember. Walker and Case used to train in the same barn where we found Case and Brody last week. I never saw them working out or anything, but Walker would occasionally come by the horses when Case was drilling and visit with me. He had this massive crush on a girl who went to a different school, and he would ask my advice on how to flirt with her. In retrospect, this had to be Walker's way of starting a conversation, because I'm the last person on earth who should give relationship advice.

Walker and I formed a pretty casual friendship. Somewhere spanning the border of more than acquaintance and less than Case. Because no one was as close as those two. But we would sometimes eat lunch together, and he always waved in the halls at school. Then I graduated at the semester break, and not long after, Walker got really sick. He stopped coming around the stables, and I wasn't in school anymore. By the time I learned he was dying, it felt too late to visit him—out of place, maybe. Presumptive. In truth, I was afraid.

I wish I'd been braver. I would have liked to tell him thank you for those moments of friendship. They were the closest I'd had to the real thing in a long time.

Case finishes up on his half of the stalls, and I see him leading a mammoth of a Thoroughbred named Moses toward the tack room. He notices my curiosity. "It's okay. He's mine," he explains.

"Wait. Really?"

Case looks sheepish. "Technically. I don't ride very often, but my dad had hopes. He bought him for my thirteenth birthday."

I whistle low, too impressed to be annoyed. "A top-dollar beauty of a stallion for a thirteen-year-old who will never ride him."

He winces. "Yeah. Well, to be fair, I did ride him a lot at first, but high school happened. Anyway, I'm fixin' to change that. Wanna join us?"

I swallow. I mean. I absolutely do. I always want to ride. And Mab could use the exercise. I have a trail ride this afternoon, but not for hours, with plenty of time to come back and prepare.

But Case Michaels and me? Alone? And not only alone but also on horseback?

Listen. I have been very comfortable with my horse girl status for at least a decade. I'm familiar with the stereotypes, and I've embraced them. Any real horse girl will tell you trail ride dates are, like, the epitome of romantic.

And while it's perfectly acceptable to offer grace to Case Michaels, I'm not a total idiot.

I shake my head. "I can't," I lie. "I need to finish up here, and then I have chores for Camilla. But have fun." I swear his face falls, as though he's disappointed. But a blink later, it's gone, and I'm not positive I didn't imagine the whole thing.

I take my time finishing what I'm working on, stalling, while surreptitiously tracking Case's progress in saddling his horse. Eventually, I can't stand it anymore. I prop my fork against the door and walk up to him, gently nudging him out of my way.

"Been a while, huh?"

I watch as a flush of color creeps up the back of his neck. I'm not used to seeing him so flustered.

"I mostly remember the steps," he admits, "but if memory serves, Moses won't suffer no fools."

I snort. "You're absolutely right about that." Moses is the kind of horse who likes to "accidentally" stand on your foot until you're begging for mercy.

I finish in short order and make a show of double-checking Moses's setup (for the benefit of his rider) before giving the handsome horse an affectionate nuzzle. I stage-whisper in his long ear, "There's an extra sugar cube for you if you toss him on his ass."

Case chuckles low, his confident swagger slipping back into place. "No offense to Moses, but I think I can hold my seat."

And after seeing him out of his element, I decide I might be hating this cocky side of him a little less.

Ten

WINNIE

That afternoon, I'm scheduled to lead two trail rides. The first, immediately after lunch, is a private ride. A wealthy local family with extended relatives visiting from Mexico.

"Looking to see the best of what Texas has to offer, Winnie, so don't be shy about taking them the long way around."

The "long way around" is Mr. Michaels's way of communicating he wants me to take them down every rocky pass, across every babbling brook, and through several gently waving pastures until they're saddle sore and looking to spend some time relaxing by the giant outdoor firepit with several bottles of our most expensive wine.

"You got it," I agree with a smile. I check my phone to make sure I don't have any messages and slip it in between my boot and my sock before climbing onto Mab's back. With a click of my tongue, we approach the gathered group, already helped into their saddles by Camilla. A quick study reveals there're at least ten of them, but a good portion seem capable enough on horseback. A familiar-looking dark-haired girl around my age is giving her mom—older sister?—a hard time about her posture, but they're laughing and the picture of ease, so I know I won't have to worry about them.

I introduce myself and explain what to expect on our ride today. I offer a short lesson on basic steering and horse handling, but it's not necessary. Our horses could do this trail on autopilot. Because the group is so large and I'm the only one leading, I ask for experienced volunteers to hit up the middle and the back of the pack, then give them a short rundown of our travels today.

And we're off.

We're near the halfway point, closing in on the creek that outlines the farthest borders of the Michaels ranch. I give the cue to slow so everyone can gather near the water's edge and take in the view. This is my favorite spot on the property, and I tell everyone that, letting them know it's a good place to take pictures, before dismounting and offering my assistance. The dark-haired girl who was teasing her mother earlier dismounts beside me. She'd been in the rear because she said she was the most familiar on horseback. And it's clear she hadn't lied. She's a natural.

I give her my most professionally friendly smile, letting her speak first.

"You're a fantastic rider. Is she yours?" she asks, gesturing to Mab.

"Thanks," I say, then shake my head. "She's on loan, but to be honest, I don't think she'd say she belongs to anyone. More of a free agent, if you know what I mean."

"Well, yours or not, you fit well together. I know it's a trail ride, but I can tell."

"Thank you," I say again, more sincerely this time. "I think so, too. She was a rescue and hates pretty much everyone, but we seem to understand each other. I'm training her to barrel race, actually."

The girl's brows raise. "You race?"

"Only in practice. You?" And before the words totally fall from my mouth, it clicks in my brain. "Holy shh-*moly* you're Maria Santos." I smack my head. "I knew you looked familiar. I watched you in the high school nationals last year!"

"I am," she says, seeming pleased to be recognized. "Were you there?"

"Just on TV. I'm a huge fan! Of you and Duchess both. She takes the barrels like a goddamn dream."

"She does. And she's gonna be pissed at me when I get home, smelling like Jose Swervo over there."

I laugh, knowing exactly what she means, but before I can say anything more, we're interrupted by one of Maria's family members asking to have their picture taken. I walk around, taking several and chatting up the guests before I'm climbing in the saddle to head back to the ranch. We take the meandering way, but not so meandering the older folks start grumbling about sore bottoms. I casually wind us back to the firepit, which is already sporting a friendly fire and several Adirondack chairs courtesy of Case. Well played, sir.

I help folks dismount and accept their thanks, while also posing for a few more pictures. Maria jogs up as I'm leading Mab back to the stables and extends a hand, face down. Clearly a tip.

"Oh, that's not—"

"I insist. My uncle Rodrigo is never impressed with American riders, but he won't shut up about you and the trail. Well worth the gratuity. Please."

I take the cash without looking and tuck it away. "Thanks."

"I know you said you don't race, but you also said you train. I could use a partner. Someone to push me and maybe even exercise Duchess whenever I'm on the road. I'd pay you for your time. Not when we're working together, mind you. But, like, whatever work you'd do with Duchess. Please say you're interested. I've had a hell of a time finding someone I trust."

I gape at her for a minute, flustered. "You want to train with me? You don't even know me."

She rolls her eyes. "I've seen plenty."

"You saw a trail ride," I demur with a chuckle. "Anyone can—"

"Okay, fine." Maria cuts me off, her expression exasperated. "Camilla Gutiérrez and my mom are best friends. Since they were kids. She's like my aunt. She's been bragging on you for months now, and so I might've used this trail ride as an excuse to finally check you out and see what all the fuss is about. Now will you say yes?"

I'm still in shock, but before I can overthink it, I nod. "Sure. Okay. But I insist you practice with me a few times first before you even think about hiring me."

Maria holds out her hand again, and I shake it. "You have a deal."

—

Maria and I make plans for her to return on Friday afternoon with Duchess so she can watch Mab and me run the clover in person, and then practice together. I still can't believe all of this, but I'm giddy at the opportunity to even get to know Maria, let alone practice with her.

So it's just as well I'm finally leading Mab into her stall when my phone buzzes, putting the kibosh on all my happy vibes. At first, I ignore it. Everyone who matters should still be at school, after all. But it immediately restarts. I slide the stall door shut and double-check the latch before removing my gloves and pulling my phone out the top of my boot. It's the high school.

I groan and walk out of the stables, past a curious Case, and in the opposite direction of where Maria's family is still congregated around the fire. I make it into the open air of the back pastures before hitting Call Back.

"Hi," I drawl in my most professional tone. "This is Winnie Sutton. Someone tried calling me? I'm at work."

"Hi, Winifred," the secretary says. "So good to hear your voice, darlin'. Hold on just a moment. I'm transferring you over to Principal Butler."

I shift my weight, waiting for the transfer, my brain spinning through all the different scenarios of why the school would be calling me. Even though I graduated last year and have never broke a single rule in my entire life, I gnaw the inside of my lip, worrying maybe it's about me.

But of course it's not about me. It's *never* about me.

"Jesse's been gone since third period, Ms. Sutton. I tried to call your home number, but there was no answer. You're next on the emergency contact. While I have no reason to suspect your brother is in any danger, he's off school property, and this is considered a truancy. And"—he clears his throat—"it's not his first. I'm not sure how much longer we can go before getting the proper authorities involved. I realize things are difficult at home and parental supervision isn't what it should be, but your brother is skipping classes, delinquent on a number of his assignments, and his grades are dropping. Last week, he served detention with Mr. Wright for disrespectful speech."

I swallow a stream of my own disrespectful speech and instead thank him for the information. I end the call with shaking fingers. I crush the phone in my right hand, suppressing the urge to chuck it across the paddock. I can't afford another one right now.

I drop to my haunches, my head in my hand, and whip off my thin knit hat, forking my fingers into my long hair and pulling until I feel the hot sting of tears burning behind my eyelids.

"Fuck!" I mutter under my breath. "Fucking fuck shit fuck fucking fuck." I fall back on the packed dirt and sniff, drawing the back of my hand over my face.

"Bad news?" Case is behind me, and I let my head fall back with a groan.

"No, I'm fine. Just . . . resting."

"That was a lot of *fuck*s for being fine."

I don't say anything, hoping he'll take the hint and leave.

He doesn't. Instead, he drops to the dirt next to me, stretching his legs out.

It's like a switch has been flipped inside of me; my heart starts racing in my chest. "What are you doing?"

"Sitting outside," he returns mildly. "Enjoying the nice day."

I scramble to stand and brush off my jeans, feeling breathless. "Well, I have shit to do."

He springs to his feet. "Okay, well, let me help. What else do you have to do this afternoon?"

I blink at him. "What are you talking about? I can't let you help me. This is my job. Your dad pays me to do this stuff."

"All right, fine," he drawls. His eyes lift to the sky. "I mean, I did help you with mucking stalls, and you didn't seem all that fussed then, but whatever."

"What? I thought your dad made you do that! I thought you were being punished for last night! For being drunk at the rodeo!"

"Wasn't drunk," he corrects with a stiff grin. "Have you forgotten already? Anyway, point being, I already helped, and no one fired you. Now. Why don't you tell me what's got you so upset?"

"Why do you care?"

His eyes widen, and he plants his hands on his hips. "Because you are *clearly* not okay!"

He's not giving up, and something inside me finally snaps. "Okay. Fine. You want to know why I'm upset? You're sure? I'm upset because my brother is apparently ditching school so often, the school is gonna have to call the police. Who will turn up at our door and start asking questions about why my dad's not home and is apparently neglecting his kids. And Jesse's gonna get kicked out of school and will probably run away. And then Garrett, who's barely ten, will be home *alone* after school because fucking Jesse can't be bothered to do one single thing to help me out and *make sure she gets off the bus safely*. Except, fuck!"

Tears spring to my eyes again, and I slump, defeated. "Except she won't be, because I will *of course* be there to pick her up. I'll leave work early and get her. And then I'll lose my job because I'll have to cut back on trail rides. And then who's going to buy Garrett her shitty Walmart shoes? Or put her through robotics camp so she can win scholarships for college? Or buy groceries?"

I'm crying in earnest now. "And the worst of it is, I don't blame Jesse for not wanting to go to school—for wanting to escape the reality that's our lives right now. To see his girlfriend and be a kid or whatever. But *come on*. What about me? When do I get to do those things? When do I get to be a kid? I've literally *never* just been a kid. And now the school is calling me like I'm his mom and I'm supposed to do something, but I have absolutely no idea what they expect me to do about it!"

To his credit, when I raise my eyes to Case's, he looks staggered. It's no wonder. I spewed a near decade of trauma right at his face.

"Okay. Hold on . . ." He rubs his hand down his face, and I swear he mutters something about Walker and lists. "So, Jesse ditched school today?"

"Apparently."

"What time is your trail ride this afternoon?"

"I have another in a half an hour."

"Great. Forty-five-minute ride should have you back here by three thirty. You do that, and I'll be here to relieve you as soon as it's done. I'll brush down the horses, and you can dash home and make sure Garrett is off the bus, okay? No biggie."

I prod for the hole in the plan, but come up empty. "That's— that could work."

"One day at a time, right?"

I exhale. "Yeah. Okay."

"Hey," he says and reaches for me. I think for a minute he's going to tuck my hair behind my ear or something, which would be . . . but he drops his hand. "I'm glad you told me. All of that," he clarifies. "Thank you for trusting me."

"You kind of goaded it out of me. I didn't mean to spill my guts."

"Close enough. As someone who literally spilled his guts recently, I can confirm it's kind of cathartic."

"And also gross."

Case smiles, and it's this fond, faraway thing.

"What?"

He shakes his head. "It's stupid. Toward the end, with Walker, he used to get super sick. The morphine made him vomit, so they had him on antinausea meds, but they made him hungry, and then his stomach would rebel. It was a literal mess. At first, it really bothered him for people to see him so sick. He was always begging his parents and Brody to leave the room. But I would stay overnight. That was my shift because, despite yesterday, I usually have an iron stomach. Walker could let it fly in front of me, and I didn't care. I used to tease him that he was saving his puking for my shifts. He would say, 'Brothers who ride together, puke together.'" Case shakes himself. "I told you it was dumb. It doesn't even make sense, but—"

"But it does. You were the one person he could be vulnerable around, because you didn't flinch when he was at his lowest."

Case's blue eyes pin me, something new in his gaze. "Exactly. Yeah. So anyway, even if you were *coerced*," he teases, "I'm glad you told me."

I press my lips together, thoughtful, before I slowly nod. "Thanks, I guess, for not flinching. I can see why Walker kept you around."

Eleven

CASE

Case Jr. finds me brushing down the horses after their trail ride. I can feel his eyes on me from the doorway, but he doesn't bother announcing himself, so I don't stop what I'm doing. I don't want to forget anything and give Winnie a reason to hand me my ass tomorrow. I told her I would take care of this for her, and I don't want to let her down.

Of the two, I'm more afraid of Winnie. I've got eighteen years of practice in disappointing my dad.

I finish with a steady dappled gray named Elvis, checking to make sure his oats and water are filled before I lead him into his stall with a click of my tongue. It's been years, and I mean *years*, since I've spent so much time in the stables and with the horses, but I've enjoyed it. It's peaceful. I can see why Winnie likes it so much, even if it *is* technically work.

I latch the door and turn to face my dad with a sigh. His expression is hard to read, and I shift my weight, feeling awkward.

"Hey."

"I didn't think you knew what this place was."

I refuse to shrink back. The thing about Case Jr. is he has little time or patience for shrinking. Or wincing. Or pain. Or grief. Or any emotions outside of good-old-boy smart-assery and deflection. Which technically aren't even emotions, but they're as close to the line as we Michaels men are meant to tread.

For example, after Walker died, we're talking the very next day, my dad came into my room, handed me a glass of scotch from his "special" cabinet, and said, "He wouldn't want to see you moping. Have a drink and wash that depressed look off your face."

I get we're not huggers or anything, but a simple "I'm sorry" wouldn't have killed him.

I scoop the saddle blanket from where I've slung it over a door. "I figured it was about time I whipped old Moses into shape."

"You're riding Moses?"

"This morning I did. I'm a little saddle sore, if I'm honest. He did not go easy on me."

At my wry tone, my dad cracks a grin. It changes his entire face, that small slip of humanity. "You thinking about riding the range?"

I barely keep from rolling my eyes, leaning back against Elvis's stall. Of course he leaps straight to that. Give the man an inch . . . "No thanks. I'll stick to the stables."

He raises a brow under his Stetson, crossing his arms. I doubt he even realizes he's doing it. "I didn't know you were looking for a job, Case."

"Do I need to be an employee to muck out stalls?"

He gives a frustrated grunt. "What are you about? You're climbing corn silos and defaulting on your rides."

Ah. Shit. I'd wondered if he'd heard.

"Is this about Walker?" he asks, dismissive. "Is that why

you're moping around the stables and messing with your future? Listen, kid. It's normal to get drunk and make dumb decisions at your age. Hell, your uncle and I got into all sorts of stupid shit when we were eighteen. So if that's what this is, fine. But I won't stand by and let you throw your career away. You're fucking around in the stables when you should be training."

"I know. I'm still training. I'm always training. It's not like I've forgotten. But it's barely been six months. I'm not okay. I'm . . ." I swallow. "I'm pretty messed up, honestly. He was like a brother. I loved him."

Tension paints my dad's face, and he's clearly struggling with whatever is about to come out of his mouth next. "Are you gay? Were you in love with him? Is that—are you—"

I bite back a snort. *Of course.* I shove off the stall. "No, Dad. You realize it's possible to love someone and not be in love with them, right?"

"So you're sad? All of this"—my dad waves his hand around—"and disqualifying last night. It's because you're still crying over your friend."

I blink, dry-eyed and sober and straight. "All of this"—I mirror his wave—"is because I realize just because my best friend died, doesn't mean I have to. I'm sorry it doesn't look the way you think it should, but it's all I got."

"I'm not paying two people to work in the stables."

Now I do roll my eyes. "In all fairness, you should pay Winnie Sutton more. She goes above and beyond. But that's whatever. I'm not looking for pay."

I can tell my dad wants to argue, but he can't find anything wrong with what I've said. I'm working. For free. I'm training for the career he wants for me.

I'm suddenly struck with an idea.

"Speaking of Winnie Sutton, have you seen her ride?"

He nods. "She's our highest requested trail ride leader. An absolute natural in the saddle."

"Not like that. Have you seen her barrel race?"

He perks up. Nothing gets to my dad like rodeo talk. "I didn't know she raced."

"That's because she doesn't. Not technically. She doesn't own a horse or anything. I don't even think she's ever taken lessons. Like you said, she's a natural." My idea is gathering steam, and I plow ahead. "But Camilla has her working out Queen Mab every Friday afternoon, and I've never seen anything like it. Her times are insane. Like she could easily go from our arena to the main event and walk away with top prize."

"What's she doing here, then?"

"Right?" I say enthusiastically because rodeo talk happens to get me going, too. It's maybe the only thing Junior and I have in common. "I asked the same thing. Apparently, no horse, no saddle, no entry fees . . . I'm not sure, but she's practically raising her two siblings. I think money is super tight."

"If that's why you were saying she needs a raise, Case, I'm sorry, but I can't give her higher wages because she has it tough at home. I have other employees, and we pay fair wages."

I scoff. "First of all, you could. You're the boss; you can do whatever the hell you want. But that's not what I was thinking. What if you sponsored her, through the ranch? It'd be great marketing, wouldn't it?"

My dad looks doubtful. "That's a massive investment."

"Dad. Just come and see her one Friday. Talk to Camilla. If you don't think she's got it, fine, but I promise she and Mab'll blow your mind. I've never seen anything like it in all my years at rodeos."

Case Jr. rubs his lips with his hand, in that way he does when he's thinking. "I'll see if John can meet with the distributors this week or next, and I'll come by. But no guarantees. I'm not looking to throw money at some girl because you've taken a shine to her."

My breath catches in my throat, and I will the heat away from my face. "That's not . . . I wasn't . . ."

My dad points at my face, victorious. "That. That look. That's what you've been missing." He turns on his heel. "I need to get back in my office for a phone call. I'll see what I can do about Friday."

With that, he's gone. I'm still standing there five minutes later when Elvis nudges the back of my head, knocking off my hat and dropping it to the concrete floor.

"What do you want?" I ask under my breath, turning and petting his nose. Mab nickers from the stall next to us and demands her own pets.

"Yeah, yeah," I tell her, reaching for her soft nose. "I know. She'd be pissed if she knew. This stays between you and me for now, all right? I'll worry about my part, and you worry about yours."

—

The next time I see Pax, we decide to skip the party scene. It's still pretty weird and stilted between us, but I can't spend the rest of my life hanging out with Walker's ghost. And I'm pretty sure Winnie would laugh in my face if I invited her to do anything outside of work. That's twice now I've tried to get her to go on a ride with me, and she's turned me down. If I go for a third, I'm gonna have to hire her for a trail ride.

Besides, I like Pax. He's impossible not to like. When he showed up the afternoon of my birthday, two 12-gauge shotguns looped under his arm, and pointed toward the sky, I grabbed my old work boots and the keys to a pair of matching four-wheelers.

I haven't hunted for small game in years. I'm doubtful I could manage to hit the broad side of a barn at this point, but we've never really hunted to shoot anything, anyway. It's always been about the experience: the excuse to mud up our tires and walk in the woods. Best of all, this is something I never did with Walker. He couldn't get into it. It was too slow, too quiet, and there was no way he'd ever be able to aim at something as cute as a rabbit.

Which is good. I need a fucking break from feeling things. Between the list and puking my guts out at the rodeo and my dad giving me shit for not drinking it off like a real man and Winnie's family stuff that isn't really my problem but also somehow is . . . I think I might be losing it.

I'm also nineteen today. Walker died a week shy of his eighteenth birthday, and now I'm two years past that. And I'll keep getting older. Every year, I'll pull a little further from him, and it's fucking with my head.

So this, today, is untainted territory. I'm not looking for his ghost, and I know with complete and utter certainty he's not going to show up. Which is better than I thought things would go on my first birthday without Walker around.

We drive the four-wheelers out to the back wooded acres and park near the edge of the trees. I toss Pax an orange vest and slip on my own, despite the fact no one else is around. People have been shot for dumber reasons.

It's blustery for April, but not cold. The air is dry, and the sky is cloudless. I suck in a lungful of breath and hold it before letting it out slowly, my head feeling clearer. Pax and I start loudly stomping over dried leaves and packed earth.

Have I mentioned we're not any good at hunting?

"How's Madi?" I ask after a few minutes.

Pax scrunches the side of his face and shrugs one shoulder. "Hell if I know. Probably fine? I guess? She got mad because she found out I was hanging out with Lexie Aldean while she was up at Oklahoma State visiting her friends for a girls' weekend."

I don't know where to begin with that statement.

"Were you *just* hanging out?"

Pax fiddles with the brim of his hat, shifting his shotgun and checking the safety again. "Mostly."

I snort. "That means no."

"It's not like Madi was sitting in the dorms alone, pining after me."

"Fair point."

"Anyway, whatever, man. I'm getting tired of this back-and-forth shit."

"It has been years," I concede.

"Two. But I love her."

My eyes bug out, and I choke on air. "You do?"

"Probably."

"What the fuck are you doing, then?"

Pax smirks, meeting my gaze. "No clue."

I bark out a laugh, and it echoes extra loud in the woods. Birds take flight above us, startled.

"What about you?" he asks. "Any women aggravating the hell out of you?"

"Too early to say," I admit. "Hopefully a friend, right now. But she's prickly."

"Pretty?"

"Very. Remember Winnie Sutton?"

"That smart chick who graduated early?"

I tamp down my sigh. I'm getting used to the idea literally

everyone else knew Winnie in high school and I was a blind fool. "I guess so. I didn't know her well in school. I think her little brother's dating your sister, though."

"Jesse. That's right. I hadn't made the connection. Walker was friends with her, too, I think."

I whip my head around. "He was?"

His eyes dance with amusement. "Yeah, I remember them talking at lunch sometimes."

"Huh." I'm quiet for a bit, mulling over what Pax has revealed. Why would Walker add *Befriend Winnie Sutton* to the list if he was already friends with her?

Walker, you meddling fucker.

"I'm sorry about Walker," Pax says suddenly. "I don't think I ever said that. But I meant to. We all were sorry about him."

I nod. And for today, for right now, I don't feel angry about Walker's passing. Just sad. That's progress, right? "Thanks."

We continue on in silence for a long while, but it's not so awkward anymore. It's normal. We don't see any cute rabbits, we never take off the safeties on our guns, and we never bring up Walker again, but that's okay. More than, actually.

Instead, we hop on the four-wheelers and rip off to the farthest fields, tearing them up and letting loose. And I make it one more day.

Twelve

CASE

I finish my workout with Brody early the next morning, just as the sun is fully coming up. Instead of heading inside to shower off, I make my way to the fence, climbing up on the bottom rung and slinging a leg over to sit on the top.

"Hello, Charles," I drawl, taking in the nearly two-thousand-pound longhorn bull that belongs to my father. He's a killer. Absolutely. His horns span at least six feet across and curl up to sharp points. These days, Charles is more of a show bull than anything else. My dad studs him out and moves him with the herd, so he's rarely this close to the barn and the tourists, but he's on rotation this week.

And so, as with every morning, I've sat out here and watched him. Walker's list said *Conquer a bull OUTSIDE the arena*, and I know Charles is the bull he meant. He always wanted to fuck around and try to get on the old crank's back, but I wouldn't let him. Told him he didn't have a death wish. And I don't either, but after defaulting on the ride the other night, I feel like I owe him this one. It's not a buckle, but it's *something*.

I just haven't figured out how to make it happen without dying.

Even if I didn't have Ghost Walker and his list of bullshit tasks pushing me to be a better human (that's the result, whether he planned it or not), Winnie Sutton's dirty looks would be motivation. Is this why he wanted me to be friends with her? Because he knew she would make me feel useless and lazy by comparison? Did he know how fucked up her home situation was all along? That the more I got to know her, the more I'd feel like a waste of time?

(Unrelated: I asked a confused Kerry to teach me how to do laundry, and I've only turned half of my clothes light blue, so I guess it's going fine.)

I don't think that was it. Walker was loyal. He always saw the best of me. It's more likely he knew *she* needed a friend, too. I lost my best friend, but she doesn't have one either.

Unless you count Mab. Which, I guess after seeing them together, I do. By my calculations, I only have to be more useful than a horse and I'm *in*, which is not as easy as one might presume.

The only problem with this arrangement is the small matter of my attraction to her. Because let's face it, Winnie Sutton is beautiful. Toned legs for days, soft hair falling to the middle of her slender back, freckles painted across her cheekbones. Dark, arresting eyes and a sexy smile. Obviously, she's not interested in me in the slightest. She doesn't have the time to be interested, and even if she did, I doubt I'm her type: useless, more money than I need, spends my free time arguing with the ghost of my dead best friend.

So that's not a thing. *We're* not a thing. Which is freeing, because it allows me to concentrate on being a good friend to her.

Or, at least, to convince her to be my friend. Or to convince her to *want* a friend in the first place, useless as I may seem. But if I'm ever presented with the option of being a friend who also gets to kiss her, I absolutely volunteer.

I'd even throw away my pigheaded one-time-only rule for her.

(Okay, okay, fine, I'll throw it away, anyway.)

Winnie Sutton makes me want to be better. Not to deserve her or anything so angsty as that. Just, I want to be okay again. Whole. Productive.

For now, I'd settle for not actively wasting away.

I've been getting up even earlier every morning and meeting Brody in the barn at 6:00 a.m. for training. This serves a two-fold purpose: 1) It gives Brody time to train *with* me, side by side, before he has to go home to clean up for work. 2) It allows me to get my training out of the way earlier so I can help Winnie in the stables.

Even if, as my dad pointed out, it's not my job and I'm not getting paid. Well, not any more than my already generous monthly allowance, anyway. I'm not telling Winnie that, though. I don't want her to get the wrong idea and assume I'm doing this to be closer to her.

Because that's only some of the truth, and I also don't want to give my dad any reason to think I'm suddenly interested in ranching after all this time.

I'm well aware that to Junior, a future in the PBR would make it okay for me to not ranch. Gold buckles and riding bulls and drinking my grief away and rubbing some dirt on it . . . those are all acceptable. Those are *being a man*. If I won't run livestock because I'm too busy making a name for myself mastering the circuit?

Well, fuck yeah, that's the cowboy way.

I raise my protein shake to my lips, finishing it in one long gulp and grimacing at the chalky dregs at the bottom of the bottle. Charles's tail flicks irritably, knowing I'm watching him again. I run the scenario in my head: waiting for him to come close to the fence, maybe even luring him over with some fresh grass, and then at the last second, jumping the top rung and launching myself onto his back. I'd need a rope. Something to loop around his neck, in a tight slipknot, and use it to hold on.

The thought makes my stomach compress and my palms sweat, adrenaline coursing through my veins at the mere thought. The timing would have to be perfect. The coast clear. My hands steady.

Not today, then. I head to the house and get in the shower. Tomorrow, I'll try again.

—

After my shower and a quick breakfast of eggs and bacon, I spot a dust cloud coming down the long drive through the window. Winnie's here. I rinse my glass out in the sink and press a kiss to Kerry's cheek. "I'm off to the stables. Thanks for breakfast."

Kerry huffs. "Hold your horses. I made you something."

"You did?"

"I made it for you to share with Winnie. It's cold out there this morning."

I raise my eyebrows, my expression bland. "Yeah, I know. I was out there for two hours already."

She waves me off, reaching into the pantry and passing me a delicious-smelling basket. I have no idea where it came from. It's like one of those picnic baskets Dorothy carried in *The Wizard of Oz*. The kind with the flaps that open and shut on top? There's no way Case Jr. had one of those lying around. "Lemon poppy seed. Winnie's favorite."

I blink. "How'd you know?"

She clicks her tongue. "The girl's worked here for two years, Case. You're the only one who seems to have missed it."

Seriously.

I take the basket and rush out the door, crossing to where Winnie's parked. I'm surprised to see doors on both sides of the car open and also Garrett's happy wave as she steps out from the passenger side. Something about her immediate acceptance of me, even after I let her down at the rodeo, gives me a sharp pang in the center of my chest.

"Hi, Case!"

"Hey, it's Little Sutton! Skipping school?"

Winnie gives a frustrated grunt as she slams her door behind her with her hip. "Apparently, it's a teachers' planning day."

Another one? I turn to Garrett. "So they plan, and you get to come hang out with us?"

"Something like that," Winnie mutters, even though I wasn't asking her. Before I can respond, offer a muffin, or anything, she's already storming off to the stables.

"Jesse never came home last night." Garrett lags behind to update me. "So Winnie drew the short straw."

Her honesty throws me, and it takes me a beat to recover. "First of all, I think you meant to say Winnie *drew the golden ticket*. You did, too, for that matter, becauuuuuuse"—I raise the basket between us and nod toward the stable—"Miss Kerry has baked us some of her special lemon poppy seed muffins!"

"Ohhh," Garrett says. Her tone is soft and wistful, and I warm at the expression on her young face. *Well played, Kerry.* "Winnie and I both love lemon poppy seed."

"Then it's fate. You're meant to be here to help me eat all of these today."

We make our way to the stables, and I lift a flap followed by a plaid kitchen towel, holding the basket under Winnie's nose. The magical pull of sugary sweetness softens her expression immediately.

"Are those lemon poppy seed?"

"See? The day's already looking up."

She grabs a muffin, immediately diving in. "I forgot breakfast," she admits.

"Take two, then. Three. However many you need. There's more than enough here. It's like Kerry woke up and decided to bake for an entire football team."

Garrett giggles, reaching for her own and taking a giant bite. I know, these girls aren't starving. They have food at home. But I'm also aware Winnie skips meals when she's busy—and she's busy all the time—and no one is making sure she is taking care of herself. Ergo, I feel like I should take care of her.

(With baked goods my housekeeper made, because I'm a douchecanoe, but still.)

(Note to self: Buy something nice for Kerry and convince her to make more muffins.) (*Or* better yet, maybe ask her to teach me how to make muffins so I am less of a douchecanoe.)

I swear I can feel the rush of air against my face as Ghost Walker gestures wildly at me as if he's saying, *See? Growth!*

We fill up on the muffins, and Winnie passes the empty basket to her sister. "Hey, Garre, take this back to Miss Kerry at the big house and make sure you say thank-you for the treat. Let her know how delicious it was."

"You got it," Garrett says, rushing off, long dark braids streaming behind her.

Winnie turns to me, but before she can open her mouth, I say, "Whatever you're going to freak out about, don't."

She wilts. "I'm going to lose my job. I can't bring my little sister to work with me! I can't babysit while I'm supposed to be taking care of the horses, *and* I have a trail ride this afternoon. It's a private tour with another rich family who will not be cool with my little sister tagging along and chirping facts about quantum physics."

I clamp down on my smile. "You're not going to lose your job."

"This is twice now I've had to bring my sister with me. It's so unprofessional!"

"Yeah," I say dryly, "because this place is the height of professionalism. You're not going to lose your job," I repeat. "You aren't going to babysit while you work, and you aren't going to take her with you on the trail ride even though I sort of wonder if Mr. Schneider would be into a discussion about quantum physics. Doesn't matter." I wave her off. "Garrett would hate it."

Winnie's eyes bug out and her nostrils flare, and I probably shouldn't find it attractive, but I do. A little scary, sure, but attractive nevertheless. I cut her off before flames start pouring out of her eyeballs.

"As much as I would love to see that temper of yours explode, hold on. I'm not dismissing your worries. I'm trying to tell you I volunteer as babysitter. Though . . ." I pause and consider, scratching at my early-morning scruff. "Is *babysitter* the correct term? For a genius ten-year-old? She could probably teach me a few things. Tutor me in trigonometry. Improve my riding form. Build a working wind turbine out of Popsicle sticks."

Winnie blinks. "You want to watch her?"

"Sure."

"You?"

"Yeah. Me."

She narrows her gaze. "Do you even know anything about kids?"

"What's to know? I have nineteen years of life experience."

"I can't."

I place my hand on her shoulder, ignoring the way my skin heats at the connection. "You don't have a ton of options here. We'll be fine. It's like two hours. We won't even leave the ranch."

She releases a long breath. Then does it again. Hell, she's really having to convince herself, which is doing wonders for my self-esteem. "Okay," she concedes.

"Great."

She tips her head to the side, considering me. "Why are you doing this?"

I shrug, lifting my hand off her shoulder. "What else have I got to do?" She presses her lips together. I sigh. "Look, it's fine. I want to help. I literally have all day open and owe Garrett after turning out at the rodeo."

"True . . ."

I try a new tactic. "It's okay to accept help. The world won't fall apart if you're not holding it."

"It feels like taking advantage."

"Okay, fine. You're right. I won't ask her to tutor me. She's too young, and it's her day off."

Winnie cracks the tiniest of smiles, and my chest might explode at the victory. "Are you sure about this?"

My heart is thudding. It feels like I've been given a gift, and the last thing I want to do is mess this up, but also, I'm me, so I say, "Absolutely. Now how does that rhyme go? 'Beer after liquor, never been sicker'?"

"Case." Her eyes are smiling, though. Her entire face is one giant relieved grin.

I did that.

"Just kidding. We'll stick to energy drinks."

"Case." Her tone is soft, and I can hear the front door slam in the distance, signaling Garrett's return.

I match her tone. "Winifred."

"Thank you."

This time, I smile. I've been a bit out of practice with smiling, but she brings them out of me like breaths. "You're welcome."

—

Winnie's on a trail ride when it all goes to shit later that morning. Garrett was outside the barn while I was brushing down Elvis and Jose. She had been sitting on the bench, doing her homework. Or maybe it wasn't homework. Maybe it was extra credit. Whatever it was, the weather was gorgeous, so she asked if she could sit in the sunshine, and I listened to her humming, enjoying the quiet, when all of a sudden, a loud screech fills the air and rips through my heart.

I drop my brush with a clunk and sprint toward the noise.

"Garrett?"

"*Case!*" She is full on screaming now, and I skid to a stop, taking in the scene in front of me. Garrett has climbed into the pen in front of the barn. The one with Charles. She's pinned against the fence, but on the inside. Charles is standing, chest puffed and nostrils flaring, eyes locked on her tiny form.

I don't even stop to think. I launch myself over the top of the fence in front of her and whip my bright T-shirt off, wildly waving it over my head like a fucking matador. "Hey, Charles.

Here, Charles!" I fling the tee. "Fetch, Charles!" He doesn't take the bait.

"Oh my god, Garrett!" Winnie's terrified voice rings out. She's back from her trail ride.

I yell, "Grab her through the fence, Win! Get her out of here!"

As soon as I feel Garrett pulled from behind me, I dart to the side, taking Charles's attention with me. He's huffing while his hooves paw at the dusty earth, and my heart pounds clear out of my chest. He plows forward and ducks his head, but I dodge out of the way, my reflexes clearing his horns. We line up, and he charges again, this time bucking a little. I need to get out of the pen, but I suspect he'll get under me if it takes me too long to climb the fence.

Winnie stands on the gate, waving her arms wildly. "This way, Case. On three!"

I rush at her, counting in my head. One, he's just behind me. Two, I can hear the rumble in his chest vibrate down to my bones. Three, his hot breath is on the back of my fucking neck. The gate swings open, and I dive through, somersaulting out of the way as Winnie shoves it closed with a mighty clang.

Charles is vicious, but he's not stupid. He pulls up short with a powerful snort, and by the time I'm surging to my feet, he's already turned away as if he wasn't just about to murder me. I slump back down to the ground, my blood thrumming and my head spinning. I shut my eyes and let out an involuntary groan.

"Holy fuck, are you okay?"

I whimper, my eyes still closed. After a beat, I say weakly, "Pretty sure."

"Garrett, what on earth? Why were you in there?"

I hear Garrett's sniff from somewhere in the vicinity of my head. "The wind. It blew my chart into the pen. I thought I could quick-jump in there and grab it and come right back out, but then I saw the bull and freaked out! Oh my god, are you okay, Case? Win, is he okay?"

"Case is okay," I mutter, even though it's debatable. But hell, I don't want Garrett to feel bad.

"Garre, I need you to go ask Kerry for a glass of cold water, okay? Tell the truth, but make sure she knows Case isn't hurt."

"Okay."

After a beat, I open one eye. "Is she gone?" I whisper.

Winnie's face above me breaks into a droll smile. "You have at least five minutes until they all come running."

With a grunt, I prop myself up on my elbows and wiggle my limbs to check for breaks, but everything seems to be functioning.

"Are you okay?" Winnie's question is soft. Softer than anything else I've ever heard from her before.

"Surprisingly, yeah. I think I am. I can't believe I did that. I've been staring down that fucking bull for fucking days, and without even thinking, I launched myself inside the pen."

"Thank you. I don't . . . I don't know what else to say. Just thank you. She could have been killed. *You* could have been killed. You almost were! I can't . . ." Her eyes take on a sheen. "Oh my gosh, look at my hands." She holds up trembling fingers. "I think it's starting to hit me now."

I drop back to the ground with a thud. "I'm just gonna rest a second. Catch my breath. Tell me when they get close?"

My eyes are closed, but I can feel the ghost of a brush of fingers across my forehead, cool and calming.

A few minutes pass before she quietly drawls above me. "They're comin'."

I sit up again, this time pulling my knees closer to my chest, draping my forearms across, attempting to look casual and not like I ache in places I don't remember the names of.

Winnie snorts. "Yeah. They'll never guess."

"Does this mean I'm fired from babysitting duty?" I ask out of the side of my mouth.

"Hell. It takes more than almost being gored by a psychotic bull to scare us Sutton girls."

I cringe at her forced lightness. I know I messed up. Royally. "I'm sorry. I swear I was watching her. She was outside the barn on the bench the entire time, and I—"

Winnie interrupts with a gentle hand to my arm. She pulls my focus toward her, and my eyes lock on hers. "Case. Stop running the analytics. Kids are unpredictable. You can never watch them closely enough. You could carry Garrett in your shirt pocket, and she'd still find a way to get hung up in the buttons."

"I told you to trust me, and I let her wander into a bull enclosure. You'll never let anyone help again!"

"Please," Winnie says lightly. "You're practically a superhero in her eyes at this point. I think you're stuck with her."

I look away from her, feeling better. "What about you? Am I a superhero in your eyes?"

She knocks my shoulder. "Super? Eh. Hero? Fuck yeah. I think you might be. But," she says under her breath, right as her sister and Kerry rush over to us, arms full of supplies. "You tell anyone I said that, and I'll have to kill you."

A little while later, after Winnie and Garrett leave for the day and Kerry finally lets me out of her sight after feeding me and monitoring me for a concussion (even though I definitely did not hit my head), I enter my room and head for my desk. I pull out Walker's list and a black permanent marker, and when I come to the words *Conquer a bull OUTSIDE the arena*, I draw a fat line right through it.

Fucking conquered.

Thirteen

WINNIE

I t's been two whole days since Case saved my little sister, and she still hasn't stopped talking about it, or rather *him*, every chance she gets. Understandably so, of course. When I think of the way he flung himself in front of her . . . Jesus. I may never sleep again.

That said, hero he may be, he's still the same self-absorbed dummy he was last week, even if I am feeling a tiny bit softer toward him. Garrett might be a certifiable genius, but she's still ten and not exactly subtle. I've already been subjected to "seventy-five things Case said that were super hilarious," and we've only been home an hour. Unfortunately, I've got bigger fish to fry than my little sister's crush.

I get paid tomorrow, so I've decided to take my siblings out to the taco truck for dinner. It's mostly a treat for me, if I'm honest. A girl cannot live on chicken nuggets alone. Jesse texted he'd be here soon, so I'm Garrett's captive audience.

What he doesn't know is I've gotten yet another call from

Principal Butler about him skipping class. Final, *final* warning and all that. The "we really mean business this time" kind. I've been thinking of ways to bring it up all day, and the best I've come up with is *taco truck*.

I tried to talk to my dad about it early this morning when he got off work, but he seems to think it's not a big deal. Or rather, it's not a big deal for *him*.

"Let him get his GED, Winnie. I can't force him to go to school. What do you want me to do?"

"How about ground him? Take away his phone? Return the calls from the school? Anything!"

"And how do you expect me to enforce any of that? We all know I can't follow up on anything with my work schedule."

"Dad, you've been working the third shift for over ten years. You have to have some seniority there. Can't you apply for a daytime shift?"

His eyes turned steely. "I like the night shift, Win."

That's what it always comes down to in the end. My dad likes the night shift. I'm sure a small part is he's been a night owl for decades, but it's more likely he doesn't remember how to be a parent, and third shift allows him to avoid it. By default of his paychecks, he puts food on the table and keeps the lights on, and that's enough to soothe his conscience. That and the extra layer of avoidance on the weekends when he pisses away the rest of his time and money at the VFW with his buddies. To be honest, it *was* fine for a while. I was handling things—until now. Now it's not fine. Now I need him to step up and be a parent, but it seems like he saw my early graduation as an end date for him. An "Oh, good. Winnie can take care of everything now."

And I just . . . always have.

I have no disillusions about my parents. My mom had big plans for her life, and kids were never in the picture. Why she kept having them is a mystery, but it came to a head when she was pregnant with Garrett. At least she waited until Garrett was born before she left. She's never even sent a postcard, like they do in the movies. She could live the next town over for all I know. It used to upset me, but I haven't had a whole lot of time to dwell on it, and why should I? She chose to leave us. Good riddance. Fuck off.

My dad is another issue altogether. He's absent for sure, but he doesn't resent us the way she did. He just doesn't have a clue what to do with three kids and hasn't ever cared enough to figure it out. Every now and again, we'll have a Sunday afternoon together and he'll be affectionate and fun and present, and for that brief period of time, we feel like a normal family. It's almost worse because you see the potential of what could be—what our family might've looked like if she'd stuck around or if he'd tried. I sort of hate those days. They fuck with my head, and more than that, they fuck with Jesse and Garrett. Every time, it takes longer and longer to recover from the tease.

I know what people think about us: *Those poor Sutton kids.* I can hear it in their hushed voices in the school office, or in the principal's tone when he calls to warn me about Jesse. I can see it in Camilla's gaze when she recognizes Garrett hanging around the stables. Even in Case's expression when I lost my shit over Walmart shoes.

They aren't wrong. It's not easy being us. But it's also the way it's always been. Do I realize not everyone lives this way? Yes. Do I wish it were different? Fuck yes. But wishing doesn't do anything. I can't force my dad to get his shit together. I can't drag my mom back here and make her care about us.

All I can do is my best: *I* have my shit together. *I'm* here. *I* care about us.

I've been doing some research, and there *is* something I could do that would allow me to have more of a say when it comes to Jesse's bullshit. But with that comes more responsibility, and I'm not completely sure I want it. It's a commitment.

But also, it's not like I'm going to leave them, anyway, so . . .

There're lights in the drive, and I see Jesse get out of a car I don't recognize. I do recognize the driver, though. It's a kid named Pax, who was in my year in school. According to Case, Jesse is dating his little sister, Chelsea. Pax opens his car door and stands, waving in a familiar, friendly kind of way. I swing open the front door, letting Jesse in.

"Hey, Winnie Sutton, long time no see!" Pax shouts from the drive.

"Hi, Pax. Thanks for driving Jesse home."

He gives me an easy smile and says, "No problem. You guys have a great night!" before turning to duck back in his car.

I turn to Jesse, closing the door behind me. "I didn't know you needed a ride. I could have picked you up."

"I didn't," he says, sullen as, well, he *always is* these days. "Pax offered to drive."

I change tack. "Any homework? I thought we'd go out for tacos tonight. Garrett is starving."

He brightens. "I'm hungry, too."

"Great," I say. "Then we can go whenever your homework is done."

He waves me off. "I'm ready now."

I press my lips together to keep from arguing with him. I don't want to start a fight before dinner. The plan is that a full stomach of tacos will soften him up, and then I can ask him about school *after*. I decide to drop the homework for now. It's not as though one day is going to make or break things at this point.

An hour later, we're huddled at a pastel-painted picnic table in Amarillo, a dozen tacos spread out in front of us. Barbacoa for me, chipotle chicken for Garrett, and grilled mahi-mahi for Jesse. I crack open a green soda and make a face at the sweet, fizzy taste bubbling up on my tongue before sipping again. I don't much care for the drink, but when in the Southwest and all that. Garrett loves them.

We devour our food while Garrett talks our ears off with more funny wisdom à la Case Michaels, and Jesse, for once, doesn't put her off. He asks her questions and even informs us Pax and Case are pretty good friends. He tells us a story of how he saw Case jump in a pool naked at a party a few weeks back that makes me choke on a fried tortilla chip and sends Garrett into a fit of giggles. Bless. I wonder if that was the morning I ran into him and we fought in the parking lot.

That feels like a year ago. Or at least several flip-flopped changes of opinions ago.

I decide to bring up school when all that remains of our dinner are empty wrappers and everyone is in high spirits.

"Hey, Jesse, I got a phone call from school today. Second one this week."

Jesse rolls his eyes. "What, they want to put up a plaque in the cafeteria in your honor or something?"

"Yeah, no, definitely not," I say humorlessly. "They said you're about to be expelled for truancy. And they will have to report our family to the police."

He pales so much I can see his baby freckles, the ones I thought disappeared years ago. "What? Why would they do that?"

"I don't know, maybe because it's illegal to miss school so much?"

He scowls. "Let me quit, then. I'll get my GED."

"My dude. You're only fourteen. That's not an option."

"Then tell them I'm homeschooling."

"That only works if you're *actually* doing school at home. With a parent or guardian to supervise your progress. You barely live at home these days, so that's not happening. What's your deal, anyway? It's not as if you aren't smart. You've always done super well in school."

"I don't care. I'm not interested in college, not that we could afford it, anyway. Maybe I want to get a job."

I raise a brow. "Really," I drawl cynically. "A job."

He shrugs, peeling the greasy wax paper in front of him. Uh-huh. That's what I thought.

"Look. As much as I would *love* for someone else in this household to get a job and help out, you're too young to be working. You need to stay in school. We can't afford truancy fines, and to be frank, we can't risk an inquiry from CPS."

I watch the little color remaining in my younger brother's face leach away. Garrett audibly swallows next to me, reaching for my hand with her small, slightly sticky one.

"I'm gonna level with you here. You're playing with fire, and we don't have a single pail of water to our names. I get it. I do. You're tired of things being how they are. Sick of struggling. I swear, I know. But if you give up on me, on *us*," I correct, squeezing Garrett's little fingers gently, "I don't think I can fix it. We don't have parents around. Legally, that's very bad."

"You take care of us," he says in a low voice. "We don't need parents."

I swallow hard at the childlike assurance in his changed voice and try not to smother under the guilt of yesterday and Garrett's dance with a longhorn. "And I always will. I promise. But I'm not your guardian. I don't have a say in what happens."

"What if you were?" Garrett asks softly. "Why can't you be our mom?"

Jesse narrows his eyes. "Because she's not our real mom."

"Obviously," Garrett says, glaring at him. "But she's the only mom I've ever known. And Winnie already takes care of us."

I sigh, raising my hand between them. This is the part I researched. What I've been researching ever since I talked to my dad and he refused to help.

"Technically, I could file to be both of your guardians. I'm nineteen. Dad would have to give up his rights, though."

Garrett brightens, but Jesse frowns. "No way, Win. You can't do that. Like you said, you're nineteen. You can't take responsibility for us. You have your own life."

I squeeze my sister's hand reassuringly but look at my brother. "You're right. I do." *Kinda.* "And I didn't want to be a parent before I even got to be a kid. But that ship has sailed. A long time ago. I won't leave you guys. So here is the way I see it: either you get your ass in gear and back into school until you're at least sixteen, when you can and will get your GED, or I'm going to file for guardianship. Because I can be your big sister, or I can be your parent, but I can't be both."

"You're insane," Jesse says, shaking his head.

"No. I care, dummy. So please, please, *please* go to school. That's all I'm asking. That's your job right now. The three of us have to stick together and help each other out. No one else is going to look out for us, so we have to do it. If you don't care enough to go to school for you, do it for the sheer fact if CPS comes, I can't guarantee Dad will fight for us. Which means *I* will have to."

And that means my dreams are put on hold for another eight years. At least.

I'd do it. But I'd rather not have to.

—

It's the rare moment I'm off the clock and don't have anywhere to be for another hour—and the sun is shining. I'm tucked behind the stables on an old workbench, sprawled on my back, boots swinging and hat tilted over my eyes when a shadow falls over me.

"Case said you might be hiding back here."

My lips spread in a smile beneath my straw hat. Maria.

"Hey, girl. You're blocking my vitamin D."

"Scooch over, then, and share the wealth."

I squirm to one side, and she settles in next to me. I slowly ease to face her, the warm sun making my movements lazy. "Were we supposed to meet today?"

She blocks the sun with one hand, squinting. "Nah. I knew today was a Garrett day. I was in the neighborhood and was hoping a certain sandy haired friend of Case's might be loitering around the ranch."

"Pax?" I ask, surprised. "I think he has a girlfriend. Ish," I correct after a beat.

Maria shrugs a shoulder as if "girlfriend" is an insignificant detail. Which, the more I get to know the rodeo queen, it probably is.

I snort, tipping my hat down again. "Hell. I'd give my whole car for an ounce of your swagger."

Maria throws back her head in an elegant laugh. "Your car is a piece of shit, no offense. You'll have to do better than that."

I elbow her in her side, and she barely reacts, but I feel too comfortable to care.

"Seriously, Sutton. I'm shocked you make it out of the parking lot every day."

"Truthfully, same. I once ran over a nail and got a flat, and the repair guy told me the replacement tire was likely worth more than the rest of the car put together."

"You know who can afford new cars?"

I groan. "Don't."

"Winners."

"Fuck you, Santos."

Maria laughs. "Just saying. A few races could pay for new tires. Or a pair of those boots you were telling me about."

"Or Mab," I say softly, imagining it so easily. Yearning surges in my chest.

"Or Mab," she agrees, turning back to me, her dark brown eyes penetrating.

I yank the hat off my face, shaking off the longing and rising to a seated position, wrapping my arms around my knees.

Maria nudges my shoulder with a small smirk. "Though, as long as you're sidelined, my and Duchess's path to the NFR is clear."

I nudge her back, pleased balance is restored between me and my new friend. "As long as *you know*, deep down, if Mab and I were there, we'd be kicking your ass at every turn."

"Deep, deep down, maybe," she concedes. "But don't you be thinking I'm gonna admit that to anyone else. Pure deniability from this point on. You want to beat me, you're gonna have to get out there and prove it." She pats my shoulder before jumping down from the workbench, brushing off her jeans and smoothing her gorgeous blue-black locks. "I think I hear my future boyfriend."

I grin, relaxing back on the bench and replacing the hat over my face. I'm glad for the reprieve. "Get 'em, tiger."

Fourteen

WINNIE

U sually, I tell myself Fridays with Mab are for her and who-ever her future rider turns out to be. It helps me com-partmentalize my feelings and remember she's not mine. Every drill, every ride, every spin of the barrels is for them and their future.

But after the last few stressful weeks, fuck it. This ride is for *me*. I'm choosing to be selfish and hog Mab to myself for one afternoon and pretend for a few hours she's mine and we're the only two souls in the entire world. I even beg Camilla to put away the stopwatch for once, and roll the barrels all the way out into the back pasture, where Mab and I can forget about barri-ers and walls. I lead her out through the other, closer pastures, luxuriating in the way the warm sun seeps into my heavy barn coat. Making a split-second decision, I pull it off, tossing it over a nearby fence post, and fold the sleeves of my worn flannel over my forearms. The breeze tangles in my hair, and I remove my ball cap to allow the gusts to toss the strands freely.

The air out here smells like green grass and open sky and

whatever the opposite of my trailer is, and my stomach does a giddy flip at what lies ahead.

It's such a change from the heavy dread that's dogged my every move recently, I barely recognize myself in this moment. We reach the edge of the paddock I've reserved, and I pull Mab over to the fence to mount. I swing my leg over the top rail and perch like a Carolina chickadee ready for flight. Mab's glossy coat twitches in anticipation. She's perpetually ready, but there's no doubt in my mind she's caught my need for speed.

I slip my hat back on to shade my eyes and reach for the saddle to pull myself over, leaning down and pressing a kiss to Mab's mane, drawing my fingers through the softness. "Hey, girl. How do you like the change of scenery?" I run her through several drills, getting her acclimated to the distance of the barrels and our wide-open setting. The ground here is soft and sandy, mimicking the inside of the arena and protecting the horses from divots or anything that could trip them up, but it's still different. The sand outside isn't as preserved as it is in the arena.

After we're warmed up and I'm confident she's plenty annoyed with me holding her back, I nudge her into a controlled trot and run her through the clover formation, paying close attention to how she feels underneath me: how she's reacting to the turns and if she's hesitating (she's not; she never does). I listen to her breaths and sync mine in turn. I work to anticipate her stride and match my own motion so I don't jar her or catch us up. We should move smoothly as one, rather than clatter along like a disjointed car on train tracks.

I nudge us into another rotation just as we finish, but this time, I press my knees and click my tongue in signal, and she takes off. That little nudge is all she needs. It's all I need, too.

We're flying. We hit the closest barrel and circle it flawlessly, my far hand out for balance since our angle is so steep. A breath later, we're on our way to the second. Slip down and in, clearing it easily. Then the third. I hold Mab's reins tightly, keeping her *just* off the barrels, but giving her enough room to angle herself comfortably and to allow her weight to shift precisely. She's the muscle, but I'm her control center. I trust her to go as fast as she possibly can, and she trusts me to keep her safe.

Equal partners.

And then it's the final pass. The straightaway when we can both let go of our control. I don't have to tell Mab to go. She understands the assignment. Has from the very first.

But today, this is for me, too. Even I get to let go.

I don't breathe. I don't blink. I'm not even sure my heart thuds in my chest. I'm weightless and worriless. Nothing can touch me.

And then, when we get to the end and catch our breaths, I lead her immediately into another round before my responsibilities can get their claws into me again.

—

I don't notice we have an audience until the final pass, when I see a flash of bright color in my periphery. My heart seems to know he's here before the rest of me. *Case.* Mab and I complete our run, and I nudge her toward him, noticing he's not alone. His dad and my boss, Mr. Michaels, are also there. This gives me pause, but I swallow back the uncertainty, reminding myself I'm not doing anything wrong. I'm supposed to train Mab. Camilla pays me extra for this.

In fact, after our "trial practice session," Maria somehow convinced me to approach Camilla with an offer: training other horses to barrel race at the Michaels ranch or even others in the arca, including Maria's. Camilla was immediately interested. I still have my original responsibilities, but this would be on top of those. A few hours extra tacked on at the beginning or end of my workday. We have a couple of boarders with racing potential, and Camilla has been considering purchasing more. A bit of a side hustle, depending on Mr. Michaels.

Presumably, that's why he's here.

I reach the fence and dismount, draping Mab's reins over the post. Not that she would dream of running away, as tired as she undoubtedly is, but I don't want Mr. Michaels to think I'm careless with one of the horses, even if she's not technically his. Speaking of, Camilla rides up on Elvis and jumps off, flashing me her reassuring smile.

"Looking good out there, Winnie," Mr. Michaels says. "Mab seems to have taken a liking to you."

I reach for Mab, giving her nose a nuzzle. "It's mutual. She's a beautiful horse."

"For Winnie, she is, anyway," Camilla says dryly. "For everyone else, she's a grouch and a half."

I tsk good-naturedly as Mab gives my hand a lick, no doubt looking for salt. "She's not grouchy. She's particular, is all."

"Well, Winnie," Mr. Michaels says, straightening from where he'd been leaning his forearms on the top railing of the fence. He's practically casual today in his jeans and Carhartt button-down. "I know you probably want to get Mab taken care of so you can head home, so I'll cut to the chase. I'd like to offer you a sponsorship. It's been brought to my attention you're wasted in our stables." He narrows his eyes. "That is to say, you still have your job, if you want it, but I think we all know you'd be better served in the arena, racing barrels."

My mouth drops open and I stare, unblinking, my brain

trying to catch up to the words coming out of his mouth. Whatever I thought this was going to be about, a sponsorship never crossed my mind.

"I'm sorry, what?"

"Barrel racing. CBM Ranch would like to offer you a sponsorship. We'd fund your entrance fees, loan you the horseflesh, including Mab, since clearly she's no good to anyone else, and in exchange, you spread our name, wear our logo, and win buckles."

I'm still struggling to understand. "But," I stutter past numb lips. "I've never even been in a rodeo before. I don't own a horse. Or even a saddle. I've never raced in front of a judge."

Mr. Michaels grins, and it looks remarkably like his son's. Down to the dimple. "All of that can be remedied with some hard work and training. I've been told this is a solid investment. After watching you this afternoon, I'm inclined to agree. If you're interested, that is."

Everything in me wants to agree. This is one of those once-in-a-lifetime, too-good-to-be-true kinds of deals, and it's literally everything I've ever wanted. Except—

"I can't. I'm sorry." And I am. I'm sorrier than I can even express. Sorrier than I've ever been about anything in my entire life. My throat is thick, and I can already feel the hot tears behind my eyes, waiting in the wings to pour buckets. I sniff, clearing my throat. I catch Camilla's troubled gaze. "I'm—I thought we talked about training? I could train horses for racing. Here. For—" I swallow hard. "For *other riders*." I shake my head, taking a deep breath and feeling calmer, my focus switching between Camilla and Mr. Michaels and back again. "It's an incredible opportunity, sir, but I can't travel. I have to be close to my family. I'm sorry for the confusion."

Mr. Michaels looks seriously taken aback. He exchanges looks with his son, who I note, looks equally gobsmacked.

"Winnie, *what are you talking about*? This is the chance of a lifetime—"

Oh, for . . . *now* I'm seeing it. The whole picture is becoming crystal clear. This wasn't Camilla. This was *Case*. Of course Case went to his dad. Mr. I-can-fix-anything-with-a-bunch-of-money. Except this can't be fixed with money. Heartache, frustration, flattery, anger all jockey inside of me, competing for attention. Anger wins.

"I'm talking about *no*, Case. As in N-O. I realize you don't hear it often, but today you will. I appreciate what you were trying to do, but I'm not your girl." I turn to his dad. "Mr. Michaels, I hope this doesn't affect my current position with your ranch, and I truly am interested in training behind the scenes, for more pay, of course. However, while I appreciate the offer for sponsorship more than I can say, I'm not in a position to accept your generosity at this time."

I lead Mab past the silent trio and wait until we're safely out of ear shot before I allow any tears to slip out.

"Winnie!" Case yells from behind me. "Wait up!"

I swipe quickly at my face, clearing it of evidence. "Go away, Case."

His long strides come nearer, eating up the distance. Hell. Can't a girl cry in peace?

"Come on, talk to me! This is a huge opportunity, Winnie! You could do this."

"I said no, Case. Please stop."

"But—"

I reach for Mab and without warning, harness my adrenaline

to swing my leg over her back and kick her into a gallop all the way back to the ranch.

Soon Camilla is there, and she takes Mab's reins from me as I dismount. Sympathy oozes from her blue eyes, and I don't much care for it, but I don't have the energy to do anything about it either. "Let me finish for you today. Why don't you head home?"

"I should brush—"

"Mab might not love me the way she does you, but we do all right. Case is headed back to try for a third time."

"I can't," I whisper, the tears surging again. And what I mean is I can't say no again. Doesn't he realize it's breaking me into pieces to say no?

But I still can't say yes. I can't leave them. Like our mom left us. I promised.

"I know, honey. Go on ahead. We'll talk later about the rest."

Fifteen

CASE

I'd have never anticipated Winnie's junker of a car could spin gravel so hard, spitting dust and fury into the sunny spring afternoon. It's the perfect visual representation of the verbal smackdown she unleashed on me. In her quiet way, she put me in my place, and I feel like the biggest fool on the planet. *Of course* she can't do this. God, she can barely manage the work she does here at the ranch, and that's within driving distance of her brother and sister.

I groan, thudding my head against the fence post. I recognize Winnie's barn coat slung over the top and pull it off the rail. That's just great. *And* she's going to be cold. Way to go, Michaels, you fucking jerk.

Minutes later, I recognize Pax's truck speeding up the long dirt drive, and I make my way over to him as he's easing next to my SUV. He rolls down his window, and I lean against the door, Winnie's coat still slung over my arm.

"Hey, man."

"Hey, yourself," he says, sounding amused. "You look like

shit. I was gonna ask if you wanted to grab some food with me, but—"

I'm already shaking my head. "I would, but I think I need to, uh, go." I clear my throat, tugging on my ball cap with my free hand. "I have to chase after someone. I fucked up."

He nods sagely. "Does this have anything to do with the way Winnie Sutton peeled out of here, Miranda Lambert screaming out her windows?"

I grimace. "Probably."

"You sure you don't want to let things settle down? I only saw her for a half second, but she looked—" He frowns. "I'm pretty sure she was crying."

If possible, I feel even worse. "Yeah, I think that means I *have* to go. And I shouldn't wait."

He nods, muttering, "Godspeed," before brightening. "D'you know where she lives? I dropped her brother off last week. He's still dating Chelsea, apparently."

"Actually, no, I have no idea. That would be great. I was gonna . . ." I trail off because I have no idea what I was gonna do. I hadn't gotten that far. I'm way out of my element, but I imagine stealing a look at her employment records for her address isn't very ethical.

A few minutes later, with Pax's directions in mind, I'm making my way across town toward the Suttons' place. I take my time, collecting my thoughts and practicing my apology while cursing Walker and his stupid list.

I'm shit at making friends. Okay, that's not true. I'm not reducing Pax to tears every time we hang out, so I can't be that bad. Maybe I'm just shit at girls. Why would Walker pick someone so pretty and hardworking and smart to be my friend? That seems counterproductive. Obviously, my inevitable crush on her would make me act like a fucking idiot. There's no other explanation for why my boot is constantly stuffed in my mouth around her: I keep trying to swoop in and play savior when she very clearly does not want to be saved.

Eventually, I find my way in front of the olive-green trailer Pax described. I pull next to a tired-looking Ford pickup and hesitate. Winnie's car isn't here, and I'm second-guessing whether I have the right place before I see movement behind a beige-and-white gingham curtain on the front door and see a familiar set of braids. The door flings open, and Garrett steps out on the stoop, waving wildly.

Silver lining: at least one of the Sutton girls doesn't hate me.

I release my seat belt and reach for the barn coat before stepping out into the cooling evening air.

"Hey, Braids," I say, using my new nickname for her.

"Hi, Case! What're you doing here?"

I raise the coat, grateful for the excuse, and offer it to Garrett. "Winnie forgot her jacket at work. But I see she's not here, so—"

Garrett steps away from my offering and instead opens the door, beckoning me. "Come on in! She's supposed to be home soon. You can wait for her."

Right. I'm sure Winnie will love me being here in her home, uninvited. I bite back my sigh and follow her sister in, my curiosity overruling my need to not piss off the eldest Sutton. Besides, I'm already in deep. Might as well make it count.

The small home is warm and cozy. I expected it to be . . . different. More desolate maybe? Or cramped. I immediately feel like a dick and decide to check my privilege at the door. Absolutely nothing about Winnie or her sister—or even her brother, for that matter—has given me reason to judge them by their presumed lack of wealth. Christine's snide remarks from Pax's party a month ago are still fresh in my mind, and I feel my face get hot at the memory.

The reality is different. The paneled walls are painted a soft, neutral color and the carpets are thin, but tidy and clear. The kitchen is small, with old laminate on the floor and generic cabinetry, but every surface is gleaming and spotless. There're candid pictures of the three Sutton kids everywhere, and while the furniture is definitely worn, it's covered in soft-looking pillows and throw blankets.

I inhale a deep, reassuring breath. *Winnie.* Everything feels like Winnie. Neat, practical, warm. I swallow hard at the implication. This is her home. She's made it a home. I have a bedroom I barely think about, but Winnie has an entire home.

Her brother is sitting on the couch, inquisitive expression on his face, his phone all but forgotten in his hands.

"Hey. It's Jesse, right?" I cross the room and hold out a hand. "I'm Case."

"Yeah. I remember. You gave me your beer." Right. Shit. Let's add that to the list of disappointing things I've done to a member of the Sutton family. "You're friends with Pax," he continues, not noticing my inner turmoil.

I nod. "I just left him. He told me how to get this to your sister," I say, holding up the excuse barn coat.

"He's a good guy," Jesse says, sounding grown. A smile presses against the corners of my lips when he stands to his full height, flexing his gangly limbs. "Winnie's not here right now."

It's obvious he's taking his measure of me, and I don't mind. In fact, I'm sort of relieved. From all the grief this kid's given his big sister, I expected him to be a selfish asshole. He might be that, but it's clear he does care. Fuck's sake, *someone* needs to.

"Braids mentioned that. I was going to drop this off, but she insisted I wait." I search around awkwardly for something to say. "This is a nice place you have here."

"Winnie," Garrett says as explanation, confirming what I'd already guessed. "Once she started working at your ranch, she saved up a bunch of money and did a full remodel. Well, aesthetically, anyway." I chuckle at her wistful expression and five-dollar word, though I suppose for a mini-genius, it's more like a fifty-cent word. "Want to see our room?" she asks, already tugging my hand. "You can't come in. It's a rule. But you can look from the door. I cleaned it because it's Friday, and if I clean my side of our room on Fridays, Winnie and I get to have a movie date with popcorn and M&Ms, and I get to pick the film."

I spend a full minute oohing and aahing at the gold and pink décor of Garrett and Winnie's room, impressed at their commitment to the theme. Sorry, *aesthetic*. I'm not a ten-year-old girl, but I think if I were, I would be pretty infatuated. I make a conscious effort to avoid studying the less glittery half of the tiny room. Too much, anyway. My eyes might linger on her simple floral bedspread and the imprint left behind on the pillow when its owner woke up this morning. But *that's it*.

"And who is this?" A deep, mild voice comes from a short hallway off the kitchen, startling me from my reverie.

"Daddy! It's Case Michaels. He rides bulls! And owns the ranch Winnie works at!"

Mr. Sutton is tall, dark-haired, and lanky with pale features and deep bags under his eyes. He looks freshly cleaned up, so I guess he must have just woken up for work. I make my way across the kitchen and hold out my hand.

"Hello, Mr. Sutton. I'm sorry to intrude. I came to return Winnie's jacket. She left it behind today, and I thought she might need it this weekend."

He takes my hand briefly and then searches the living space. "Where is she?" he asks, as if it's only now occurred to him she's not home.

Guilt creeps up my throat, but before I can confess anything, Jesse answers, "She just texted. She had something come up but is grabbing a couple of pizzas and will be home soon."

Mr. Sutton glances at the clock and runs a tired hand through his hair. "Cutting it close," he mutters.

It takes me a beat, but I realize he means about dinner. He was waiting for her to bring him dinner before work, and my stomach squirms uncomfortably.

"Well, I'd better hit the road, then. Don't want to be late. Let your sister know I grabbed something on the way." He reaches to remove his coat off a hook by the door and turns to me. "Nice to meet you, Case."

And with the slapping of a screen door, he's gone.

The fuck? That's it?

Jesse closes the heavier door before sitting at the table and looking at me.

"So, was . . . Is that—" I cut off, feeling disrespectful.

"Winnie gets annoyed when we leave the door open. Lets the heat out."

I close my mouth, clenching my jaw. That's not what I meant, but okay. That, too.

"Right," I mutter, forcing myself to remain impassive. "Kerry yells at me for that all the time, too."

Garrett snickers, pulling up a chair and offering me a seat. "I like Miss Kerry."

I sit down. "She likes you, too, Braids. You'll have to come back soon for more muffins. I can't eat them all by myself. I'll never fit on the bull at this rate."

"What happened at work?" Jesse cuts in.

"What do you mean?"

His eyes narrow. "Why isn't Winnie here? What'd you do?"

My breath leaves in a gust. "Oh, well . . ."

"Jesse!" Garrett practically hisses his name, clearly horrified.

His glare doesn't budge. "Winnie texted me she needed some time and would be home soon. She knew she'd be too late to catch Dad. She never does that."

I purse my lips and nod. "It's okay, Garrett. He's right. She did leave work upset, and it was my fault. Though, in my defense, my intentions were good." I shift in my seat. "I was trying to help."

I choose my words carefully, trying to give Winnie privacy but also realizing I'm in way over my head here.

"Have you ever seen Winnie race?" I start with a question.

Jesse shakes his head, but Garrett says, "A few times. She's like the wind."

I nod. "Exactly like the wind. She's excellent. More than. And there's this horse at our stables—"

"Queen Mab," Garrett offers.

"Yes. Mab. See, Mab hates everyone, and I mean everyone, but not your sister. They're like this power couple on the ranch. It's like they can read each other's minds or something. And Winnie's been training Mab to barrel race. Not for herself but for a future owner. And in doing so, she's unlocked Mab's potential. Camilla, our stable manager, has timed them on multiple occasions, and let's just say your sister and Mab could easily sweep every competition in barrel racing, local or otherwise. No one's heard of them yet, but I promise she could be the best there is."

"You're talking rodeos?"

"I'm talking *the rodeo.*"

Jesse looks thoughtful and settles back in his chair. "What happened? This all sounds like good stuff. Why would she be mad about any of that?"

"Right? Except," I hesitate, because this is where I want to be careful. "Rodeo can be very expensive."

Jesse and Garrett are silent.

"So," I exhale. "I talked to my dad and asked him to come and watch her race, just once, and see her potential. See if maybe he would want to sponsor her—like have the ranch sponsor her. That's a common thing in professional sports competitions, you know? Sponsorships."

The siblings brighten.

"What did he say?" Jesse asks.

"Obviously, he was all in once he saw her," Garrett says.

I can't help my grin at her matter-of-fact tone. "Obviously."

"So why is Winnie mad? That sounds awesome."

I pause, trying to think of a way to say it without actually saying it, because while I've come to realize Garrett and Jesse are her reason for saying no, she'd never in a million years want them to feel that way.

But also, maybe they need to know that? Why is she the only one making sacrifices? Maybe she should accept help? This is definitely not my decision to make, though.

"Fuck," Jesse says before I've come to a decision. "I know."

"Jesse!" Garrett's eyes are wide.

He looks at his younger sister, his expression chagrined. "Winnie won't leave us. She promised she wouldn't leave." He turns to me. "She'd have to tour around to compete, right?"

I raise my head and dip it once, slowly.

Jesse slumps. "Our dad sucks," he says and raises a hand to

gesture at the closed front door. "As you can probably tell. And we don't have a mom. Well, technically, we do somewhere, but hell if we know *where*. And, um, I was cutting school a lot. I stopped!" he insists at my raised brows. "But it's only been a few weeks and the school told Winnie they would have to call the police and the police means CPS and so Winnie was thinking she might have to file for guardianship if that happened to keep us together. In conclusion, this is my fault."

Garrett glares at him and looks so much like Winnie I almost laugh. "It sure is."

His face is so pale and stricken. I'm struck with a pang of sympathy. The kid is fourteen, after all. I made a lot of shitty choices at fourteen. Hell, I make them at nineteen.

"Regardless," I say. "She's mad at me, not you. *Never* at you. Okay? And your sister is a grown woman who can make her own decisions."

"So she's upset because you tried to help?" Jesse asks finally, his brows scrunching.

"I'm sure she wouldn't see it as helping," I explain wryly. "More like steamrolling her and offering her impossible choices my rich-kid brain can't even comprehend. To be honest with you, I messed up. To be extra honest with you, I keep messing up. I want to be her friend, but I'm not very good at it."

Something indiscernible dances in Garrett's eyes, and it makes me fiddle with the collar of my shirt. The trailer is feeling a little *too* warm and cozy all of a sudden.

Jesse studies me again. "Just her friend?"

I clear my throat. "Yeah." What temperature does Winnie have this place set at?

"Whatever you have to tell yourself," he says finally. "You know, I was there when you jumped in that pool buck naked."

I choke on air. "Yeah?"

He smirks, somehow knowing he has me by the balls. "Yeah. It was awesome."

I work at not looking at Garrett. "I wouldn't say that. It was cold. And I could have drowned. You should never go swimming after drinking. Not that you should drink in the first place, since you're way underage, but if you do . . ." I trail off, feeling extremely uncomfortable. "Anyway," I say loudly, straightening. "Now you can see why maybe it's best I go. I've done plenty of damage for one night. You guys can pass on the coat and let her know I came by."

"Not a chance," Jesse says. "I want to see her reaction to your being here."

I wince. "I don't need to ruin her night." To Garrett, I say, "Besides you have a movie date, right? And pizza."

"Movie date can be tomorrow. I agree with Jesse. Besides, you owe us. You made her mad, so you should be the one to make her happy."

"How?" I choke out. "I'm a disaster at this."

Garrett is beaming. "Keep trying."

Sixteen

CASE

We don't have to wait long for Winnie to show up, two hot pizzas in hand. She doesn't seem surprised by my presence at her table, likely because she saw my SUV in the drive, but that doesn't keep her from scowling at me.

"You left your coat."

She rolls her eyes, but her face is flushed. "How'd you know where I live?"

Right. I invited myself over to her house.

"Um, Pax came by after . . . after you left, and he offered to tell me. I planned to drop off your coat, but you weren't here, and then Braids, um, I mean Garrett, invited me in."

Winnie's face is even pinker, but she still manages a scary glare. "And you decided to make yourself at home?"

My eyes dart to Jesse and Garrett for some assistance, but the former isn't even trying to hide his glee at my discomfort and the latter has eyes only for her big sister.

"I didn't—"

She mutters a curse under her breath and gestures to her

brother. "Get some plates and set the table. Make it for four," she directs in an overly polite tone. "We have a guest."

"Oh," I say awkwardly, making to stand. "That's okay. You don't have to feed me."

She levels me with a look. "Sit your butt down, Case. We have plenty."

Her tone is as brisk as ever, but there's something warmer around the edges I've only recently learned to recognize, and I decide to take the offering for what it is. "Okay."

The Sutton siblings chat during dinner, and I listen. It's captivating the way their conversation flows round and round. Everything is familiar and easy. I'm a little envious, which is a mind fuck, considering everything else at play here.

"Case was telling us about barrel racing," Jesse eventually blurts.

I choke on a piece a cheese sticking to the back of my throat. I reach for my glass of water and drain half of it in a single gulp.

Winnie doesn't seem too fazed, however. She sighs and glances at me. "He did, did he?"

"Garrett says you ride like the wind," Jesse continues, his tone a little accusing and a lot exasperated.

The corner of Winnie's lips quirk. "Well, sure I do."

Have I ever mentioned how hot her confidence is? Like, if her siblings weren't right there, and also, if I wasn't trying to be a good friend . . .

Jesse nods thoughtfully. "I think I'd like to see it sometime."

Winnie's eyes soften, and she focuses on her brother. Something private passes between them, and I don't want to intrude or interrupt. Much.

She clears her throat and nods. "That can be arranged. After school, of course."

Jesse nods, picking up a slice of pizza and eating as if nothing's happened. I watch the siblings, chewing in silence, feeling like I've missed something. It's like they have their own version of sibling speak. A secret language.

I only eat two small pieces. I know what Winnie said about them having plenty to share, but I can't shake the feeling that I'm taking from them, and anyway, this entire day has been pretty unsettling. I'm not that hungry.

After they finish eating, I'm trying to figure out a way to make a graceful exit when Winnie turns to me. "I could use a walk. Wanna join?"

My eyes grow wide, but I keep them on her. "S-sure." I think I hear a snort coming from Jesse's vicinity, but I ignore it. A walk. Alone. Yes.

Unless. Oh, shit. Is this where she murders me for interfering in her life and inviting myself into her house, spilling her secrets to her siblings?

Well, Win, your ten-year-old sister insisted, so it's not like I had a choice but to insert myself into your private life . . .

Walker's ghost snickers in the back of my mind. *I'm so happy to provide you with endless afterlife entertainment*, I think.

Great list, by the way. Totally killing it.

I help the siblings clean up dinner and then move to the door. "I have a coat in my truck," I say. "Meet you out front?"

Winnie nods.

I wave to Garrett, and she walks up to me, throwing her arms around my chest. My breath leaves in a quiet *oof*, and I squeeze her back, tugging a braid before releasing her.

Jesse gives me a nod over the top of her head. He seems less pissed than when I first walked in, so that's something, I guess.

A minute later, I'm tugging on my coat, my breath hissing

as the freezing material hits my skin after I'd left it in the back seat. The porch light flips on, bathing the night in a subtle glow, and Winnie walks out, her arms slipping into the sleeves of her barn coat.

"Thanks for bringing this," she says. "It's my only coat, so I would have had to steal from Jesse, and all his clothes smell like Axe body spray."

I huff a laugh. "Ah yes, I remember those days. Kerry used to 'accidentally lose' mine whenever she cleaned my room."

Winnie's eyes widen. "She cleaned your room?"

I freeze. "Not always," I hedge. "But probably more than she should have. I was gone a lot."

"You're not one of those guys that doesn't know how to do your own laundry, are you?"

"No! I can do my laundry. *Technically*," I admit, thanking Christ I'd asked Kerry to show me how to run the washer and dryer a few weeks ago.

Winnie gestures to the left with a point of her chin, and we start down the road. She stuffs her hands in her overlarge pockets, and her head falls back as she looks at the sky. "It's so clear tonight."

I hum my agreement, and for a little while, we walk in the silence. It's darker than dark out here, but the inky night is interrupted occasionally with a porch light from neighboring homes. Some are trailers like Winnie's, and others are small single-level ranches. No one's outside. Springs in the panhandle aren't horrible, but it still gets dark and chilly early.

"I met your dad," I offer. "He seems nice enough."

Winnie shrugs. "Nice enough is about right."

"Did he give you a hard time about being late?"

She shakes her head. "He never gives me a hard time." Her

lips curl in a humorless smile. "If he wanted to complain about me being late with his dinner, he would have to also acknowledge he could make dinner for himself before work."

She's silent a beat, then, in a low voice, she says, "We don't have a Kerry. We have a Winnie."

I swallow hard, my apology bubbling up and overflowing inside of me. "I'm so sorry, Winnie. You were right. I shouldn't have gone to my dad. I wasn't thinking. I didn't mean to over-step."

Winnie shakes her head, not meeting my gaze. "It's okay. I've cooled down. I know you didn't mean anything by it. But you see why now, don't you?"

"Jesse told me about the guardianship thing."

Winnie doesn't look surprised, only resigned. "Yeah. That happened."

"Do you think you'll have to do it?" I can't even imagine. I can barely take care of myself, let alone be responsible for two other lives.

But I suppose Winnie's been responsible for two other lives for a long time.

She releases a breath into the night air, a misty cloud pouring from between her lips. "I don't know. Maybe not, if Jesse can get his shit together. I'm kind of banking on his indignant fourteen-year-old conscience to motivate him into staying in school."

"He said he was done skipping," I offer.

"It's been a week," she says blandly.

I make a face. "Well," I say. "Forward progress, I guess?"

"Forward progress," she agrees, releasing her hands from her pockets. Our arms swing between us. I resist the urge to make a grab for her hand.

Be a friend. Friends don't hold hands. Friends don't kiss.

I think back to Walker. *Friends don't flinch.*

I take a deep breath, psyching myself up to say something unflinching.

"I know what you're doing, and while I don't understand what it's like to be in your position, at all," I say, "I think you're wrong."

In the near silence, her breath catches, and she takes a step away from me. Immediately, I feel colder.

"Just—" I pause. "Please listen for a second. Hear me out."

I can tell listening to me is the very last thing she wants to do, but she's not running away, so I plow ahead. *Please don't let me fuck this up. Again.*

"You have to have faith in other people. You're not alone. Remember what I said? The entire world won't fall around your ears if you aren't holding it up. You have more reason than anyone I've ever met to distrust people. You've been let down a thousand times by people who should be the first to line up and support you. I get that. It's—God, Win—" My hands clench and open compulsively. "I wanted to punch your dad earlier when I met him."

She stops short, mouth gaping. "What?"

I cringe. "He's just . . . doesn't he realize how incredible you are? He walked out of his room, all ready to be taken care of. He didn't even blink over the fact a strange man was in his living room with his kids."

I raise a hand, stalling her. "I know what you're thinking. Real rich coming from the kid with a housekeeper cleaning his room. I'm . . . Listen, I'm realizing a lot of ugly things about myself these last few weeks, and I'm not sure how to reconcile that, but I *am* learning, and I want to think I'm going to do better. I don't want to be like him."

"Case," she starts gently. "You're *not* like him."

I pull a skeptical face. "On the surface, I kinda am."

Her eyes search between mine, her face open and her freckles glowing in the streetlight. "You're not, though. You took care of Walker when he was sick. You've done nothing but take care of me and even my sister these last few weeks. It's annoying how much I've had to rely on you, and you keep showing up. Hell, you saved Garrett's life! Even today, with your dad, I know that was you trying to take care of me. Misguided, sure, but still. I have no idea what I did to earn your efforts, but I'm grateful."

I nail her with a knowing look. "How can you even say that? I've made you cry like three times."

She snorts, nudging my shoulder and walking ahead. I follow. "Oh, please. Two times, tops, and I'm pretty sure the first was actually the school and Jesse. You were conveniently nearby."

"That's not going to change," I tell her. "Unflinching, remember? Let me help you. I want to help. I want to be your friend."

"You do?"

I throw back my head, exasperated. "Come *on*! I'm so desperate to be your friend, I'm beyond embarrassing at this point."

Her lips spread into a full smile. "As it happens, I could use a friend."

Relief floods through my bloodstream. "Thank God." I swipe at my forehead. "You, Winnie Sutton, are more intimidating than Ballbuster."

She barks out a loud laugh. "Who?"

"He's, like, the worst bull on the circuit. Total nut-crusher. Throws everyone in less than four. His real name is Inferno, but that's too high-brow for a fifteen-hundred-pound beast."

She's overcome with giggles. "Oh my gosh. I don't know whether to be flattered or mortified to be worse than *Ballbuster*."

"Flattered," I insist. "For sure. Walker would love this—watching me fumble around after you. He'd say I deserve it after giving him so much grief about Taylor."

Winnie calms down. "You know, he used to tell me about her. Did things ever work out with them before . . ."

I shake my head, catching her drift before exhaling. "Well, kind of. She died a few months before he did. They knew each other from their hospital stays over the years."

Winnie's expression falters. "Oh. Oh no."

"Yeah, it sucked. He did get to tell her how he felt, and she did, too. But the timing . . ."

Her breath rushes out in a sad sigh. "Jesus, that's the worst thing I've ever heard."

"Right," I agree grimly. "Except I like to imagine they're going at it like rabbits in heaven."

Winnie gasps, laughing, her watery eyes wide. "You like to imagine that, huh?"

I nudge her shoulder. "You know what I mean. Seems only fair."

She nods. "It does."

We turn back for her house, and I change the subject. "Don't hit me, but you know there *are* local rodeos, right? Like, you have to start there, anyway, and create a name for yourself. Not that I don't think you'll fly through the rankings, but you have some time before you have to tour. Season doesn't even kick off until early summer. We have months to whip you into shape and figure things out."

Winnie sighs.

"Forward movement," I remind her.

"I know," she says. "I'll consider it. That's as much as I can promise. It depends on Camilla and your dad and whether or not

Jesse stays in school." She flashes a smirk in my direction. "You realize you said 'we' right?"

"Yeah, well, I'm not out of it yet."

"Will you come no matter what? To watch or whatever?" She blinks up at me, her dark lashes fluttering, and my heart stutters in my chest. I swallow hard and nod, definitely not pointing out she's already asking me about coming to see her race when she just said she would only consider it.

Nope. Just gonna roll with this.

"You couldn't stop me. That's what friends do, right?"

"Right," she agrees, turning to walk again. "Friends."

Walker never wrote *Fall for your friend* on his list, but maybe this is like the situation with the corn silo. Maybe it's meant to be taken more in the spirit of things.

In which case, I have every intention of making Winnie Sutton my friend.

Seventeen
WINNIE

May arrives on the heels of a thunderstorm. One of those expansive ones that spin down from Oklahoma and settle for a while. They're rare enough we don't bother fighting it too much. Just let it roll through and green things up a bit. Since our trail rides were canceled for the day, I texted Maria, and she drove out to join us under the guise of "practice."

And by *us*, I mean me, Case, and *Pax*. I thought there might be some issues because last I heard, Pax was still off and on with Madi Wallen, but clearly, I understand nothing.

Enter Maria Santos, and suddenly, everything is well and decidedly *off* for poor Madi.

It's been an interesting few weeks around the ranch. Case has been making himself at home in the stables for months, but now it's stables in the morning, training in the afternoon, and the occasional evening practice when Maria's feeling pushy and Jesse's able to stay home with Garrett.

I've gone from zero social life to nightly plans in the course of three weeks. I'm still mega hesitant about competing, and to his credit, Case has kept up his end of the bargain and isn't forcing the issue, but Maria is another story. Give the girl an inch . . . I can't find it in me to be annoyed. I sort of like the change. Jesse hasn't missed a day of school in over a month, and I've been making more money than ever with the new horses Camilla has me working with: Risky Business and Pistol Annie. They're two longtime boarders whose owners are friendly with Mr. Michaels. He and Camilla have been talking me up while also discussing the grand adventure (and solid investment) that is *rodeo* and have convinced the owners to let me train their horses to race. Maria is positive she can find us riders looking for fast, well-trained horseflesh, and Camilla has even invited me to come on a trip down to Fort Worth in two weeks to check out a couple of other potential candidates we can train up and sell.

"Or," Camilla offered in a too-casual manner, playing with her leather work gloves, "you know, maybe even keep, in the event you decide to take Mr. Michaels up on his offer of sponsorship. You'll need more than Mab."

I didn't respond.

Things are going unusually well, but it feels precarious. As if at any moment, all these plates I've got spinning are gonna wobble and shatter on the ground. It's the way it's always been, after all.

It's like Mab. When we first got her from that horrific auction, she was skin and bones. Her ankles and fetters scarred, her coat dull and oily. She was skittish to the max. She still stutter-steps over new ground textures, but when she first came, it was as though she was deathly allergic to concrete and closed-in spaces. Her previous owners didn't have stables or even a shed, and consequently never allowed her inside, even in extreme weather. They kept her tied up in their backyard. I don't know if they ever struck her, but I *am* acquainted with neglect, and there's something fucked up that happens after being told no so many times. The hope dies. It hurts too much, and eventually, self-preservation kicks in. You stop trying to escape. You stop asking for more than what you have. You learn to be grateful, even, for the little you're given.

Eventually, you become protective of that tiny, muddy, shit-filled backyard. Because it's *yours*, and because all you love in the whole world is in that space.

The less you have, the tighter you hold on.

It's hard for someone like Case Michaels or Maria Santos, with their gobs of money and security, to comprehend that, but I'm pretty familiar with the concept. It's not as though I don't *want* the sponsorship or I don't think I could win. I do, and I would.

It's that I don't have any faith it will work out for me. Faith, hope, belief, whatever, it's all the same hurtful bullshit wrapped up in pretty sentiments. I lost all of that somewhere around Garrett's first birthday when neither my mom nor my dad made an appearance, and we kids ate a box cake made by a nine-year-old.

I can do anything except depend on someone else.

Mab's the same. Fuck if she's ever going to ask for permission again. She belongs to no one. I'm convinced she only works for me because like attracts like. Two neglected and tired souls, living for the moment.

And this moment is a good one, preceded by weeks of equally new and different, good moments. Four almost-adults sitting on a covered wraparound porch watching a rumbling storm roll in over the plains. I've never done anything like this before, and being casually a part of something so mundane makes me feel off-balance, but not in an unwelcome way. Here I am. Sitting with other people who aren't related to me, watching weather. "Shooting the shit," as Pax likes to say.

"D'you see that one, Michaels?" Pax asks, referencing the lightning strike none of us could miss.

Case grunts his response and Pax continues, his tone definitely up to something. "Looked like it nearly took out the grain bin—excuse me, *silo*—out at my place."

I stiffen, but Case just shakes his head, the dimple closest to me popping in and out of view.

"Reckon it's about . . . what? Thirty feet in the air?"

"*Reckon* that's the grain bin," Case says, honey-thick Texas accent in place. "The silo's a good seventy-five, hundred feet."

"Right, right. I always mix those up. Easy to do."

Maria finally cuts in, exasperated. "Okay. What're we missing?"

Case raises a brow at me, and I press my lips together. I know the rumors, of course, but if he's willing to share the facts firsthand, I won't stop him.

He lets out a long-suffering sigh, but I don't think he's really mad. This feels like a schtick between him and Pax. "Well, Maria," he drawls, "you see, a long time ago, when I was a child . . ."

"March," I pipe in, amused. "Barely two months ago. Tell the story right, Michaels."

"When I was *much* younger and more irresponsible than I am now," Case presses on, "and truthfully, fucking sad and also drunk, I found this list—"

Ooh. A list. I focus my attention, intrigued.

"—from my dead best friend, Walker Gibson."

"Ah. I knew Walker. From rodeo," Maria says. "I'm sorry for your loss."

Case's expression tightens ever so slightly, but he shakes it off and continues, "Right. Thank you. So as I was saying, Walker, the meddling fucker, made this list before he died. I don't know when," he rushes to answer the question before I ask. "Sometime, and when he was dying, he gave it to me. He said they were all these things he'd wanted to do but didn't get the chance, and maybe I could do the list without him."

Even the storm seems to go quiet around us, and the only sound is the low, sloping cadence of Case's voice. The air is at once static and expectant. "Oh god," I whisper.

Case turns to me, his eyes meeting mine. "Yeah.

"Anyway," he carries on, a little louder, a little gruffer, the electrified space between moments lost. "This list runs the gamut. There's your typical *Go on a road trip* and *Sing karaoke* kinds of tasks, and then there's far stupider shit like *Jump off a corn silo*."

My voice strangles. "*Jump off?*"

"A fucking corn silo," Pax says. "Damned city boy."

"He meant grain bin," Case explains.

"Apparently," Maria says mildly.

"But of course, I didn't realize until I was already at the top. And I was stuck, because it was fucking high and I'd been drinking."

"So the fire department came and got you down," I finish for him.

"Pretty much."

I lean back in the painted wooden rocker and imagine Walker as I knew him. "In the spirit of fairness, he didn't mean to almost kill you."

"Not with that one," Pax says darkly.

I stiffen, halting my rocking. "What does *that* mean? What else is on the list?"

Case rolls his head to the side and raises a single dark brow.

"I'll tell you, but first I need you to know it's already done, and also remember I wasn't hurt."

"Case!" I smack his arm, and he grins sheepishly.

"Conquer a bull outside the arena. Which, as you know, worked out fine in the end. Though, admittedly, I was sweating that one for months. Wasn't exactly sure how I was supposed to conquer Charles. Turns out I needed the proper motivation."

I surge to my feet. "Are you kidding me? Case! What were you thinking?"

He remains sitting and shrugs. "In all sincerity, Win, I was looking to *feel something*, and fuck if it didn't work. But also, I wasn't thinking. For the first time in my life, I didn't think something through, I just acted—and thank Jesus I did, or maybe things would have ended a little differently. So let's drop it."

It's as if we're the only two on the porch. I'm alarmed at how shaken I feel at the memory of Case in front of that bull.

He gets to his feet and reaches for my shoulders, so I am forced to look him in his eyes. "It was reckless. One hundred percent Walker and not at all me. It's not *my* list; I didn't write it. I wouldn't do something like that normally, and I'll never be repeating it, because it scared the shit out of me. But I did it and it's done, and it worked out for the best, and neither Garrett nor I died in the process."

"Where's the list?"

His brows draw together. "What?"

"Do you have it still? Is it inside? Go get the list," I demand. "I wanna see it."

His arms drop, and he exhales. After a beat, he seems to notice the curious stares of our friends and makes a decision. "Okay, follow me."

I've never been inside the big house before. From the outside,

I knew it was luxe. Tiered landscaping with plenty of fancy lighting and pretty furniture. There's an in-ground pool and one of those outside kitchen patios. Some nights in the winter, when it gets dark early and I work late, I see it all lit up, softly glowing, and it is like something out of a romance movie.

But none of that prepared me for the *inside* of Case's home. The foyer (because he has a whole-ass foyer) is paved in soothing sandstone and white marble. The ceilings pitch to a high point with open skylights and are accentuated with enormous wooden beams. There's a massive stone fireplace with a cowhide spread before it, bookended by giant squashy leather couches. In fact, everything is big and imposing and clean. We pass the kitchen, where Kerry is stirring something that smells delicious on the stove. She's small, but she looks miniscule in the sprawling space. My entire trailer would fit in here. Garrett's and my room is the size of his pantry, easily.

Case grabs my hand, interrupting my gawking, and tugs me up the stairs. "Just grabbing something, Kerry!" he yells over his shoulder.

He walks through the landing to where it splits in opposite directions, then turns right. I follow, catching a glimpse of a photo of a beautiful woman I don't recognize holding a baby, standing next to a young version of Case's dad. This must be his mom. I have no idea what happened to Case's mom except that Mr. Michaels is a widower.

"Is that your mom?"

Case stops at the door he was about to open and walks back. "Oh yeah. That's Mom. With me and my *dad*. She died a few months after. That picture, right there"—he points, tracing the lines of her lovely smile—"sums up about all I know about her."

"Oh no. I'm so sorry."

He looks genuinely unbothered. "It's okay. She died of an aneurysm in her sleep. Kerry's been taking care of me ever since."

I focus my attention on the old photo, not meeting his eyes. "My mom left us after Garrett was born. I was nine, so I remember some stuff about her, but I think I've blocked most of it out. But Garrett and Jesse? They have zero memories."

"You haven't seen her since?"

"Nope," I say, popping the *p*. "She left to get cigarettes after coming home from the hospital and presumably never looked back. I don't know if it was the baby blues or what."

He grimaces. "I'm sorry, too, then. That's awful."

"Good riddance," I say and mean it. I turn to him. "So. The list?"

"Right." He leads me into his bedroom and immediately heads for a large desk situated in front of his window. I try not to look like I'm memorizing the details of his room. The unmade and rumpled California king. The pile of familiar clothes in front of a walk-in closet. The collection of gold rodeo buckles and trophies lining his dresser. A framed photo of him and Walker.

Case holds a paper in front of him, but when I grab for it, he swipes it away. "Before you read it, there's something I need to tell you."

"Okay."

"You need to remember Walker made this list. Without me knowing."

"Right."

He crosses his arms over his chest, pulling the short sleeves of his T-shirt distractingly tight across his shoulders and biceps. "And for a long time, I assumed it was for him, like he said. Stuff he'd never gotten to do. A bucket list, you know?" I nod. He continues. "But then Pax told me *you* knew Walker."

I blink, confused. "Oh. Yeah. Kinda. I mean, we were friends. He would talk to me here at the ranch while I worked sometimes. And if he saw me sitting alone at school lunch, he'd keep me company. I liked him a lot. He was a good guy."

Case nods. "The best. He was the best guy. So, remember that when you see this, okay?" He hands me the folded piece of notebook paper.

I pull it open and read through the list. Case is right. There's a lot of the typical bucket list stuff. Also plenty of things Case has already crossed off, including, I note with a snicker, *Jump into a pool naked (at a party)*. Well, that makes sense. Still stupid, but makes sense. I skim my eyes over the remaining items until I get hung up on the last.

Befriend Winnie Sutton. My breath catches in my throat, and hot tears surge to the corners of my eyes. "Gah."

"Yeah."

"He wanted you to be my friend."

"Correction: he wanted *us* to be friends. There's an important difference. He was already your friend. He put that on there for me. He knew you and liked you, I know that. I can't tell you how many times you do something or put me in my place, and I think, *Walker would love this shit*."

I stare at the list, blinking but not seeing.

"Winnie? Say something, please."

"I've always wanted to learn French."

"Huh?"

"It says here, *Learn a language other than English*. Spanish would be more practical, especially in Texas, but I don't care. I like how French sounds. It's sexy. Want to learn it with me?"

"Winnie . . . ," he says warningly.

"Look. It's fine. Do I feel extra pathetic your dead best friend basically assigned you the task of being my friend? Sure. It's pretty mortifying. But I know he meant well, and he likely never counted on you being so honest and showing me the list . . . so."

"It was for me," he cuts in quickly. "All of this stuff is for me. To survive losing him. After the bull, I kinda figured it all out. He was trying to give me directions. A contingency plan or whatever. I like plans. And maps and lists. Formulas, equations. He knew that about me and knew I was going to need a friend who could put me in my place. Please don't be embarrassed. I'm glad he did it, and I'm glad we're friends."

I take a deep breath, releasing it slowly. "Okay."

"Okay."

"So, French?"

A single dimple pops. "*Oui.*"

I pass the list back to him. "No more stupid, reckless stuff?"

He tosses the paper on the desk behind him. "You mean more reckless than facing down a bull? It's all gravy from here."

Eighteen
WINNIE

CASE
Qu'est-ce que le grille-pain a dit à la tranche de pain?

I open my phone and squint at the text, huffing a quiet laugh from where I'm riding in the back seat of Camilla's pickup truck. It's been two weeks since the big List Revelation, and I'm officially on my way out of town for the first time in, well, ever. Camilla invited Maria and me to tag along on her day trip down to a ranch outside Fort Worth to check out potential horses.

It's also been two weeks since I offered to learn French with Case. Of course, I wasn't aware Case had taken four years of French in high school and apparently specialized in dirty jokes. I've downloaded Duolingo onto my phone in an effort to catch up, but it's been slow going.

Thank goodness for Google Translate.

I study the foreign words again, identifying *pain*, which I know is bread, and *le grille-pain*, which is presumably a toaster?

Which makes no sense. I give up, copying the words into translate.

What did the toaster say to the loaf of bread?

After a minute, I cave.

WINNIE
I honestly have no idea, but I am sure it's salacious . . .

CASE
Je suis désolé. Réessayez en français, s'il vous plaît.

That one, I know. Fucking know-it-all.

WINNIE
Je n'ai aucune idée!

CASE
Mieux.

A frustrated growl escapes my throat and catches the attention of Maria in the passenger seat. She turns around. "You okay?"

"*Oui.*"

She snorts, turning back to the front. "It's only Case," she explains to Camilla as if I'm not there. "They decided they were going to learn French together."

Camilla arches a brow in the rearview mirror. "Really?"

"Kinda," I grumble. "Except Case sees it as an excuse to send me dirty jokes in French."

Camilla's eyes widen, and I rush to clarify. "Not like that."

"Oh, *exactly* like that," Maria says.

"No!" I say, sitting up straighter and ignoring the buzzing of Case's return text. "You're acting like it's flirty or something, and it's definitely not. It's annoying and purely a friend thing."

"Sure. I wish Pax paid half as much attention to me as Case Michaels spends on you. Come on, Winnie. You *fascinate him.*"

I roll my eyes. "First of all, Pax is on you like white on rice. It's adorable how that boy follows you around. Tell me he didn't offer to oil your saddle yesterday afternoon and it wasn't even a euphemism."

"It needed it." Maria pretends to pout.

"And second of all," I continue, undeterred, "I work on his family's ranch. He helps out with Garrett and Jesse. So of course he pays attention to me. *That's what friends do.* Friends also recognize when their friend has a recent history of being a fuckboy and they know better than to get their boundaries crossed."

"Is that what the kids are calling it? Crossing boundaries?" Camilla says with a painted smirk.

My phone buzzes again, and I choose to ignore my present company.

> **CASE**
> (Okay, you give up?)

> **CASE**
> Je te veux en moi.

> **CASE**
> JE TE VEUX EN MOI!

Oof. That's unfortunately cute. A dirty joke about a toaster. Who knew?

> **WINNIE**
> Oh mon Dieu.

> **WINNIE**
> C'était horrible!

> **CASE**
> How's the drive going?

WINNIE
Long. Maria has commandeered the radio, and it's been nothing but Olivia Rodrigo since we left.

CASE
You know, someone once got mad at me for belittling OR.

CASE
Not that I'm hung up on it or anything.

WINNIE
OR has a place and that place is on call for when I'm mad about a boy or maybe a breakup.

CASE
So not recently . . .

WINNIE
Aïe, merci pour ça.

CASE
Ha.

CASE
Gardez-le juste reel.

CASE
You're just mad there's no Tim McGraw.

WINNIE
I mean. I don't think that's asking too much.

"Earth to Winnie!" I drop my phone in my lap and look up, immediately wiping the smile off my face.

"What?"

Maria's grin is all-knowing. "You hungry? We're thinking of stopping early to eat, since there's a long stretch ahead that won't have much outside of fast food."

I consider the money I have in my wallet and nod. "Sure, I could eat."

—

We're on our way back to Amarillo, two stunning new quarter horse stallions in tow, when my phone rings. I'm sitting in the passenger seat this time, though Maria is still in charge of music because *"No one under the age of thirty listens to Shania Twain unironically, Winnie."* But I've opened my window wide to let the dry, hot air blow through my hair, so I quickly move to close it and turn down the radio.

"Hey!" Maria protests. I hold up a finger, seeing a number I don't recognize.

"Hello?"

"Winnie!"

"Garrett?" My heart thuds. The warm feeling from a moment earlier is gone, and it's as though icy water has been poured over my head.

"Winnie, I'm okay," she reassures me quickly, but goddamn it, she doesn't *sound okay.* "It's . . . all right. . . . Don't be mad. It's okay. We're okay. But, um, Dad didn't show up after robotics practice today, and I didn't think I should stay by myself at the school . . ."

"Wait, why didn't the teacher stay with you?"

She sounds apologetic, and without seeing her, I know her little eyebrows are scrunching together. "I thought I saw Dad's car, and Mrs. Gunner had to pick up her own kids, so she left, but it wasn't Dad. And the school was closed since it's Saturday, so I tried to walk home . . ."

"What?!" I yell into the phone, my words strangling. "You walked?"

I can hear the waver in my sister's voice, and I swallow down a curse and make my voice even. "Garrett, I'm sorry. Listen, honey. I'm not mad at you. I promise. Not at all. You were stuck. I get it. So where are you now? Are you home?"

I glance at the clock on the dash. It's well past two, and Garrett was supposed to finish with her robotics club at noon.

"No." She sniffs into the phone, and I feel sick. "I'm at the Stop and Go on Fuller Street. A nice lady saw me walking and is letting me use her phone."

I clutch at my hair, pulling it taut, to keep from losing my shit. *One day.* I left for one fucking day.

"Okay, honey," I say. "Can you put her on the phone?"

I hear some shuffling and some garbled words and then a quick, "Hello?"

"Hi there. This is Winnie Sutton. You have my little sister there with you. I'm sorry to ask this of you, but can you wait there with her for a moment while I try to get ahold of my dad so he can pick her up? I'm so sorry about this."

"No problem, hon. My name is Jenny Carter, and this is my personal phone number, so you can call me right back at it. I'm in no hurry. I'm gonna run in real quick and get Garrett something to drink, if you don't mind. It's awfully hot out."

I swallow hard, embarrassment and inadequacy working to suffocate me.

"I'd appreciate that, ma'am. Thank you so much. I'll call you right back."

I end the call with a shaking finger and allow myself a single moment to let my head fall back as I swallow convulsively to get myself under control before scrolling to my dad's number and hitting Send.

It rings and rings, and I get nothing.

I try Jesse.

He picks up on the first ring. "Hey, Win."

"Where are you? Is Dad there?"

"I'm at home. And not yet. He must have stopped to get—"

I cut him off. "He forgot Garrett, Jesse. She's stuck at the gas station on Fuller. Sh-she tried to walk home. Alone."

My brother curses. It sounds like he throws something. "God, Winnie. I'm *so sorry*. I knew he was supposed to get her, but I thought maybe he took her to lunch or something. Shit," he curses again. "Want me to call the VFW?"

I rub at my temples, thinking fast. "No. Even if you reach him, I'm not sure he's in any state to drive her. I'll try finding someone with a car and call you back."

I hang up and scroll to the first name that comes to mind.

"You back already? How was it?"

Just the sound of his voice, and I nearly lose it. "Case, I need your help."

His response is instant. "Anything. What's wrong? Are you okay? Did you get in an acc—"

"I'm fine. I need you to go to the Stop and Go on Fuller and pick up Garrett, please. Right away. Can you do that? She was supposed to be picked up hours ago, and my dad—"

"Yeah." I can hear the jangle of his keys. "Yeah. Winnie. It's cool. I'm five minutes out. I'll get her and call you as soon as I have her, okay? It's going to be fine."

"Yeah. Okay. I'm gonna call the lady who's with her and let her know someone is coming."

A minute later, I end the call, and I realize Camilla has pulled over the truck and she and Maria are watching me. I look up into their concerned faces and immediately burst into rib-busting sobs.

"I t-told youuuu. I told y'all! It's not about me. I can't ever leave them because if I'm not there, shit like *this* happens. He doesn't take care of them. She's fucking ten years old, and she was walking home in ninety-degree weather *alone*. A stranger stopped her. God. What if some pedophile stopped instead of Jenny fucking Carter? What if she got hit by a car? I'm two hours away! I told her I would take care of her, and I'm not there!"

"Oh, no, Win—" Camilla starts to say, but my phone is ringing in my hand, and I answer it.

It's Case. "I got her. She's all hopped up on Dr Pepper, and she and Pax are starting a burping contest in my back seat. She's fine. Everyone is okay. Jenny Carter seems very nice, and she said to let you know Garrett was extremely polite."

I shake my head. "Thank you, Case. I don't know what I would have done—I'm so sorry to interrupt your—"

"Winnie Sutton, stop that shit right now." He lowers his voice. "I know you're beating yourself up, and this is not your fault. Understood?"

"Sure," I lie.

He sighs. "We'll revisit this when you get home. Jesse's at home?"

"Yeah. I need to call him. He's probably freaking out."

"Call him and tell him Pax and I are coming to get him. I promised Garrett some ice cream. I bet the kid could eat."

"Oh," I rush to assure him, "you can just bring her home. You don't have to—"

"Too late. Already turning down your street. No need to call Jesse. I'll send Pax in so he can scare the shit out of his little sister's boyfriend."

I can't help the strangled chuckle that slips out.

There's a smile in his voice when he says, "That's better. See you in a few hours, Winnie. Be safe, okay?"

"'Kay. Thank you."

We hang up, and I gesture for Camilla to keep going in a "nothing to see here" kind of way. Which is rude, but I'm exhausted, and all I want is for this trip to be over now.

"All worked out?" Maria asks hesitantly.

"For now. Case and Pax got her."

"Well, that's good, then. I bet she'll be excited to spend time with—"

But I lower my window again and turn up the radio. Within minutes, I'm asleep.

—

I sleep the whole way back to the ranch. We woke up early, and I'm feeling fuzzy from the emotional roller coaster of a day, so when Camilla waves off my offer to help her unload the horses, I don't argue. It's not until I arrive at a darkened house I realize Case still has my siblings and my dad's never even been home today. I shoot Case a text to let him know I'm in town and then grab my keys and hop right back into my car. I drive to the VFW in silence and park next to my dad's old truck. It's Saturday, so that place is hopping as much as any small-town bar can be, and I wave at the bartender, a big-bellied, nosy sort with more hair on his face than the top of his head.

"Hey, Jer. Is my dad in the back?"

"Winnie Sutton, as I live and breathe! Girl, you're all grown. Haven't seen you in an age. What can I get you?"

"Still only nineteen, Jer, and I'm not thirsty. Dad's in the back?"

He nods, and I wave before moving past several pool tables, booths, and neon signs toward the loud crowd of men surrounding the electronic dartboards. I recognize my dad, sitting with his back to me on a stool. He's got a handful of bottles on the tall tabletop in front of him, but I doubt he's drunk. My dad's not a big drinker; he just likes this place. He hides in here with these guys, slinging beers, bullshitting over darts, and reliving the glory days. I tap on my dad's broad, flannel-clad shoulder, and he spins on his stool, smile dying on his lips when he sees it's me.

"Hey, Dad. Been here all day?"

"You're back! I thought you wouldn't be back until late afternoon."

"It's six o'clock, Dad."

He sputters around the sip he'd been taking. "No kiddin'?"

My arms fold over my chest. "You forgot to pick up Garrett from camp, Dad."

He frowns, puzzled. "Was that today? Did you get her?"

"No, I didn't, as I was somewhere in the middle of Texas when a complete stranger called to say they saw your ten-year-old daughter walking home alone in the heat. I called a friend to go and get her for me. *Where the hell were you?*" By the end, I'm dangerously close to shrieking.

He looks around at the heads turning toward us and lowers his voice. "I was here. Like always. You knew that. You could have called me, and I would have gone and got her."

"I didn't have time to call around and hunt you down, Dad! Garrett was at a gas station with a stranger! She could have been kidnapped or run over or had heat stroke. All while you were sitting here avoiding your responsibilities!"

"Garrett's fine, though?"

"No thanks to you," I say.

My dad takes another pull from his bottle and makes to turn in his chair, his dismissal clear.

"That's it?" I ask, feeling the childish urge to stomp my

foot or swing at something. "You have nothin' to say for yourself?"

He spins back around, his face older than I've seen in a long while, his tone resigned. "What would you like to hear, Winnie? I fucked up. Nothing new. I've never claimed to be father of the year."

"I don't need you to be father of the year," I insist, frustration burning in my chest. "I just need you to be a father."

"I'm doing the best I can, Winnie. Christ, you turned out okay." This time, he gets up and takes the darts from another guy, and I know we're done talking.

I spin on my heel, stomping out to my car, kicking at the gravel as I go. I end up picking up a fistful of rocks and chuck the stones one by one at my dad's tailgate. Not that it matters, dinged up and ancient POS that it is.

"Please tell me that's your dad's truck."

I pick up another handful and whip at the rusty letters that spell out CHEVY.

"I'm, like, ninety-nine percent sure it's his."

"Close enough for me." Case is standing against my car, arms folded across his chest and denim-clad legs crossed at the ankles. "Your brother thought you were probably here. Said he'd stay home with Garrett and get a frozen pizza going for you in case you were hungry."

My chest squeezes at the thought of my fourteen-year-old brother making me dinner. Frozen pizza, but still.

"Did it help?"

I make my way to Case and lean against the hood next to him. "Not as much as I'd hoped. I knew it wouldn't make a difference." I sigh. "But I'd thought it might be, I don't know, cathartic or something. Instead, it made me feel like shit."

"If it's any consolation, I think Jesse has been affected for the better these last few months. He's grown up a lot."

I shake my head, smiling sadly. "That doesn't make me feel better. He's not the one who needs to grow up. That's just perpetuating the cycle."

"Maybe so. But I also think it's okay for an almost fifteen-year-old to have some responsibilities, and he's learning that from *you*. He wants to help. He doesn't want you to do this on your own. And, for that matter, neither do I, nor Camilla, Pax, Maria. . . . We all want to help."

My fists clench impotently against my sides. "I'm so fucking sick of needing help, though. I don't want help! I want to be able to leave my house for one fucking day and know everything will still be okay while I'm gone. This right here is why I can't ever tour, Case. At least not until Jesse can drive and Garrett can stay home alone."

"But why should you always be the only one sacrificing? Why are you the one left waiting for your life to start?"

"Why should *they*? What makes my life more important?"

"I'm not saying that," Case says, impatient.

"I know," I say softly, pushing off the bumper and turning to face him. "I know you're not saying that, and I know you mean well. You've done so much for me, and I'm so thankful for what you did today. You didn't hesitate. I can't tell you what it means to know I could count on you with them."

"You can count on me with *you*, too, you know."

I shake my head again, so tired. "I can't count on anyone with me, but if I could, I'd want it to be you."

His expression is fierce, and I want to kiss him for it and say fuck-all to my boundaries. "That means something," he insists.

"Not enough," I whisper.

"Not yet, maybe," he concedes. "But I'm gonna wear you down, Winnie Sutton."

"I hope so." And I'm a little surprised to find that I mean it. For the first time in a long time, I *hope* so.

Nineteen
CASE

I didn't figure I'd ever be back at the St. James Medical Center after the solid month I spent there visiting Walker last fall, but I'm relieved to note the cloud of dread I used to feel walking to the pediatric ward has all but disappeared.

I'm sure it has to do with the fact I'm not coming here today to watch my best friend fade away. Instead, I'm here to visit a friend who is recovering from a bone marrow transplant. Ryder's a thirteen-year-old cancer patient who was in the hospital at the same time as Walker, recovering from an infection caused by his most recent bout of chemo. Their rooms were close, and sometimes when I stayed overnight with Walker and he'd be asleep, I'd stop in to find Ryder awake. Ryder's a massive rodeo fan, so we had lots to talk about. His parents called me this morning to ask if I'd come by and visit him while he's stuck in bed recovering.

I'd be lying if I said I hadn't felt any trepidation about coming back, but I figure visiting someone who's sick isn't half as bad as being the actual sick one. Plus, I've been holding on to something that was Walker's, and I think it needs to go to Ryder.

I stop at the front desk and give my name and get a sticker with today's date in return. The friendly voice behind the glass asks me if I need directions, but I wave them off and make my way directly to the elevators. I ascend, and before long, a *ding* rings out and a recorded child's voice announces, "Seventh floor!" I swallow back the memory of how, toward the end, Walker would cringe at that voice. It's so cheerful. It's meant to make kids feel safer, but when you're a dying seventeen-year-old, it feels mocking.

Maybe I should fill out a comment card or something.

The doors open, and I'm greeted by a chorus of cheerful exclamations from the front desk. "Case! What a surprise!"

"Hey, Maggie, Donna, Craig." I nod at the older gentleman in his perpetual bow tie. "How're y'all?"

Good, goods and *Can't complains* are exchanged, and a moment later, I'm buzzed through the security doors. I reach the nurses' station to another round of smiles and friendly greetings. This time, they ask about Kerry and how bull riding is going. They ask if I'm away at school yet. One shy-looking younger nurse asks about Brody Gibson, and I make a note to give him shit about it later.

I visit for a few minutes, feeling a little weird about how *not* weird this is. It's been seven months since I was last here, and yet they are just as pleased to see me as if I were here yesterday. Eventually, I break away, promising to stop back before I leave, and I make my way to room 118. I knock on the door, and Ryder's mom startles before brightening from where she's been asleep in a plastic recliner at the foot of the bed.

"Case! Oh my goodness! Ryder." She shakes a blanket-covered foot gently. "Ry, look who it is!"

I school my features just in case before walking the rest of the way into the room. It's something I learned with Walker. No matter what you have going on in your own life, in your own headspace, you drop that shit at the door because they are already taking on enough on their own.

This time, though, I needn't have bothered.

"Bro!" I exclaim. "I don't even recognize you! Is that a Mohawk?"

Ryder runs a hand through his neon lengths and beams. "Mom and Dad said once my hair grew back, I could do whatever I wanted with it."

"His dad promised," his mom says wryly, "but it suits him."

I move closer and pull a chair from the wall to sit at the side of his bed. "It really does. I'm mad jealous. You look taller, too. Even sitting down. How is that possible? It hasn't been that long! You're like a whole-ass middle schooler now!"

Ryder's face flushes with the minor cuss, but I know he's loving it. The pediatric intensive care unit was pretty empty during the month he and Walker were here last fall, so Walker and I made it our mission to make sure Ryder always felt like one of the guys. That meant teaching him cuss words and all the right rodeo lingo.

"I know. Doc says if I keep up the good numbers, I might even go to school in the fall. Seventh grade."

"Ah." I lean back in my chair and close my eyes. "Seventh grade. I remember seventh grade. Lots of cute girls, if memory serves. And you know the ladies love a rebel. They're gonna be all over this." I wave my hand at his hair.

Ryder smiles and tells me more about his plans for after he's discharged, and his mom fills in the gaps about his treatments and how successful the surgery's been.

"Provided there's no infection," she tells me, "he could be home by the end of the month."

I shake my head. "Awesome, bro. I'm so impressed. You're kicking cancer's ass."

"I was thinking I might want to try some riding after I get better," he tells me. "Maybe learn some roping or"—he shrugs, his shoulders still bony in his gown—"even try to sit a bull."

I swallow the emotion threatening to ruin my careful composure. "Ryder, man. I've no doubt in my mind you can do whatever you dream up. You want to ride a bull? Or a horse? Or learn to rope a calf? Any of it—you bring your mom and dad and you come to my ranch, and it's on the house."

"Oh, you don't have to do—"

"On the house," I insist to his mom before turning to Ryder. "I have a friend, Winnie Sutton, who's the best barrel racer you've ever seen. She's working on training a couple of horses to race, and I'm sure she'd love someone to come out and test out her stock. You'd be doing us a favor if you're really serious about this."

Ryder's eyes flicker to his mom, who grins at him and then at me. "If the doctor agrees, we'll give you a call," she says.

"Speaking of rodeo," I tell Ryder, "I've been holding on to this for you and almost forgot all about it." I reach into my backpack. "So I'm glad your mom called."

I pull out the shiny gold buckle and pass it to him. "It was Walker's from his last rodeo. I'm not too proud to admit he handed me my ass to win it. Rubbed this buckle in my face for weeks. Wouldn't take it off. I'm positive he'd want you to have it.

He thought the world of you and talked about you all the time. Always asking how you were. He'd be super stoked to see how well you're doing, and he'd choke over that haircut."

Ryder takes the buckle from my hands and holds it close to his face to read it. His eyes are bright and watery. "I can't take—"

"Please," I insist. "It's yours. At least until you can win your own."

At the challenge, his expression becomes fiercely determined, and while you can't ever know for sure, I feel deep down the little dude's gonna be okay.

I visit a while longer, telling them stories about some of the stupid stuff Walker and I got into over the years, until Ryder's eyes start to droop and a nurse pokes her head in to get lunch orders.

Ryder's mom walks me out of the room. She closes the door behind her for privacy, smoothing the wrinkles in her button-down and wrapping her cardigan around herself. It may be summer outside, but hospitals are always cold, no matter the season. "Thank you so much for coming by. I know you must be busy, but Ryder's been talking about you so much, and I thought a visit might break up the tedium of waiting to heal."

"Thanks for telling me he was here. Can I come back to visit, or would you rather me not?"

"Oh! If it's not too much."

"Not at all. This was good. Ryder looks strong. So much better than last fall, even."

"He is. Of course these things are never certain, but his team is very optimistic."

"Great. Good. Glad to hear it."

She puts a hand on my arm, and her look is maternal. "It's good to see you, Case. You seem to be doing okay?"

"I am."

"Don't think I didn't notice how you played off Ryder's questions about the PBR."

I feel my face get warm, and I shift my weight. "Yeah, well . . ."

"I always thought you would be a good nurse or doctor," she presses on. "Something in the medical field."

That stops me in my tracks. "Really?"

She hums an affirmative. "You have a gift—a way about you. I've been in a lot of hospital rooms and doctors' offices in the last decade, and I've seen it all. A lot of people come in here and don't know how to act. They're awkward and too careful. They make patients restless. Or they pity the patients and make them feel miserable. But not you. You've always just been yourself. Toward Walker and Ryder, and I've talked with a few of the other parents and they've all said the same. During those weeks you spent here with your friend, you made an impact in a lot of young lives."

I clear my throat, trying to repress the surge of emotion. "I don't know what to say. Thank you, Mrs. Jones."

"Just something to think about. It takes a special person to come in here and take care of these kids day after day, riding out the inevitable storms with them."

I nod, my thoughts tripping over each other. "Yeah. Maybe . . . I'll definitely consider it. Thanks."

Someone is heading for us with a cart of lunches, so I let Mrs. Jones get back to her son. After a quick stop at the nurses' station, where I promise to bring some of Kerry's cookies with me next time, I leave.

———

Hours later, I'm still thinking over what Mrs. Jones said to me and remembering this one moment back when Walker was still alive.

It was one of his last good nights, when he was lucid enough to hold a conversation—when he was still *himself*. Walker had looked terrible. A shadow of his former strong and wiry self. His eyes were watery and yellowed with jaundice, his skin was pasty and stretched thin over his bones. I'd just finished cleaning him up, and he said to me, *"You know, you're not terrible at this taking-care-of-people thing."*

"Shut up," I said, snorting.

"I'm serious. I never realized it before. You're kind of made for this."

"I have a strong stomach is all."

"It's more than that."

I don't know. Maybe it *is* more than that. Like when I talked to Winnie about being *unflinching*. That's what it all comes down to, right? I've always been good at school. Math and science come naturally to me. But I'd want direct contact with people. With kids, even. Pediatric patients. Nursing.

I nearly scoff. A "murse" is what my dad calls them. Male nurses. But I don't know. Nurses do all the hardest shit, really. Doctors would come in and out of Walker's room, holding their clipboards and checking the charts. They would read the numbers reported by the nurses and then skip out again. Not that doctors aren't extremely important. But nurses are the ones on the front lines.

"Riding out the storms," as Mrs. Jones said.

I think I'd like that. No. Scratch that. I think I'd fucking love it.

I wander down to the kitchen, still lost in my thoughts, and find myself sliding onto a stool while Kerry is elbow-deep in an uncooked chicken. Trisha Yearwood is playing softly over the Alexa speaker. Winnie and Kerry share a taste in music.

"Hey, kiddo," she says, not bothering to look up from where she's rubbing copious amounts of seasoning in between the skin and meat. "How was St. James?"

"Not as bad as I'd thought," I admit. I reach for a corn muffin, peeling away the paper wrapper and taking a bite. "Ryder looked great, and the doctor said his numbers were nice and healthy. They think he might even be discharged by the end of the month."

"Oh, that's great news," Kerry says, sounding relieved. "Did he like the buckle?"

"About shit his pants," I tell her with a smirk, and she shakes her head at my crassness. "He's interested in rodeo," I carry on. "I invited him out here to train with Winnie sometime."

"Not with you?"

I shrug a shoulder, popping the rest of the savory corn muffin in my mouth. Kerry puts jalapeño in her corn bread, and the spicy-and-sweet combination is heaven-sent. "I mean, yeah, sure, me, too. Unless I'm away at school."

Kerry stiffens, using her free shoulder to nudge her reading glasses back in place, right below her line of vision. She narrows her eyes at me. "Are you planning to go to school this fall?"

"I'm thinking about it."

Her soft features brighten. "Really? That's wonderful. Studying gen eds or what?"

"I don't know. Maybe nursing?"

"Oh, Case," she exhales. "You'd be a great nurse."

"You think so?" I ask, playing with the paper, smoothing it on the cool marble top. "You don't think it's, I don't know, kind of feminine? Not that *I* feel that way," I rush to assure her. "Just . . . you know what Junior'd say."

Kerry levels me with a look, plopping the whole chicken in

a baking dish and stuffing a bunch of leafy, green stuff around it. She shoves it in the oven and moves to the sink to wash her hands. Then she turns back to me, drying them on a small towel.

"Yes. I know what your dad would say, and I'm sorry for it. But you're a grown man, Case. You can make your own choices—different choices, even—than your father would make, and while he may give you grief for those choices, in the end, it's you who has to live with them. So," she says with a small smile, the one that tells me she already knows what the answer will be. "Can you live with being a nurse?"

"I think I could."

"Then you should consider it."

I sit back. "I could be a nurse. A pediatric nurse."

Kerry beams at me, her eyes watery. "I can see that."

I can't believe how right it feels. More right than anything has felt in a long time. Which instantly fucks with my head, growing a pit in my stomach. For so long, I adopted a different kind of dream, and that future looks nothing like college and a nursing degree and working with kids. I stuff down the feeling and nod at Kerry. "Yeah. I think I'd like working with kids like Ryder." And Walker.

Is that shitty? Would Walker hate me for it? That instead of chasing the thrill of the arena for the rest of my life, I would take care of sick kids. Would he feel like I'm an insult to his memory? Would he feel like I've given up on him and our dream—*his* dream of a buckle?

I feel a hot flash of impatience at the last part. Because Walker's not here, and this is my life, not his. In the same breath, I can tell Winnie she needs to think of herself for once and not put aside her dreams for her siblings, and there I go doing the fucking opposite with regard to my dead best friend?

And there's the guilt.

Kerry hums to herself, ignorant of the storm inside of me. "Good. That's good, Case. You should check out the University of Texas. I hear they have an excellent nursing program, not to mention a nationally competitive rodeo team."

I force a grin. "You just happen to know that, huh?"

She flutters her hands at me dismissively, hiding a pleased expression.

I jump off my stool, feeling the need to get some fresh air and think. First, I round the island to give her a kiss on her cheek. "I love you, Kerry."

"I know," she replies with a chuckle. "Now get out of my kitchen."

———

I drive for a while with my windows down, long enough for the sun to set and the air to turn slightly cooler, before somehow turning up at the Fareway Freight train trestle. Another task off the Walker list. One of the last. I haven't been putting it off, like I did with Charles. Not exactly, anyway. There's a lot of history here because we used to fish underneath it as kids during the offseason. A lot of memories of long talks and big dreams. Maybe that's why I'm here. This is where we originally hatched our plan to go into the PBR together. Maybe I'm hoping there's something magical about this place. That being here will give me clarity, or maybe I just want to get this fucking list over with and move on with the rest of my life.

I'm stagnant. I'm literally standing on the precipice. Do I follow the path he laid out before me, or do I swerve?

It's a stupid dare. Trains are rare and the trestle is rickety as fuck, but kids used to walk across it all the time until last summer when two sophomores from the football team got hit by a freight train in an initiation gone tragically wrong.

I don't know if that was before or after Walker made this list, but everything seems pretty quiet now, so I jump out of my car and hike up the steep hill in the darkness toward the tracks. I stand at one end and stare into the tunnel. It seemed shorter from where I was parked. I shine my phone's flashlight and count the railroad ties. Fifty-four in total. The trestle isn't as high as the corn silo, but it's still a good twenty-five feet in the air over Rock River. I take a step. Tiny pebbles grate against the metal, scratching and squeaking under my Jordans. I take another step and another until I'm in the dead center of the narrow bridge. Twenty-seven ties in. Wrapping my arm around the cold metal, I lean out into the open air. The cool night presses and pulls at my sweat-damp button-down, making me shiver. I gulp the air into my lungs, past the tightness in my throat. Beneath me, inky black water rushes over massive boulders, drowning out the noise of my breaths. The air pricks at my cheeks, and I realize I'm *crying*.

What am I doing? I slide down carefully to a squat, still gripping the metal, even as I curl in on myself. I can't seem to catch my breath. I can't feel or see or hear anything but rushing water. I don't know how long I stay like that; I only know all of a sudden, the metal beneath my palms is shaking. No. Not shaking. *Vibrating*. Every atom of my being instantly charges as if I've been zapped with a cattle prod, and I spin on my heel to see the telltale pinprick of lights rapidly growing in the distance.

A train.

You have got to be kidding me. I calculate the numbers. Do

I have time to make a run for it, or do I have to jump? The water is fucking cold.

Run it is. Make it a sprint.

The rumbling is louder, but it's still a ways off. Twenty ties. Eighteen. Thirteen. Twelve. Eight. The train is louder now. Really loud. Too loud to look. Just run. Keep running. Don't stop running.

Six.

Five.

Four.

Three.

Two.

One.

I scramble off to the side, sliding on the dewy grass and rolling painfully over gravel and debris. My body comes to a stop just as a mighty gust of wind and painful roaring assault me—the train flying past. I reach for my chest as if I could grasp my heart, thudding painfully inside of me, trying to escape. Train car after train car rushes past, and still I sit, rubbing at the beating muscle under my fingertips. It finally passes, and I fall back against the ground, staring at the star-filled sky and laughing.

Fucking laughing.

What just happened? I can't believe that just happened. I almost died. Fucking Walker and his fucking list almost killed me. Again.

With a groan, I get to my feet and climb back up toward the trestle.

Because of course, I have to do it all over again to get back to my truck. This time, though, I don't mess around. I don't count the railroad ties, and I don't stop at the halfway point to cry. No trains come, and I make it back to my car in one piece. The trembling has stopped, and my adrenaline has melted away. It's been seventeen minutes since I left my car, and now I'm back, and I'm just me again.

Nothing has changed. I'm still the same as I was when I stepped onto that trestle. I still have the same problems, the same misery, same loneliness, same uncertainty.

But also, *everything* has changed. Because that's it. I'm done letting Walker's memory guide my life. I won't survive it. I need to start living on my own.

Twenty
CASE

The night after the train trestle, I watch a Rangers game with my dad for the first time since I got my driver's license. We don't typically do that kind of father-son bonding. He's always working late, and to be honest, we don't have a whole lot in common. I have to imagine I'm a lot like my mom, though he's never said. I know he loved my mom, so much he can't bring himself to talk about her even, eighteen years after the fact, and I've always told myself he has to love me that much, too. Like deep down inside. Or maybe that's not something men talk about with their sons. Walker's dad was super affectionate with the both of us, but that could be because his kid was sick. Maybe this is typical if no one's actively dying.

I've never given it much thought. Not until recently, after being exposed to Winnie's dad. The thing is, my dad and I don't see eye to eye on much, but he *has* always seen me and taken care of me. He's always been a dad.

The bar is admittedly low, but still.

We eat our roasted chicken in the media room with a screen

so enormous, it makes the players look life-size. My dad doesn't ask about my day and I don't ask about his, but we sit in the same room without fighting, and he doesn't force any bullshit life advice about "sucking it up," so I count that a win. He does ask about Winnie, with a twinkle in his eye I've only seen one other time—the last time she came up between us. He still likes to give me shit, and somehow *that* feels so normal, I don't even mind.

I realized something last night, sprawled on the ground, my heart pounding out of my body and my life flashing before my eyes. I told myself I didn't want to live by Walker's list anymore, but I also don't want to live by my dad's expectations. I don't want to care about failing to meet his manly standards. I don't care if he thinks my grief is a failing. Or that I should drink coffee black and drown myself in the good whiskey when I'm feeling too much. I don't even care if he calls me a murse. So what. I'm alive, you know? And as long as I'm breathing, I'm going to live the way I want.

—

After the game is over and my dad goes to bed, I set out through my dark house, to the back porch. There's something I need to take care of.

I walk over to the firepit and turn on the propane, igniting the flame and lighting up the night. The rest of the ranch is a heavy blanket of navy and pinprick stars, impossible to make out beyond the reach of the flickering blue fire.

I stand in front of the flames, feeling the heat press against my legs, and reach for the folded paper I've tucked away in my pocket.

The list.

Ghost Walker stands across from me. I know he's not real, but he's so vivid at this moment, in the firelight, he could be.

He sighs, tucking his hands into his pockets. He gives me a nod. The kind of nod he might've given me from across the arena after a rough ride. The kind that says, "Sometimes shit just doesn't go your way."

"Let me start by saying, I still miss the fuck out of you."

I suck in a deep breath, releasing it past trembling lips, willing myself to keep it together. "And that list was mostly a fucking disaster. I could have died at least three times. I'm not sure what the lesson was supposed to be." I laugh, shaking my head. "Actually. That's not right. I do know what the lesson was supposed to be. It's to not put so much stock in ideas that came from a dying almost-eighteen-year-old, even if he's the best friend you ever had."

Ghost Walker smirks, and I stand there watching him a long time. Memorizing the way he looks: young, healthy, full of shit. For the rest of my life, this is the way I want to see him, not sickly thin, gasping for breath. When I go to college, get married, start a career, have kids, whatever happens, *this* is who I want to see.

"I should let you go," I say, swallowing thickly. "I *need* to let you go."

I hold the worn piece of paper covered in his handwriting over the flame, letting it catch, watching the embers chase through the crossed-off tasks one by one, turning them to ash. A soft breeze spurs the flame faster, and a heartbeat later, it's gone.

And so is Walker.

—

I apply to nursing school a week later without telling anyone except Kerry and Pax. Kerry for obvious reasons, and Pax because I've been compulsively checking my phone ever since hitting Submit on the application and he thought I was texting Winnie.

He'd started giving me even more grief about my friendship with Winnie than usual, so I caved in a backward attempt at self-preservation, which, I'll admit, did not have the desired effect. Now, every time he's in the vicinity when my phone vibrates, he's instantly alert and ready to give a smirk (Winnie) or curiously raised brows (college).

I used to think Walker was the most obvious human on the planet. I was wrong.

But it's not so bad. Better than waiting for the application results alone, and anyway, Pax isn't completely off base about Winnie. I can fully admit to having a massive crush on her, even as she's becoming one of my best friends. She's fun, cute, and talented. Smart as fuck and tough. I admire her. She holds it together in a way I'm not sure I could. The other weekend, I fully expected to find her sobbing in her car in the parking lot of the VFW. Instead, she was dry-eyed and chucking rocks at her dad's tailgate. I've no doubt she was devastated. I could hear it in her voice on the phone, and Camilla said she cried herself to sleep on the ride back from Fort Worth. But by the time I saw her, she'd put herself back together again.

Do I wish she didn't have to?

Well, sure.

But just because I wish life would go easier on the Sutton kids doesn't invalidate how impressive they are for handling it as it is.

And anyway, Winnie doesn't want me to make things easier. She's been abundantly clear on that front. My new tactic is to go along for the bumpy ride.

WINNIE
Qu'est-ce que l'ouragan a dit au cocotier?

I glance up from my phone at the arena, where Winnie is currently on one of her backup stallions, Risky Business. How on earth did she manage to text? I watch her, puzzled, until she catches my gaze and smirks before dropping into a perfect canter, leading her steed closer and closer to the barrels.

"Yo! Case!"

I drop my gaze, giving my attention to where Pax is spotting Brody as he's bench-pressing.

"Sorry, what?"

Brody grunts with effort, and Pax gestures at him. "Switch places with me. I can't spot Brody. I can barely spot you."

I swap positions as my phone buzzes again. My fingers twitch to check my phone, but I train my focus on Brody lifting beneath me. My phone vibrates again. Pax snorts.

I narrow my eyes at him. "What did the hurricane say to the coconut tree?"

"Is that what you're doing all day? Knock-knock jokes?"

"They're not knock-knock jokes. Did I say, 'Knock-knock'? But yeah, in French."

"Hold on to your nuts," Brody says. He comes to a sitting position, and I pass him the towel.

"Huh?" I say.

He scrubs his face and neck. No matter how many fans we bring out here, it's still hot as blazes. I also hand him his water bottle. "The joke," he says. "The hurricane tells the coconut tree to hold on to its nuts."

I blink. "Genius. Please hold."

CASE
Trop facile.

CASE
Accrochez-vous à vos noix.

WINNIE
. . .

WINNIE
Cheater! Brody told you.

I groan out loud and can hear the echo of laughter in the arena. Over the half wall, I can see Maria doing a little dance.

"Your girlfriend gave me away."

Pax looks entirely unbothered by this news. "Well, you did cheat."

Brody gets up from the bench, and we trade places. I lie down while he removes some weight from each side. Not a lot, and not nearly as much as we remove for Pax, but enough so I don't kill myself.

I reach up and remove the bar, completing my sets. We go through the routine one more time with Pax and then move on to squats. Once again, Brody starts us off.

He stands beneath the bar, hauling it to his shoulders and stepping clear from the supports. Then he executes a perfect squat.

Bastard.

"Hey," I say, "been meaning to ask you. I was at St. James last week to visit someone, and there was this nurse . . . or maybe she was a tech? Young, cute, with curly hair? She asked about you by name."

His face turns red, and I can't tell if it's the exertion or something else.

"You were on the seventh floor?" he asks, his brows drawing together as he stops at the top.

"Yeah. Remember that kid Ryder? Cancer patient? His mom called. He's back in after a bone marrow transplant. She asked if I could come and see him."

Brody nods. "Little guy?"

"Middle schooler."

"Shit." Brody starts squatting again. He finishes his reps and places the bar with a clank of metal. "I don't know how you can stand going back. I hate that place. I don't ever want to see it again."

I move to redistribute the weight. "Well, it's not like I was there to sit in Walker's old room and reminisce. I was visiting someone."

"Yeah, another sick kid. No thanks. I've had enough to last a lifetime."

I line myself up underneath and meet Pax's eyes. He's watching me in silence, and I can't tell what he's thinking.

"Yeah. I guess I get that," is all I say.

"That's why we're here, right? Get qualified and get the hell out of the panhandle. Put it all behind us."

"Sure." I do my reps, letting the conversation tumble around in my brain. I've been preoccupied lately, but it's occurring to me Brody's gone from my coach to a sort of equal partner in this training. It used to be "you and Walker," and then it was "you," and now its "we're" and "us." When did that change?

Pax does his squats, and then we move to the medicine balls for balance training while I'm still puzzling over Brody's words.

—

Later that afternoon, Winnie invites me on a trail ride. "On the condition we stick to English," she requests.

"*Je suppose,*" I say with feigned reluctance, though, if I'm honest, her half-Texan, half-French accent is so awful, it's cute. She definitely feels more comfortable with French texting, but that's because she can cheat with Google Translate (and I can pretend not to notice). (I can also pretend to not freak out about the fact Winnie is inviting me on a trail ride after turning me down every other time I've asked.)

Brody had to get to work at his day job, and Pax and Maria took off for "date night," which apparently consists of dinner followed by parking in some open field. Not that I have room to talk. I wasn't exactly treating girls to fancy picnic dinners a few months ago. But that was kind of the point, wasn't it? And anyway, I've stopped that. I haven't so much as hugged a girl since the corn silo, unless you count the times I've held Winnie, which . . .

Well, she doesn't count that, so I'd better not.

We saddle up Moses and Mab and take off for the farthest reaches of the ranch. I've come a long way in my riding in the last few months. Winnie and Maria would never let me live it down if I didn't earn a horse like Moses. And Winnie practically lives on horseback. If I want to spend time with her, be her friend, learn what makes her tick, I need to be more comfortable on horseback, too. Logic, right?

I've always been good at logical reasoning.

I look around, taking in the golden plains spreading before us, miles and miles in every direction. The sun is still plenty high in the sky, being summer and all, which buys us time to explore.

"I forget sometimes how much I like it out here—how lucky I am."

"It's pretty unreal," she admits, settling back into her saddle and taking a deep breath. I mirror her. Most days, the air is so warm that every time you stop moving, you start to sweat, but out here in the open grass, the breeze is constant and comfortable. I lift my cap and spin it backward, letting the wind cool me.

"Do you think this is what heaven looks like?" I ask.

She considers carefully, no doubt knowing what I'm really asking. Mab dances in place, probably scenting the creek up ahead, but Winnie doesn't acknowledge her. "I think for Texans, it must."

"You're probably right. Though I wouldn't be shocked if Walker's not waiting in some arena chute right now, ready for the ride of his afterlife."

She smiles fondly. "Always *just* qualifying by the skin of his teeth to keep things interesting."

"But for me, this would do," I say.

"Horseback and all?" she teases.

"It's growing on me." There's something different in her expression. Easier, maybe. Her eyes flicker down to my mouth and back up. My hands are full of reins, so I dip to my shoulder to swipe at my lips. I ate a CLIF Bar after my workout. I probably have chocolate on my face. Winnie flushes and turns her attention back to the copse of trees in the distance. She closes her eyes and lets her head fall back, soaking up the sun and making my chest ache.

I clear my throat. "What about yours? Is this enough, or maybe you'd prefer something with a clover course and a trio of barrels?"

I'm baiting her, I know, but she seems so relaxed it's worth the risk.

"Maybe," she says, not bothering to open her eyes. "Or maybe I agree with you. This is pretty ultimate right here."

I don't say anything. I can't think of anything to say that wouldn't put an abrupt end to this safe bubble we're in.

Instead, I click my tongue, urging Moses on to where he and Mab have been yearning to go since we stopped. Winnie's right on my heels. We bring the horses to rest in the shade and tie them close enough to the water's edge so they can drink all they want.

"Maria and Camilla want me to do North Texas Open next Friday night. Late entry, but it's small-time enough it's not a big deal."

I school my features, keeping them casual-but-reasonably-excited. "Really? And what do you want?"

The corner of her mouth quirks in a way that tells me she sees through my effort but appreciates it, anyway.

"Thank you for asking," she says, amused. "You're the only one who does, you know?"

"I'm trying."

"I can tell." She turns to lean against a tree trunk, facing me, and sighs. "I want to do it. Which probably makes me a glutton for punishment, but I want to see how Mab and I'll fare in the arena when it's for real. Even if it's a local competition, Maria will be there on Duchess."

I rest against a trunk opposite her. "And since Maria is the reigning national high school champ, this is a good way to test it out."

"Right. I mean, I've ridden against her in practice. And Mab and I always do well, but Mab's never competed. She's a rescue, after all. She's got, um, some baggage. So for all we know, she could get out there in the loud crowds and totally choke."

Or you could, I think. Not that I, personally, think Winnie will choke. There's no way. But I can see the excuse for what it is.

"I don't know it this means anything," I say, "but North Texas

Open is set to be my first rodeo, post Walker. Well, technically my second, but you know what I mean. So maybe we can do it together?"

"You and Mab?" she jokes.

"Right. Of course. Me and Mab. You can be our support cowboy."

Winnie rolls her eyes theatrically. "Ugh. Fine. If I have to do everything."

"You really do."

She presses her lips together a moment, her eyes doing that easy thing again. That's twice in less than an hour. Not that I'm keeping track.

"You'll watch me race?" Her tone is vulnerable; all pretense dropped.

"I'll be there the entire time, if you want. Will you watch me ride?"

She exhales, her shoulders drooping in relief. "The entire time, if you want."

"Unflinching, Sutton." I hold up a fist.

She taps it with her own. "Unflinching."

Twenty-One
WINNIE

I take back every time I've given you shit for nearly puking on Brody's boots last spring," I say.

I can tell Case is trying to hide his smile, but his dimple is, as always, a dead giveaway.

"To be fair, I deserved at least ninety percent of that. However," he says, nudging me with his plaid-covered elbow, "I reserve the right to cash it in and return the favor a hundredfold if you upchuck off this tailgate tonight."

I inhale through my nose, releasing my breath through tense lips. Clasping my clammy hands between my knees, I tuck my chin to my chest and concentrate on not puking. I don't want to give Case ammunition to hold over my head for the next year.

Yes, it's a double standard. What's your point?

He wraps a reassuring arm around my shoulders and speaks in a low tone that's saturated with reason. I've heard him use it on Moses and the more persnickety boarders, and I'm not sure the comparison is very flattering. "It's just a race. You and Mab could complete this clover blindfolded and still blow away the competition by at least a full second."

Case and I are sitting next to each other, denim-clad legs dangling off the back of his dad's tailgate. My very first rodeo. It's a local thing, a county fair. Typical stifling summer night in the panhandle. Whenever the wind shifts from the direction of the livestock tents, it smells like a deep fryer made babies with a doughnut factory perfumed with a whiff of fresh manure.

Usually, I find eau de county fair intoxicating and nostalgic, but this afternoon, it's wreaking havoc on my already-twisty stomach.

I lean into Case's hold and allow my head to drop on his broad shoulder for a moment before mumbling into his sleeve, "I can't believe I let them talk me into this."

"Me neither," he quips back. "I thought for sure you'd re-nege."

I slug him, but his thick leather protective vest muffles the impact. I groan in exasperation.

"I almost felt it that time," he offers. His tone is teasing, but these last few months of training and working alongside Case Michaels have given me a chance to get to know him better, and I can tell he's tense.

I raise my head to look in his eyes. Just between us, lost in the ruckus of a gathering rodeo crowd, I check, "How're you doing? You ready?"

He doesn't bullshit me. That's something I've learned about Case. His first instinct is to make some self-deprecating, sarcastic remark. Which, hey, sounds like me! But we won't do that with each other anymore. Not when it counts.

No flinching.

He exhales, pulling his arm away from my shoulders and clasping his own hands together in his lap.

"Physically, yes. I'm readier than I've ever been. Mentally, I'm almost there. Emotionally, I'm fucked."

"That good, huh?"

He chuckles low. "I won't puke, if that's what you're asking."

"Brothers who ride together, puke together," I remind him quietly. For a split second, his pained eyes drill into mine, but then he blinks and nods, releasing a long breath.

"Good point. This might be like ripping off a Band-Aid, ya know? Like once I get the first ride over with, I'll be all right."

"That makes sense. Same here."

"He'd be over the moon you're doing this," he says, breaking the tension that's settled around us.

"He probably would, wouldn't he? I don't think I ever told him about my racing ambitions. I never said them out loud to anyone before you. But he would have appreciated the reckless life choice, I think."

"A hundred percent," Case agrees. "Reckless life choices were his specialty. And the wardrobe improvements," he adds with a smirk, looking me up and down in an exaggeratedly lascivious way. "He would have dug that, too. There ain't a pair of flame-painted chaps he didn't love. But," he concedes, "we can work up to the flames. For now, let's just say rodeo suits you, Win."

My face burns, but I let him look his fill because the truth is, I picked this getup with him in mind. The problem is, I friend-zoned myself because I've been completely freaked out about my family, but since then, things have settled down. Jesse's finishing out the school year, strong, and Case, Camilla, and even Maria take turns watching Garrett at the ranch whenever I need to train.

It's not perfect and I'm not ready to tour if I ever got to that point, but no one's died or called CPS yet, so we've got that going for us.

And now I've gone and completely fallen for this cowboy next to me. Turns out spending almost all my free moments with Case Michaels just makes me like him more. Which is both amazing and awful at the same time.

So when Maria told me I needed to shop for something new and colorful to wear tonight, I decided I was going to try to catch the attention of my closest friend while I was at it.

Try being the key word. I've never tried to do anything like this in my entire life—never had the time for hooking a crush's attention.

My boot-cut jeans are snug around the hips and flare over my new boots. My button-down is a bright coral that pulls out the color in my eyes. It's slim fitting around my waist and, for once, shows off my figure. More than my oversize barn jacket ever did.

Sure, it's not Prada, but I feel like a shinier version of myself—you'd have thought I *was* wearing a ball gown with the way Case's eyes bugged out of his head when he picked me up this afternoon.

It was like for the first time, Case might see me as a woman and not the girl he mucks horse manure with.

Lord knows his tucked-in plaid shirt and fitted vest are doing all sorts of tingly things to my insides.

Of course, I've known how good-looking he is all along, and it's impossible not to notice the way his jeans stretch over his muscular thighs and how his shirt spans his wide chest. His attractiveness is not a secret, nor is my reaction to it.

However, the last months of working with each other have made me want to shove him into an empty stable stall and kiss him senseless. It's not only how he looks anymore. It's how he *cares*.

I'm completely gone for him, and I'm very sure he has no clue.

Idiot.

Attractive, considerate, charming, funny, sweet *idiot*.

Brody and Camilla choose that moment to walk up. Which is for the best. As much as I want to kiss Case, I do have other things to worry about right now. Both of us do.

———

Less than an hour later, the other barrel racers and I have drawn our racing order. I'm in the waiting pen brushing down Mab, whispering comfort into her ears in the hopes some of it trickles into my own subconscious. The sick feeling in my stomach has been replaced with the itch for the chance to prove my worth. So much is riding on our performance today, and I don't want to let anyone down. I know it's my first race, and no one expects perfection. And yet I feel like they're expecting a miracle.

Jesse and Garrett are here, sitting with Case and his dad. I was reluctant to let Case leave my side. Standing here, surrounded by competitors, is intimidating as all get-out. Everyone seems to already know everyone. They're all huddled in groups while Mab and I are on our own in our stiff new duds. We stand out like a sore thumb, which, for the record, is my least favorite thing. The fact I want to race so badly I could cry is the only reason I'm here, feeling like the most awkward human on the planet while everyone squeals and chatters around us.

But then I considered my sister, hopped up on rodeo crowds and cotton candy, spewing mathematical theorems or—*shudder*—family secrets to Mr. Michaels. I knew I wouldn't be able to concentrate until I was sure Case was up there running defense.

"Here you are! I shoulda known you'd be hiding away in a corner. I half expected you to ditch me completely." It's Maria. Over my shoulder, I glimpse voluminous dark curls and sequin detailing on the bright pink blouse I helped her pick. She's astride Duchess, a lovely painted mare who, even after several introductions, eyes up Mab as though she's also sizing up the competition.

I stop compulsively grooming Mab.

"I considered it, believe me. Case talked me off the ledge." I swallow and straighten my shoulders. It's okay to be confident. Maria said competing in rodeo is all about swagger. *Don't let them see your fear*, she told me. "It's just a case of first-race jitters," I admit. "Mab's unbeatable. This ain't new; the location's just changed."

Maria's eyes widen, impressed. "Fighting words. I love it. Don't let Duchess hear you talking smack."

I let Mab's reins drop for a moment and reach over to stroke Duchess's caramel coat. "I'm sorry, Duchess. You know I love you." A little louder, I say, "Second place ain't nothing to be ashamed of."

"Oooh, Santos, looks like you've stumbled on a rookie," another voice singsongs.

I lift the brim of my hat, and recognition passes over Christine Reynolds's face. She smirks, but not in a friendly way. I lower my brim again, though I can still see her fine, unfortunately.

"Winnie Sutton, is that you? My mistake." She looks to Maria. "Does she work for you?"

"Hey, Christine," I say to my former classmate. "I didn't know you rode." Or if I did, I forgot.

Christine is effortlessly pretty and has the cowgirl aesthetic down to a tee. If you typed "girl from a country song" into the search box on Instagram, you'd be flooded with a thousand girls who look like Christine Reynolds.

Not that I've done that. Specifically. But when I was shopping for my new competition wardrobe, I may have researched a little to try to fit in.

Something I doubt Christine has ever had to do in her entire life.

My former classmate flips a long blond ponytail over her shoulder. "I don't ride. I race. And I win. I didn't even know you had a horse," she snips, all pretense gone.

My face burns. I swallow and shift back toward Mab, reaching for her shoulder and finding her steady heartbeat underneath her coat. I take comfort from her calm. "Technically, I don't. But Mab's adopted me, and she has a need for speed, so"—I shrug—"here we are."

"Does that patch on the back of your shirt say CBM Ranch?"

"Yeah," I say, bemused. "I work there."

"And they're sponsoring you? I didn't know the Michaels brothers were so into charity."

Maria gasps above us and dismounts. "Okay, that's enough of that. Christine, don't you have somewhere else to be? Like, anywhere but here? They'll be calling your name soon."

Christine narrows her eyes and turns on her heel, marching back to her horse.

Maria watches her leave with a furrow in her brows. "Reynolds is plenty competitive, but that was something else. What'd you do to her?"

I shake my head. "Nothing. We've never, ever spoken before today. We went to the same high school, but ran in different crowds." As in Christine *had* a crowd and I didn't.

"Hmm." Maria looks uncomfortable. "I have a theory, but I don't love it."

"Oh yeah?"

"You remember a few months back when Case was doing his whole 'sad-sap fuckboy thing'?"

"Vaguely." I mean, I'd guessed.

"I heard a rumor Christine and Case . . . you know."

Now I'm really red. "Oh. Well, what's that got to do with me? I'm guessing they had a bad breakup?"

"Oh, no. Nothing like that. Case didn't do commitment. That part I know for sure. It was his deal. One time and that's it."

"Yikes."

"Yeah, but you know he's not like that anymore, right?"

I think about the last few months we've spent together. "Yeah, I know."

"Whatever Christine's problem is, I have a feeling she doesn't like seeing you with his last name on the back of your shirt."

I ignore the way my heart thumps at the implication and shake off my nerves. "Well, that's too bad. She's gonna have to get used to seeing my back."

Maria's laughter rings out. "Damn straight, Sutton." She slings up onto Duchess's back. "Good luck out there. I look forward to seeing your name right under mine."

It takes a second for her words to register, but before I can respond, Maria and Duchess are already trotting off. I return my attention to Mab, hiding my grin.

"It's on."

Twenty-Two

WINNIE

Soon, I'm astride Mab, waiting for my name to be called over the echoing loudspeakers. Adrenaline courses through my bloodstream, the effect making me nearly dizzy. I have to consciously work to focus. Mab is practically skipping beneath me. I grasp her reins tightly as she jerks and hops within the small square of space of behind-the-fence realty I've allowed her.

I know how you feel, girl. Wide-open spaces sound really tempting right about now. I calculate the distance to the exit. Worst case, we make a run for it and never look back.

But for now, the arena will have to do. There are two heats this evening, and the average of all our times, minus any deductions, will give us our final scores in the rankings.

Up until thirty minutes or so ago, I could not care less about my rankings. I wanted to do well and represent the ranch, of course, but I already know as long as I don't fall off, Mab and I are golden. I just need to not make an ass out of myself and let everyone down—and to be honest, that was enough of a challenge.

There're a lot of curious eyes in the stands, way more than I've ever faced in my life.

Then Christine Reynolds showed up like a black fly buzzing around my past. She flipped her perfectly curled hair that I bet she didn't even have to research to get right and called me a charity case. And now I'm pissed. Even if she's technically correct.

But I've swallowed back my pride over and over the past few months to do this. It's worth it.

Even if it means Christine's derision, it's *worth it*.

My hands are shaking so badly I can barely hold the reins in my clammy fingers. I inhale through my nose, holding my breath tight inside my lungs. I relax my shoulders and tilt my head side to side, loosening my neck muscles. I wipe my hands down my denim-clad thighs one at a time and recalibrate my grip. Mab's muscles twitch beneath me, and she shifts her weight impatiently.

"Steady, girl," I murmur.

My name is finally called over the loudspeakers, but I barely hear it over the loud rush of blood pounding in my ears. I press my knees, giving Mab the slightest nudge. She's bursting to go, but I hold her back, so we appear to literally dance our way up to the starting alleyway. Mab high-steps like true royalty. Once there, I take one last breath and kick her into gear.

Mab shoots out like a lightning strike, and we're off to the first barrel. I'm uncharacteristically stiff on her back, adding an extra bounce out of rhythm, and she's uncharacteristically reluctant, slowing more than necessary before the turn, but still we clear it. The second barrel is a little better. The third catches the toe of my boot, causing the barrel to wobble. Mab does a small jump-skitter away, but my hand shoots out, automatically righting the barrel just as I've done in practice without bothering to see if it's left standing. I click with my tongue and give Mab an extra jab to shift into high gear, but she's way ahead of me. We've caught our groove by now and blessedly move as one unstoppable force across the finish line.

I don't even look up at the scoreboard. I know it's not as fast as I wanted, and that's my fault. *My* jitters. That off-stride bounce at the start. My toe catching the barrel. Mab's skitter. I caught the barrel, thank goodness, because that saved us from a deduction, but I have ground to make up in the second ride.

I lead Mab back to our corner, not making eye contact with anyone else, and dismount. I round to Mab's front and touch my forehead to hers. Both of us are still working to catch our breaths, though not from exertion. We've conditioned for this plenty and could easily complete that course several times over without batting an eyelash, but there's nothing like the feeling of fire in your bones and electricity in your veins. It'll change you; it's already changed me.

Because I can tell after one race, I'm a different person. I know what it feels like to ride the wind and chase the buckle, and I'm pretty sure I can't ever go back.

(Which is too bad, because I wouldn't mind turning back the clock to the third barrel so at least then I could have tucked in my boot and avoided the tip.)

After a moment, Mab jerks her head. I raise my eyes to hers, and she gives an impatient flick of her tail as if to say, *Get a grip, Winnie.*

"Oof," I say to her in a low voice, scratching my fingertips against her shoulder. "No rest for the human. Give me a quick second to pick my heart up off the ground and recalibrate."

"That was pretty good, Sutton," his deep voice drawls from

behind me. "I mean, I've seen better, but for your first effort . . ."

A huff of laughter escapes before I say, "Fuck off, Michaels."

His large hand wraps around my arm, and he gently tugs me
to face him. His expression is determined as his eyes dart back
and forth between mine, checking to make sure I'm okay. Always checking. I've wondered if maybe it should annoy me that
he's so determined to take care of me, except, well, it doesn't.

I've never had someone check in on me before, so I'm in zero
danger of feeling stifled by the attention.

"In all seriousness, you did really well, Win. More than
well, even. You two shot out of the gate, and you could hear
a pin drop. You're all anyone can talk about right now. You're
in th—"

I cover his lips with my fingers, and his warm breath tickles
against my skin. "Please don't say. I don't want to know."

He nods, his blue eyes lit in understanding.

"Because I can do better."

Case grins. "You can."

"I'll do better this time."

"I've no doubt," he says. Then, dryly, "Maria told you to
tuck your toes on those turns."

I narrow my eyes and smack his chest. "Lord, I *knew* you
were gonna say that."

"I'm not done. Did you take deep breaths beforehand?"

"Yes, sir, Life Coach, sir, I did."

"You sure? You looked a little stiff. Granted, you still looked
better than anyone I've ever seen on horseback, but . . ." He
trails off and licks his lips, and I follow the movement along
with the sudden appearance of his dimple.

I clear my throat, feeling caught. "We both know that's a

big fat lie." I lower my voice, and he leans closer. "Maria and Duchess are pro level."

Case pulls back, grinning ear to ear. "And I bet you gave her an eyeful today. Just like you did my dad and your brother and sister and, oh yeah, Camilla, who's practically floating on cloud nine. Besides, Maria's been around as long as Walker and I have. That was your very first race ever, and you nearly—"

I cover his mouth again, feeling my cheeks warm. His lips twist under my fingers, and he holds up two hands in surrender.

"Right," he murmurs against my skin. "Sorry."

"Did you see who else is here?" I ask, my eyes darting to where Christine is grooming her horse across the way.

He follows my gaze and nods. "Yeah, I saw her." He's extremely casual as he asks, "Did she say anything to you?"

I shrug. "Nothing I can't handle."

His gaze turns intense. This close, I can smell the leather of his vest and the soap on his tanned skin. "Good."

"Hey, there's the power duo!" Camilla says, walking up to us and giving Mab a happy pat on the rump.

Case steps back, mouthing the words *cloud nine*. I grin, pleased, and try not to notice the way his absence leaves me feeling cold. Am I cold, or is he just hot?

Heh. Is it okay to think your new best friend is hot? I mean, I thought he was before we became friends, and I like him more now.

"I should leave you to get ready for your second run. I'll be watching in the stands." He moves to Mab, caressing her forelock and saying something in a low voice for her ears only. The secrets that horse must hold . . .

He struts off with a salute over his shoulder and yells, "*Sans broncher*, Sutton!"

Don't flinch.

Camilla instructs me to climb back into the saddle and gives a few hands-on instructions on my form. She leaves, and my name is called to line up once more. I start working on my breaths. Mab's still skipping around, but she feels more in control. She knows what we're doing now. She's gotten accustomed to the noise.

"Such a smart girl," I croon, rubbing her neck. "We can do better this time, can't we?"

"I hope so," Christine says, walking past on a gorgeous Thoroughbred. "You embarrassed yourself with that barrel slip."

"Ignore her," I say to Mab in a loud voice. "She's just jealous you're prettier than she is."

Christine flutters off, and by the sheer volume and force of the crowd's reaction approximately thirty seconds later, I know she did well.

But not as well as we're about to do.

Our names are called and once again, I direct Mab to the long, narrow alleyway leading into the arena. This time, I tune out the noise and distractions. I will away the roaring in my ears and home in on the course in front of us—on the feel of Mab's muscular frame. I pay attention to the way her sides rise and fall with her breaths, and I slow mine to match. "Just me and you," I tell her. "Just me and you." Then I nudge her into movement.

This time, we're in sync from the start. No bouncing. No skittering. No mistakes. One barrel, two barrels, three barrels, *fly*.

And fly Mab does. I press forward, feeling her breaths, feeling her steps. Her hooves barely touch the ground, and my body barely touches her. We're both weightless.

When we cross the finish seconds later, I collapse across her neck, rubbing down her shoulders and pressing a kiss to her mane.

"Just like that, Queen. Just . . . like . . . that. Good girl," I say. "You did so well."

The final scores come in, and we don't get first. As Maria predicted, my name is directly under hers. It's so close, I'm left wondering if I hadn't nudged that barrel in the first run, we could have beaten her and Duchess.

Which feels wild to even contemplate, but still.

Regardless, I couldn't care less, because my name is above Christine's and nearly an entire second separates us. From this moment forward, she'll have to live with the knowledge she was beaten by a trailer girl on a borrowed horse racing in her very first rodeo.

And that ain't a bad feeling at all.

Twenty-Three
CASE

Walker's competition intro song was "Thunderstruck" by AC/DC, which is both the best song of all time and also the worst. But he fucking loved it. Had since that very first competition when we met. He played it for me over the tinny earbuds of his iPod. Said it made him feel all prickly, which, thinking back on it, was a weird thing for a kid to say. But the truth is, Walker was a weird dude sometimes. Like, you know how kids will kind of tamp down their quirks in middle school and high school for the sake of fitting in? Walker never got into that. He was always exactly how he wanted to be, and somehow it worked for him. Everyone loved his weirdness. I think because secretly we wanted to be able to own up to our own individuality. We were all mad jealous of him.

At any rate, it could be argued strapping yourself to fifteen hundred pounds of raging, spastically bucking muscle inside a chute the size of a closet is plenty *prickly* enough, but as we know, Walker was a rare breed.

Most rodeos play intro music for every event under the

lights, but not usually by request. I had to call in a favor for tonight. Before drawing bulls, I slipped the request to Brody and asked him to perform some county fair public relations magic for me.

Walker Gibson is gone, and he's never going to ride with me again, but that doesn't mean I'm alone. I've chosen to live my life the way I want—I've applied for nursing school and burned the list. I thought long and hard about getting into the arena again, if this was what I wanted. And I decided it is. To an extent.

I want to qualify for the NFR in Las Vegas this spring. I made a promise, and I want to see it through for Walker and me both.

But I'm not going for the pros. This isn't how I want to spend the rest of my life. I have bigger dreams now.

The crowd is thick—thicker than when Win stole everyone's hearts and second place in the barrel-racing competition. There's the familiar buzz of excitement in the air I've been missing. An energy found in the reckless abandon of people doing impossible things. The air is overly warm and heavy with grease and tobacco smoke. If there's a breeze, I can't feel it down here. I sit on a side rail a little apart from the rest of the guys. Some of them I recognize from years past; others must have jumped into the ring during my time away. The whispers are stifling. Low mutterings of the usual too-simple explanation.

Yeah, that's Case Michaels. Yeah, he and Gibson used to be inseparable. Yeah, he died. Nah, he was sick. Something with his lungs.

We weren't sure Michaels would be back.

How Walker died was one of those things that will always haunt me because it comes up constantly.

"Did he die bull riding?"

"No, he was terminally ill."

"Oh. Well, that's still sad, but at least . . ."

At least what? When someone dies at seventeen, is there a better way for it to happen? Is a tragic accident any less horrible than a long illness?

I'm not sure it is. For the ones missing them, they're still just as *g-o-n-e*.

I clasp my helmet between my knees and pretend I don't hear them, concentrating my entire focus on the printed letters of my name.

I pull out my AirPods and plug them into my ears, drowning out the crowd and the unwanted voices in my head with some heavy hip-hop. I don't pay attention to the lyrics, just practice my breathing and let the rhythm lull me into a relaxed state. I glimpse something bright orangish-pink in the stands and know Winnie's found her seat. She raises a hand in a gentle wave, and I nod in response, feeling more grounded already. Then she pulls up a big glittery sign she and Garrett made, and I see the familiar words SANS BRONCHER in bold, block letters.

Don't flinch.

Just because Walker's gone doesn't mean I'm alone.

———

This time, I make it to the chute. It was a close thing—a hands-shaking, knees-buckling, stomach-rebelling kind of thing—but every time I felt the urge to turn out creeping along my spine, I'd look up and see Winnie. Her reassuring smile meant only for me, floating over the sea of people and tucking itself into the place inside of me where I keep track of all of Winnie's smiles.

Un-fucking-flinching.

And then I'd see Braids bouncing in her seat, still holding that sign. And my dad would lean toward Jesse, probably explaining something about the scoring, and I would swallow my panic and visualize my ride because I cannot let them down. Not again.

Walker never believed in visualization or prep work of any kind. I had to bribe him with Dr Pepper and cheese pizza to sit with me and watch films. He would say he liked to be surprised.

I would say he liked to eat sand and dodge hooves.

I'm too cerebral for that. To me, the rides have always been a problem to solve. I'll spend hours watching footage and imagining how I would have responded in each situation.

So that's how I spend my time until they announce my event. I'm still a handful of names down, so I find the bathroom and then make my way to the makeshift locker room for my bag. I buckle on my chaps, fingers brushing against the embroidered flames Walker talked me into getting. Then I grab my gloves, mouth guard, and helmet and return to the fence to watch the first few riders.

They're good. Better than my memory serves, but not as good as Walker and not as good as I am. That's not me being cocky. Well, okay, Winnie would say it is, but truthfully, I know my skills. This isn't like me bragging about having an expensive car. I didn't earn that. But when it comes to this? I'm one of the best around. I might be an emotional disaster with an overreactive upchuck reflex, but I know how to ride a bull and keep my seat. That's never been the issue.

My name is next, so I hop off the fence, and with one last lingering look to Winnie, I line up outside the chute. My heart is racing, but so far, everything is staying down. Brody's nearby, but something in my expression or maybe the green tinge to my skin must tell him I'm a loose cannon because he only slaps my shoulder once, hard, before sauntering off into the mass of coaches, bullfighters, and riders.

I hear my name over the loudspeaker, followed by the Suttons screaming for me. I slip my mouth guard between my teeth and pull down the V of my vest. I step my boot onto the rung and haul myself into the chute, hovering above the bull I've pulled for tonight. His name is Percival, and he's a fucking maniac.

Nothing like jumping right back into the deep end.

The familiar guitar riff of "Thunderstruck" plays, and the crowd instantly gets into it. I slap my vest in time with the beat before slipping my hand into the grip, face up. I carefully lower myself onto Percival, who immediately tries to rub me off, shoving my knee against the wooden chute. It doesn't feel great, but the leather chaps do their job. The chute boss grips the back of my neck and holds me steady, passing me the rope cinched through the grip and around Percival. This rope is how I stay on the bull and my ticket off when shit goes south, so I make sure I prepare it right. I wrap the rope and rewrap the cinch around my gloved hand as securely as I can manage. I double-check the feel, opening and closing my hand around it before squeezing tightly enough to lose feeling in my fingers. Not that I'll be holding on long.

And then it's time.

Let's go.

I curl myself low and tighten the one arm I'm allowed to use to hold on, and the chute pulls open.

Percival twists and bucks like he's been stung by a thousand fucking hornets, but I'm ready for him. I've studied his style. He's all over the place, so I am, too. I use my free hand to counter his movements, careful to keep it high and away from any kind of contact, and keep my center of gravity. When the buzzer sounding eight seconds rings, I flip rearward off Percival's back, midbuck, over my connected hand, and land out of the way of his hooves. It's not the prettiest ride, and I'm positive I'll see ways to improve when I watch the footage later, but I get the job done.

Garrett is screaming, and Winnie lets out a whistle I didn't know she was capable of. I remove my helmet and mouth guard in time to catch Brody as he wraps me in a firm embrace.

"He would have loved that shit."

I laugh. "He would have been bucked off in the first twist." Being left-handed, Walker would have been completely spun out by Percival's surprise left spins.

Brody beams. "That, too."

I glance back at the scoreboard. With five riders left, I'm in the lead, and because I made it to eight seconds with zero deductions, I'll be back for round two tomorrow night. Local rodeos typically only have two nights of events, which is good. More than good. I did it—I finished my ride without Walker and made it on to the leaderboard. Assuming I don't completely fall on my ass tomorrow, I'm in position to be just as good as I was before I took a year off.

But . . . as good as the ride was, it wasn't what it used to be. I don't think it was Walker being gone or my nerves at facing an unknown future. I think it might be . . . growing up. I liked it, but I didn't love it.

All I know is I will never forget the look of pure fire in Winnie's eyes as she rode this afternoon. Like racing was the only thing that mattered in the whole wide world, and the only thing worth doing with her life.

And after tonight, I know I don't feel the same about riding bulls.

And that's just fine.

Twenty-Four
CASE

The second night, there's a scheduling conflict with a local Amarillo Summer Kickoff festival, so Winnie and Brody are the only ones who stick around to watch my final bull-riding event. It's the rare night Winnie doesn't have to watch Garrett, and I'm flattered she's spending it with her butt in the stands watching me.

I told everyone it didn't matter if they came tonight. It's just a local show. I've ridden in a hundred others over the last decade. What's one more? I meant it, but that doesn't mean I don't appreciate looking up and seeing Winnie's encouraging smile. She's waving that same hand-printed sign with unbridled enthusiasm, blocking the view of at least four people behind her. It's a good look for her. No barn coat, no siblings, nothing to prove. Just Winnie being Winnie.

God, I love her.

I know I'm not supposed to. It wasn't on the list and things are complicated, but oh fucking well. I do.

Tonight, the nerves are less of the puke-inducing variety

and more of the typical "I'm about to hop on fifteen hundred pounds of unpredictable bull." Brody manages to get Walker's song playing again, and this time, it spurs me on instead of gutting me. NFR or no, tonight, I'm just a guy doing something reckless to show off for the girl he secretly loves. As luck would have it, I pulled a dead ringer named King Kong. He plays by the rules, bucking enough to score us some solid style points, but not enough to cause me to bail ahead of the eight seconds. By the time I'm flinging myself off his back and safely ducking to the ground, I already know I've won.

Case Michaels is back.

For what it's worth.

I collect my prize, take some pictures, and answer a few questions for the local paper, keeping an eye on where Winnie is waiting for me. I can tell she overhears the reporter asking me about my "impressive return to riding," because she rolls her eyes.

Keeping it real. Like when I told her she could have ridden better yesterday afternoon. Hell, she rode great. For her first time, it was practically perfection. But I'll never say that. It's not what she wants from me. She can get that from everyone else, and so can I. But to each other? We don't flinch. We tell the truth. We press buttons and challenge the status quo.

I respect her too much for anything less, and she matches me in that.

Eventually, I make my way over to where she's standing.

I gesture to the sign in her hands and the bag over my shoulder. "Maybe we can drop these off at my truck? Unless"—I smirk—"you want to carry that around with you through the carnival?"

Winnie raises the sign and smacks me lightly upside the head with it. "Are we walking through the carnival?"

"I thought we could. If you want." *Please want.* I never get Winnie to myself.

Winnie lifts a shoulder, all casual, but she looks pleased with the invite. We walk through the dusty field turned parking lot and drop our things in the trunk of my SUV. I reach for a water bottle from a small cooler I keep for rodeos and pass her one before turning to sit on the tailgate in the twilight.

"How'd it feel out there tonight?" she asks.

"Familiar," I say. "Minus the obvious, of course."

She takes a sip of her water, holding the cap in the opposite hand. "You looked comfortable. Super relaxed. Is that something you cultivated over time, or have you always been that way?"

I consider that. "Been that way as long as I can remember. High-stress situations calm me, and straddling a bull is about as stressful as it gets. It's not that I don't take the danger seriously. I'm aware of the risks, but something in my brain clicks when the adrenaline kicks in and everything gets extra clear."

Winnie nods. "I've heard about that kind of thing before. It's rare, but not unheard of. Like fighter pilots. They have to be able to turn off the chaos around them and zero in on the target."

"Not that I would compare myself to a fighter pilot, but yeah."

"You're a good person to have around in a crisis."

"That's me."

She takes another sip and swallows, pressing her lips together.

"Go ahead."

"What?" she hedges, turning pink in the dim light.

"I can tell you're gearing up to ask me something. Just ask. I'm an open book." I point my bottle toward her. "With you, anyway."

"Okay." She stops and restarts. "Okay. It's only that . . . you don't seem . . . like . . . you've been training for months and months, like me, and you won top place tonight after all that hard work, and I guess . . . you don't seem very happy?"

I look away from her, staring off into the humid night. It's not supposed to rain, but heavy gray clouds cover the sky and smother the stars from sight.

"It's not that I'm not happy," I say softly. "I am. But maybe I'm not as happy as Walker was, or as you are. Or maybe *happy* isn't even the word. Enthusiastic? It's given me a lot to think about. This isn't me keeping secrets from you or anything. I don't mind you asking. I'm just not sure what my answer is."

"That's fair. I could tell, you know." She tucks a wave of hair behind her ear. "You were missing your spark."

"Really?"

"Yeah, but I don't think other people would notice. You aren't obvious." She turns even redder. "I mean. You know what I mean. There's a difference. When you pay attention."

My gut instinct is to give her grief for being so tongue-tied, but somehow, I know I shouldn't. Not over this. The months of being Winnie Sutton's friend have taught me a lot of things. She's the capablest person I've ever met, and Winnie is *not* the kind of girl to get her words tied up over a guy.

I'm honored.

I know better than to say that, though. So instead, I wrap my arm around her and tug her close, planting a kiss on the top of her head. Then, before she can overthink it, I jump off the tailgate and hold out a hand. "Come on, Sutton. Let's go find some corn dogs. I'm hungry."

I drop Winnie off a few hours later, after I stop myself from kissing her at least four different times over the course of our night together:

1. When she beats me in the ring toss and does her stupid-cute little victory dance, shaking her butt and miming the words to some as yet undetermined Taylor Swift song.

2. When a little girl walks up to her and asks for her autograph on a napkin, and she couldn't stop smiling for a solid twenty minutes straight.

3. When she squeals and automatically reaches for my hand on the Bone Shaker, breaking all the tendons in my fingers.

4. And every moment in between.

I deserve a medal for my efforts.

Off the record, I'm 99 percent sure she's interested in more than friendship between us, but also, I'm 99.9 percent sure she doesn't actually *know* that.

Or maybe she does and we're both idiots.

My house is silent when I get home, except for the rumbling snores coming from my dad's bedroom. I creep up the stairs after dropping my rodeo bag in the laundry room to be dealt with tomorrow. My bedroom is dark and cool, and I decide against turning on the light. After spending the last two days surrounded by booming loudspeakers, flashing neon lights, and roaring crowds, the darkness and silence soothe the aftereffects of sensory overload. I change out of my jeans into a pair of old basketball shorts and switch my shirt out for something that doesn't smell like fried food. After brushing my teeth and scrubbing the sweat off my face, I collapse into my bed without bothering with the covers. I'm pretty wired right now, but I don't feel like Netflix or music, so instead, I pick up my phone and scroll aimlessly. Eventually, I wander to my inbox and, swallowing hard, click on an email I'd first opened this morning.

It's an acceptance letter to Texas Tech University in the fall. Early admittance to their nursing program. Pediatric nursing, to be precise.

I'm filled with a sudden feeling of peace. Of rightness. *This* is what I want to do. I want to help kids in the hospital. To take care of them and keep them comfortable and make them laugh or let them cry or whatever they need to do that they can't around their family and friends.

As Kerry pointed out, Texas Tech also has a rodeo team. This isn't the end of the line. I could probably qualify for a scholarship—likely will have to once my dad hears about nursing. And as an added bonus, the campus is close enough I can come home on weekends to see Winnie or, if she needs, help with Garrett and Jesse if she's touring. I can be around to keep them in line, so she doesn't have to worry.

I haven't told anyone about the acceptance. Pax and Kerry know I applied, but telling them about the acceptance makes it feel more real. And I haven't told Winnie anything yet.

I want to tell Winnie more than anything. Of everyone, I feel like maybe she would understand. I almost told her tonight, but I couldn't get the words past my lips. I don't want her to think I'm a quitter. Disappointing her would be hard to come back from, especially since I've decided I'm in love with her. And while I know she's nothing like my dad, I'm not super confident leaving the masculine world of bull-riding fame for a quiet job as a male nurse is especially attractive. Especially if she's spending all her time touring on the circuit with cocky, self-sure cowboys and I'm left back home learning how to put IVs into toddlers.

I know how toxic that sounds, and on paper, I know it shouldn't matter. But it does. Not enough to make me change my mind, but enough that, when my guard is down, there's this pang of awareness that keeps me from spilling the truth.

And then there's a part of me that worries Winnie might get scared away from racing, too. Like if I left and she was on her own, she might decide she needs to stay home after all.

After yesterday, those particular fears, at least, have been put to rest. There's no way she could walk away now. I'll have to convince her we have her back, but we have all summer to worry about that. Three months to get her to fall in love with me and trust she can follow her dreams without the rest of us falling apart.

One summer, and I plan to make the most of it.

Twenty-Five
WINNIE

Two weeks later, I'm collecting my prize for yet another second-place finish just behind Maria and Duchess.

I accept the check with a giddy flip in my stomach and smile as the flashes of multiple cameras temporarily blind me. A photographer for a local paper motions for me to move closer to Maria, who throws a long arm around my shoulders, holding her blue ribbon nice and high.

She tsks, teasingly, through her smiling teeth. She manages to speak without moving her lips and ruining the shot. "Second place yet again, Sutton."

I snort, keeping my own good-natured grin in place. "I don't suppose you're getting tired of local rodeos. Maybe you're thinking it's about time to move on to something more exciting . . . maybe out of state? I hear Oklahoma is real nice this time of year."

She raises a sculpted brow. "You mean to tell me you're still planning to stick around here?"

Heat floods my face as the crowd moves on and leaves us

standing alone with our winnings and horses. "Welllll," I say. "I don't know. You know it's complicated with my family."

Maria waves her hand dismissively. "You nearly caught me and Duchess tonight. Practically too close to call. You deserve to shoot your shot in bigger arenas than county fairs and livestock shows. While I don't relish the thought of coming up against you all summer long, I'm not one to shirk a challenge, and you and Mab are the closest thing to competition I've had in two years."

I don't know what to say. Of course Camilla and Mr. Michaels and even Case have said the same thing, but it's different coming from Maria. Like she said, we're competitors. She doesn't owe me anything.

Maria must suspect what she's said has thrown me because she waves an impatient hand in the air between us as if swatting away any awkward tension. "Enough of that serious stuff. I can see I've given you a lot to think about, and if you do turn up on the circuit, I'm probably gonna regret all these weeks I've spent encouraging you."

I snort at her rueful tone.

"You coming to my party tonight? I hold it every year, and it's the tits." She flits back to Duchess and fiddles with her buckles. "It's just a bunch of rodeo kids drinking too much, dancing to terrible music, and causing a commotion out at my ranch. My parents hide next door at the neighbors' to have plausible deniability."

I blink, stunned. I've never been invited to a party, not even a birthday party at the bowling alley in elementary school, let alone one that promises terrible music *and* commotion. Maria is my friend and we've been hanging out in arenas and ranches these past few months, but never without horses around. This feels like a big deal.

"Oh. Um . . ."

"Please say you'll come," she begs. "It's so rare to find a girl my own age that doesn't annoy the living hell out of me, never mind a stellar barrel racer. Bring Michaels, if you must. I'm sure Pax'll want him there as a familiar face, so bull riders are welcome, I *guess*," she drawls. "Just as long as your boyfriend doesn't break the good china."

My mouth drops open to protest, but she's going like a freight train.

"Sorry. That was a terrible pun. You know what I meant. Like a bull in a china shop?"

I snap out of it and shake my head. "Yeah, Maria. I get it. But Case and I aren't dating."

Maria's smile is triumphant, and my belly drops like I've missed a step. "That's what I hear," she says, her tone cajoling. "But the fact you assumed I was talking about your handsome cowboy bestie is all the confirmation I need. In fact"—her eyes flicker over my shoulder—"don't look now, but he's on his way over."

"Maria," he drawls out evenly, making the little hairs on my arms stand up straight.

His gaze hesitates on my features, and I have no doubt he's noticing my flaming face. Smooth, Sutton. Just once, God, I'd love it if you could give me a winning race and five minutes of not feeling like an idiot around Case.

Five *measly* minutes.

"Convince Winnie she has to come to my party tonight. Better yet, you should bring her." Her dark eyes are sparkling with trouble, and I nearly roll mine in exasperation. Subtle she is not. She and Garrett have been hanging out way too much. I knew I shouldn't have let her help pick up my little sister from school.

Case looks at me. "Jesse's at home tonight, isn't he?"

"Yeah, and even if he wasn't, my dad's supposed to be."

"It's up to you." *Always*. Ever since Case went behind my back to ask his dad to sponsor me last spring, he refuses to make *any* plans without asking me first. It warms me to know he's so determined to stick to his promise. But also, *my dude*, it's fine if you want to buy me a lemonade. Not everything needs a consult. I'm gonna have to sketch a Venn diagram illustrating the difference for his nerd brain.

I think my crying jags have scarred the poor guy, unflinching or not.

"I've never been invited to a party before," I say in a low voice only for his ears.

His eyes widen. "In that case . . ." He turns to Maria. "What time do you want us?"

They exchange information, but I'm completely distracted from their conversation. I don't even know what to do at a party. Do I dress up? She said it was at her ranch. And there would be drinking! Like, alcohol? I'm assuming alcohol. She probably wouldn't bring up drinking if it was water or soda. That'd be like saying, "Hey, I'm having some people over, and we'll be dining on water, lemonade, and Sprite, so don't worry if you get thirsty."

I bet I could ask Jesse about this.

Oh my god, am I even hearing myself? I could ask *my fourteen-year-old brother how to party*? Gah.

Maria starts heading out, and I wave her off, lost in my musings until I'm interrupted again by Camilla and Mr. Michaels. The pair saunter up to congratulate Mab and me, and Mr. Michaels does one of those manly shoulder squeezes to Case. I pull out my check, passing it with a flourish to Camilla. It's not my first winnings—the first went to much-needed car repairs. But this one's special.

"A down payment on Mab," I say, and I can almost feel the heat from the pride shining out of my eyeballs like little happiness lasers. I'm gonna own my own horse one day—and not just any horse, but Queen Mab, the best horse in the entire world.

Camilla beams and tucks the check into her shirt pocket without even looking at it. "You got it. I'll write up a contract, and we can keep track of the payments until she's all yours. Which"— she winks at me under her ever-present Stetson—"should be in no time at this rate."

Maria's earlier comments about touring spring back. If I could tour bigger rodeos and keep collecting prizes, I wonder if I could make a small living at this. I shove the thoughts away for later when I'm alone and lying in my bed trying to budget out groceries. No point in going down that road right now. Who's to say I could even keep up in a larger field? Considering my dad's complete failure to be dependable, I'm not comfortable risking the time away to try.

Case's dad and Camilla offer to meet us back at the ranch, and I turn to Case, finally alone. He ruffles his hair thoughtfully, lifting his ball cap and fidgeting with it.

"You sure you're up for this tonight? Maria was being a little pushy. I can totally make up some excuse—"

"No!" I cut him off. "I want to go."

He looks relieved. And cute in his rodeo plaid and vest, but what's new? "Good. When you said you hadn't been to one before—"

"Not just been to one, I haven't even been *invited*. I'm not sure I could've gone even if I wanted to, but Maria's the first person to think of me."

"That's not true," he hedges.

"Eh, Michaels, it kinda is. I'm not blaming you or anyone else, but it's not like I've been turning down plans over the last six years. The truth is, my little brother has more game than I do."

"But also less responsibility," he points out.

I release my breath, conceding. "Also true. At any rate, I like Maria, even if I wish she'd hit the road so I could win for a little while."

His lips quirk in a half grin, rewarding me with his dimple. "You were so close."

"Close only counts in horseshoes and hand grenades."

He laughs. "Fair enough. Maria's a good friend to have around the circuit. A friendly face from home and all that."

My good mood slips. "Case, I'm not sure I'm ready to—"

He cuts me off, pretending to button his lip. "I know. I haven't forgotten. I'm not gonna say another word."

I make a face and start to remove Mab's tack for the trailer ride back to the ranch. "But you'll be thinking it."

He groans theatrically, throwing back his head. "You can't hold my thoughts against me, Win. Unless you're my father. Then I'll take it like a man or whatever, but between you and me, I'm allowed to think what I want, and if I want to think about you kicking ass across the national circuit and coming home to an ever-loving parade where you get to throw your hundreds of thousands of dollars in winnings in Christine Reynolds's fake eyelashes, then—" He drops his hands to his sides with a thwap against the well-fitting denim. "Then I get to and you can't stop me."

Oof. I want to kiss him sooo badly right now.

"Well," I say. "That's okay, I guess. Though I wouldn't say Christine's eyelashes are fake."

Case reaches to pull the heavy saddle from Mab's back. "Whatever. You aren't the boss of me."

We get Mab settled in her stall at the ranch with plenty of extra carrots and sugar cubes for a job well done, and then I head home to get ready for tonight. Case has been to Maria's before, so he's going to pick me up at eight and drive us over.

Because it makes sense he drives if he already knows the way. That's *all*.

I walk in the door, and Garrett and my dad are sitting on the couch watching some old cowboy movie. Not black-and-white old, but close.

"Did you win?" Garrett asks, bouncing to her feet.

"Second again," I say. "But I was able to put my winnings down toward owning Mab! I suppose at this point, I own her tail? Maybe her mane?"

Garrett snickers. "Save her lethal chompers for last."

"If only."

"What about Case?"

I nod. "He did well. First heat done, with another in two days. He's definitely in the top three contenders."

"Can I come and see him on Monday?"

I drop my bag by the door and walk to the sink, filling a glass. "Of course. We can ask Jesse, too. Where is he, by the way?"

My dad answers, his gaze still on the TV screen, "Out with his lady friend."

I bite my lip. I was hoping Jesse would be around in case my dad flaked on watching Garrett.

"I've been invited to a rodeo party tonight, Dad . . ."

My dad looks away from the TV. "Oh really?"

"Yeah. Do you think it would be okay if I go?"

"Oooh!" my sister says. "Can I help you get ready?"

I don't look at Garrett, pleading with my eyes at my dad. *Please don't let me down. Please be the parent tonight.*

"You're an adult, Win. You don't need my permission to go."

I'm irritated at his casual response. Like I'm the one being overcautious in asking.

"I'm not asking permission, Dad."

He grunts and returns his gaze to the television screen. "I'm not going anywhere. Garrett and I have a box of microwave popcorn and a *Lonesome Dove* marathon ahead of us."

I wince at Garrett theatrically. "I'm sorry to hear that."

"It's okay," she tells me in a very grown-up voice before stage-whispering, "We all have to make sacrifices." She adds, "You know, there's a way you can make it up to me . . ."

I pretend to look annoyed when the truth is I'm anything but. "Fine, you can help me get ready."

Twenty-Six
WINNIE

That's it. Case Michaels is trying to murder me. He shows up at five minutes to eight with a fistful of wildflowers and wearing cowboy boots. Not manure-covered working boots. Not broken-in bull-riding boots. No. He struts in wearing shined-up cowboy boots under his dark-wash jeans and a fitted gray T-shirt that hugs his biceps and makes my heart skip directly into palpitations. He holds out the bouquet as if it's an offering, and I blink at him, completely frozen. My every molecule has seized in *oh shit!* levels of uncertainty.

His countenance is sheepish. "Um. I brought these for you."

I still can't move. My vision is hyper-focused on the way his tanned forearms seem to wink at me. Despite losing sensation in my limbs and apparently my brain, I can feel that sexy flicker of smooth muscle definition deep inside my soul.

"Winnie!" my sister sings. "Hello! Case brought you flowers!" Under her breath, she mutters, "I think she's glitching."

I want nothing more than to melt into a puddle on the floor, but he's still in front of me, waiting for my response like he's not sure if he's made a huge mistake and, God, I'm so embarrassing. "Sorry. Uh. I think I blacked out there for a sec." I clear my throat. Twice. "You brought me flowers?"

"Is that okay?" he says. "Blink once for yes. If you blink twice, I brought them for Garrett, and we can forget the last five minutes ever happened."

A snicker bubbles out of my throat. I take a deep breath and meet his glittering eyes. "And she's back," he drawls.

I reach for the stems. "*Merci.* I don't . . . I'm not sure I even have a vase!"

"We do!" Garrett shouts, producing a dusty one from under the sink. Her expression is straight gooey as she takes in Case and his chivalry.

Taking a minute to calm down, I busy myself with washing the vase and carefully trimming the stems on an angle. Then I set to arranging them perfectly and placing the entire effort in the center of our kitchen table. It's so large and our table is so small, it takes up most of the surface area, but I don't care. Later tonight, when I'm recovered from my abject humiliation, I'll bring the entire thing to Garrett's and my room, where I can gaze at it uninterrupted.

"They're beautiful, Case. I'm speechless. Obviously." I laugh, still nervous. He looks pleased and maybe a little relieved as he meets my eyes. We're suddenly locked in a staring contest spanning across my kitchen, and I would break first except: 1) I don't want to, and 2) I can't.

"Should we go?" he asks after a beat, his eyes still on mine.

"Hmm?"

He smirks. "To the party, Sutton? I'm under strict orders

244 OF ERIN HAHN

from the former national high school barrel-racing champion
I'm supposed to, quote, 'get the new celebrity rider to her party
and show her off.'"

My eyes widen. "Me?"

A snort comes in the direction of the couch, where my dad
is sitting watching some white cowboy negotiate terms between
equally white and definitely offensively portrayed Native Amer-
icans on the TV.

"G'night, Winnie. Have fun," he says, not bothering to shift
his attention.

Case holds out a hand. "*Pret?*"

With this boy, I think I can be ready for anything. I put my
hand in his. "*Absolument.*"

—

We get in his car, and he puts on some Tim McGraw. I glance
out the window at my own reflection in the setting sun as he
reverses out of my driveway.

This is him trying, right? That's why this feels different. Not
that he's trying *too* hard. Just maybe a little nicer? A little more
planned? I smooth my hands down my jeans. Is this a *date*?

"I should have told you right away . . . you look really good,
Win," Case says. And the nickname makes me flush head to toe.
Get a grip, Winnie. It's not the first time he's called you that.

But never like this. Not in that low, grumbly way that makes
him sound like he just woke up. And then he's dragging his
gaze extra slowly from my curve-hugging boot-cut jeans and
cropped snow-white tank top. I stick my hands under my thighs
to keep from covering the tiny slice of exposed midriff. They're
not the fanciest duds, but I was going for "casually hot." Garrett's words, not mine.

Again. Why are my siblings better at this than I am?

God. What if they aren't? Who takes fashion advice from a ten-year-old Mensa candidate?

Oh, for fuck's sake. Case thinks it's hot. *Clearly.* He can barely keep his eyes on the road. He brought you flowers and he's wearing cowboy boots and he's playing your favorite songs. *You're not this much of an idiot. Buck up, Sutton.*

"Pull over, please," I command, concentrating on keeping the breathlessness out of my voice.

Case doesn't hesitate, turning down the next dirt road and pulling off onto a wide gravel shoulder.

He spins to me in his seat, the low, evening sunlight painting his handsome face. "Are you okay? Did I freak you out? Was it the flow—"

I'm already flinging off my seat belt and lunging across the center console, cutting him off with my lips.

It's probably not pretty, but I make up for it with enthusiasm and, I don't know, graceless horniness? This boy has flipped me inside out these past months, and all I want to do is kiss him until he knows exactly what that feels like. What he's done to me. I want to steal the breath from his lungs and inject fire into his veins. I want to disintegrate into him. I want our atoms to smash together until there's nothing left but Us— capital *U.*

Case grips me tighter, his tongue slipping past my willing lips and twisting with mine in a way that's anything but graceless. It's intoxicating and stokes something inside of me that leaves me frustrated at the distance between us. He must be, too, because suddenly he's dragging me across his lap and into the driver's seat.

Okay, then.

I straddle him, and his fingers trace my sides, up, up, nearly *there*, to where I long for his hands to find me before mad-deningly sliding back down and pressing against that expanse of bare skin at the small of my back. There's not a whole lot of room to maneuver between his lap and the steering wheel, and that's probably for the best. Just enough space to press my body against him and lose myself in his taste and the feel of him, strong and solid beneath me. In his small panting breaths against my lips. In the ache low in my belly.

Eventually, he pulls back, brushing my hair off my forehead.

"I'm sorry," I whisper once my breathing calms to normal levels.

He chuckles low, and it tickles against my throat before he drops his head to my collarbone and takes several breaths.

Finally, he straightens so his eyes are level with mine. "Are you really sorry?"

I shake my head. "Not really. That was a lie. Unless you are . . ."

"I'm definitely not," he says. "I've wanted to do that for months."

It's my turn to be surprised. "You have?" I squeak.

His hands gently lift me off his lap and nudge me back to my seat.

"I can't concentrate with you, um . . . It's . . ." His chin sinks to his chest again, and he closes his eyes, taking more breaths. I crack open a couple of windows, and he laughs.

"Good idea. I need more oxygen in my brain."

I squirm a little in my seat and take a deep breath. "Me, too."

"You *kissed me*," he says.

"I did," I confirm. "You're sure it was okay? I kinda attacked you."

He turns his head to look at me. "You kinda did. I've been killing myself trying to come up with smooth ways to orchestrate a move, and you . . ." He trails off, smiling and shaking his head back and forth in disbelief. "That was probably the single hottest thing that's ever happened to me in my entire life. So yeah. Plenty okay. Feel free to do it again whenever the mood strikes."

"Just to confirm," I say, before I lose my courage. "Did you see that as a 'friends kiss' or, like, more?"

He quirks a brow. "What did you see that as?"

I lick my lips, and he watches the movement. I hold back my smirk. "I don't kiss my friends like that."

"I've never kissed anyone like that, for the record," he assures me with an adorably earnest expression. "But my feelings are definitely in the 'more than friends' territory. I'd classify them as pining? Pax calls it my 'puppy dog devotion.' Whatever you want to go with."

I press forward again, taking his face in my hand and kissing him soundly to shut him up. After losing ourselves for several more minutes, I slip back into my seat, turning my head toward him, laying it back on the headrest.

"I don't want to take away from our friendship, because you're the realest friend I've ever had."

He tips his head toward me, against his own seat. "Okay."

My stomach clenches at what I am about to say—what it will reveal. Case's face is openly curious save for the little crinkle between his brows. The one that tells me he's listening intently and committing himself all over again.

Over and over. He's been so determined to be there. He's winning me over, and that scares the living shit out of me. Six months ago, I would have never believed it possible. "And I feel like I've come to seriously depend on you. More than anyone else in my life, even."

He doesn't flinch. "You're mine, and I'm yours."

"We belong to each other," I say. "Equal partners." Rolling the words around on my tongue and testing them against the thumping of my heart.

"Is that okay? I mean, for simplicity's sake, you can call me your boyfriend. If you want."

"And you'll call me your girlfriend?"

"Every chance I get."

—

"I have something to tell you."

"Yes, *fine*, we can go back to your obnoxious car and make out some more."

Case chokes on the sip he was in the middle of swallowing, coughing and sputtering his drink down his front. Thankfully, we're sitting outside and away from anything expensive, unless you count, oh, Maria's entire house. Are *all* my friends rich?

"You're trouble."

"Sorry," I apologize and half-heartedly wipe at his front, trying not to be distracted by how warm and firm he feels under his T-shirt. "What were you going to say? I can be serious."

"Can you?" he jokes. His eyes drift down to where I'm still feeling him up. I pull my hand back and grip it around a lukewarm beer bottle. Turns out, I don't like the taste of beer. I sort of wish Maria *had* been talking about water or lemonade.

It also turns out while I do like Maria and obviously, I'm crazy about Case, I prefer horses to people. Shocking, I know. I tried. I spent the first hour inside with the air-conditioning and the music and all the people draped over all the furniture talking about all the things and making all the moves, and I thought I was doing a pretty good job of hiding my awkwardness until Case held out his hand and dragged me outside to this little patio area. The table was taken by people playing a drinking game, but we've claimed a cozy corner of the waist-high brick wall.

I don't hate it. The temperature has cooled to somewhere around *bearable*, and I don't have to shout small talk at anyone. I put down my bottle with a clink on the wall and turn to face Case. "Okay, you have my full attention, and I will refrain from touching you for at least the next five minutes. Go."

His eyes light with amusement, and he takes a deep breath before pulling out his phone. "Okay, so you know how I wasn't sure about the PBR."

"I do know, yes."

"Well," he says, lowering his voice. "I'm not going to the PBR. I'm going to college."

I can feel my jaw drop open and wildly gesture for his phone. "Did you apply already?"

He nods, showing me an email. "And was accepted."

My eyes race across the screen, snagging on a few words halfway. Raising my hands to my lips, I look up at him, blinking through watery eyes.

"Case." My tone is soft. "Nursing?"

He shifts his feet, lifting his shoulder in a shrug and tucking his free hand in a pocket. "Yeah. Well, I was thinking I could work in pediatrics."

"God." I sniff, swiping under my eyes. "You would be so good at that. Taking care of kids, helping them feel less miserable or alone in the hospital? Case—" I shake my head in wonder. "This is brilliant. I don't have words. I'm so proud of you." Then I smack his shoulder. "I can't believe you didn't tell me!"

Always the good sport, he makes a show of rubbing at his shoulder. "I wasn't sure if you'd think it was stupid. I mean,

I haven't lost a rodeo this summer, and everyone assumes I'm headed to the PBR, including my dad and my coach. On paper, it makes the most sense."

"But in your heart"—I hold up the screen—"this makes the most sense."

He shrugs again, and my chest squeezes. He seems so unsure of himself, even though I know his mind is set. "Yeah."

"Yeah," I agree.

"You don't think this is a massive mistake?"

"Absolutely not."

"And you're okay with me leaving for college? It's close enough to come home on the weekends, and I promise I can still come and help with Garrett if you ever need me . . ."

I hold back my sigh. My family already holds *me* back; it doesn't need to hold him back, too. "Case. This is important. This is your *life*. Of course I'm okay with it. I'm over the moon for you! Have you once told me I should stay back from touring so I can be closer to you?"

"I would be furious if you did."

I wave my hand. "There you go. If you don't go to college and fulfill your dreams of helping sick kids, I will be furious with you."

"Unflinching."

"Unflinching," I repeat and press my lips to his.

Twenty-Seven
CASE

The hardest shit seems to hit on Tuesdays. I don't know why. Walker's double pneumonia diagnosis was on a Tuesday in August. He died a month later on a Tuesday in September. Because of some fluke of planning at the funeral home, his viewing and funeral were an entire week after on yet another Tuesday.

I'm not a superstitious person, but that doesn't mean I haven't been wary of Tuesdays ever since. Today has confirmed why.

I never used to collect the mail. Nothing ever comes for me, and after misplacing some important something or other meant for my dad back in the fourth grade, I've never craved the responsibility. However, that was before I applied and was accepted to a university. The acceptance process itself was online, but that hasn't stopped the onslaught of marketing mailers I've received since. Not to mention a recruitment letter for the rodeo team. I'm still getting every email, too, but it's as if Texas Tech is actively *trying* to out me by doubling down on the spam.

Which means it's way past time to let my dad know my

college plans, but things have been pretty quiet the last few months. I don't feel like rocking the wagon and reminding him I'm not making choices he'd approve of.

I'm living my life the way I want, but I don't feel like explaining myself yet.

I'm thinking after July 31. That's a good deadline that's still a few weeks off but is also plenty of time before the first day of school.

It's just ever since Winnie and I became official, we've been busy. Work, obviously, and training whenever we're not working, but also, it's as though that first kiss in my car set off a fuse between us. Either I'm tugging her into the tack room, or she's pulling me behind the barn, or on one extra memorable night last weekend, Winnie stayed late after work and agreed to go night fishing with me down by the creek.

I've always had this fantasy of skinny dipping after dark with the crickets calling and fireflies sparking up the sky. Like Nitty Gritty Dirt Band–style. The reality wasn't as great. Lots of mosquitos, actually. And Winnie refused to get in the water if she couldn't see the bottom, which was fair. So reality was more like kissing in the grass under the light of the moon, which was still one of the greatest moments of my life so far.

I'm off track. The mail. I was talking about the mail and fucking cursed Tuesdays. I saw the dust trail of the mail truck while exercising Moses in the closest pasture, daydreaming about the way my girl glows in twilight. After cleaning Moses up and stowing him away, I went to retrieve the mail and grab some lunch from Kerry. Resting on top of the stack I'd retrieved from our giant rust bucket of a mailbox was an envelope with my name on it with a return address from a ticket vendor. Which was weird because I haven't bought tickets to anything maybe ever. Rodeo has taken up most of my free time the last decade. Curious, I'd walked over to a bench outside the stables and tore it open.

Inside, waiting for me, was a gut punch from my late best friend.

Two tickets to Headbangers Ball this coming weekend in Austin.

I sank to the bench, staring unseeing at the paper in my hands, blurring out my surroundings.

And that's where I've stayed.

Walker bought them a year ago. I remember the conversation— can still see him clearly in my mind. We were driving in my car after a run-of-the-mill field party. Walker was drunk as fuck, and some old Guns N' Roses song came on the radio, so he cranked it up. That was one of the hallmarks of Drunk Walker. I wouldn't let him listen to the radio in my car, because he always turned on his '80s arena rock garbage. "Thunderstruck" and AC/DC was only the tip of the iceberg when it came to Walker's obsession. But it was late, and I was sober and tired, so I didn't fight him on it. Thinking back, I'm glad I didn't.

The windows were down, and the night smelled like fresh-cut hayfields. This was months before he got sick. Not like Walker was ever healthy, in the strictest sense of the term, but he wasn't always *dying*. He was in this in-between period, borrowing years, perpetually waiting for the other boot to drop. Live fast, die young, that kind of thing. But back then, "die young" was mostly hyperbole. If things went well, he could live a happy life for a long time. But then the world went to hell, and people like Walker, who depended on everyone else to take precautions, found themselves constantly at risk.

Anyway, that night after Guns N' Roses squealed their last,

the DJ announced a concert that following weekend in Austin called Headbangers Ball. They were a touring cover band of '80s arena rock. It was sold out, so Walker went and signed up for the mailing list. He was determined *this* would be our year.

Case, he'd pleaded with me, his eyes wild and animated under thick black brows. *We have to do this. I'll make the arrangements. But we have to go.*

I'd assumed that was the ramblings of Drunk Walker. He'd just lost his girlfriend to a yearslong battle with leukemia, and I was on this mission to make him forget for a while. I went along with it at the time, assuming in the hungover light of morning, he wouldn't remember.

Except he did. The fucker had actually done it. He'd reserved two tickets for this weekend, and then he went and died on me. What am I supposed to do with these? I don't want to go. I hate this shit.

Without permission, my vision goes watery and I swipe at my nose, sniffing loudly.

I hate this shit.

I don't know how long I sit there. Long enough for Winnie to find me after returning from her trail ride. She doesn't say anything, just sits beside me. Eventually, I pass her the tickets. I can tell by the way her breath catches she's found his name, but still, she doesn't ask anything of me. Which is good because I'm a dried-out husk, so tired of crying and angry that, once again, I'm crying. I don't want to do *any* of this anymore. I burned the list; I applied to college. I'm healing. Why can't I stop this fucking sadness from sinking me over and over and over again?

How long is someone supposed to feel this way? How can a person possibly live like this, being fine one minute and the next feeling as if happiness is impossible? Like I'm grasping at a concept I'll never understand again.

Winnie leans her head onto my shoulder, and the golden warmth of her body sinks past my defenses. I still don't have any words. I might never, at this point. Thankfully, she doesn't seem to need them.

—

Four days later, I'm getting out of the shower when there's a ringing at the front door. Kerry's around, so I let her answer it while I finish getting dressed, but just as I'm pulling down my T-shirt, she's yelling my name from the bottom of the stairs. Thinking it's likely Pax, I don't hurry. This is becoming a theme with him since the tickets came, and he's been by every single afternoon to sweep me away for tacos or burgers or whatever. I don't know where he learned this maternal need to press food into my hands and feed me all the time, but I'm gonna have to convince him to start liking bookstores or the batting cages or something, because I can't keep eating like this.

"Pax, it's barely ten, how can you even be hungr—" I stutter to a stop at the bottom of the stairs. "Winnie! Hey! Sorry! What are you—" And then the rest of her appearance sinks in. You have to understand. Winnie has one style, and it's a good one. It suits her and is cute as hell and really, *really* works on a ranch kid like me. Boot-cut jeans faded to perfection, fitted button-downs to look professional for the guests, dusty work boots, and a baseball hat to keep the sun out of her eyes.

Like I said: classic, sexy, ready to kick ass, and shovel manure.

Aside from Maria's party, that's been the uniform. Which is why I'm gaping like a fucking trout this morning: she's wearing *cutoffs* and a fitted T-shirt with the words I LOVE ROCK 'N' ROLL printed in slasher font.

"Too much?" she grimaces. "I found it at Target on clearance."

"Um, no? But—" *My girlfriend is wearing cutoffs.*

"Is that what you're wearing?" she asks me, taking in my T-shirt with the sleeves carved out and worn barn jeans.

"Y-yeah?"

She exchanges a friendly smirk with Kerry, who walks out of the room, laughing under her breath. "Well, okay, then. Is your bag packed?"

I blink at her, trying to comprehend what's happening. Is it our one-month anniversary already? Did I forget something?

"Let's pretend I'm an idiot and not because I can't stop staring at your legs," I drawl out nice and slow. "What are you talking about? Did I forget something?"

"Headbangers Ball, Case. Hello? It's starting in like"—she looks at her watch—"ten hours, and the drive is eight hours, not including stops, so we need to get a move on."

"We're going to Austin?"

"Yes."

"You're taking me to Austin? Right now?"

"Well, technically, *you're* taking *me*, because I seriously doubt my car would make it out of the panhandle. But yes. I already checked with your dad and Kerry and even Pax. The point is: we're going. If you want."

"I'm—I'm not—but I haven't—" I stutter, slipping my hand into my hair and trying to make words make sense.

Kerry is there, handing me my duffel with a beaming smile. "Here're your things. I took the liberty of packing you an overnight bag. Don't you dare try to drive home tonight."

"Don't worry. I made reservations at a hotel outside Austin," Winnie says.

Kerry nods her approval. "I packed some snacks. I know

you'll fill up on junk food at the first Valero on your way, but I figured it wouldn't hurt to have something with a little more substance."

"We're going to Walker's show," I say, finally managing to coordinate the words coming out of my mouth with the ones in my brain.

Winnie takes a step closer and lowers her voice. "Are ya cool with that? I'm sorry to throw this all at you, but really, Walker did all the planning a year ago. I just went to Brody—"

"What? You did?"

Her smile is shy. "Yeah, who went to his parents because I initially wanted to pay them for the tickets. They flat-out refused the money. And before you ask, they're also paying for the hotel room. Insisted on it. They got all emotional and told me to tell you this is what Walker would have wanted—for you to still go. So I went to my dad and told him I would be leaving town, and he needed to be there for Garrett. This couldn't be like the last time when he flaked. And then I programmed Camilla into Jesse's speed dial, because let's face it, I don't trust my dad not to fuck this up, but I *am* trying to trust others. Anyway, he promised, so we'll see. But, Case . . ." She takes a deep breath, placing her hands on my shoulders.

"It's completely up to you. We don't *have* to do this. I just thought, maybe you secretly wanted to, and it could a good way to, like, I don't know, honor your best friend. For that reason, I want to do it, too. Because he was my friend, and I never got to tell him that." Her voice gets a little wobbly, and she takes a second to clear her throat. "What do you think? Want to go on a road trip and eat lots of gas station sugar and listen to hours and hours of obnoxious arena rock?"

I sink onto the steps and drop my head into my hands. It

actually sounds fun. I'm sure if it were Walker at my doorstep, I'd have given him shit for years over this, but he's not. The concert does seem like the perfect way to remember him. And getting away sounds nice. And a night in a hotel room with Winnie away from our families and coaches and coworkers . . . *well*. It's probably too early in our relationship for *that*. This isn't one of my sad distraction hookups. But still. Being with her, uninterrupted, sounds cool.

"Okay."

"You're sure?"

"Yeah. Let's do it. Um, can I change really quickly? I look like a farmer."

"But, like, a hot farmer. The kind they use in ads for those online farmer dating apps. I'm kinda digging the exposed biceps."

I snort, turning to run back up the stairs. "I wouldn't want to be too much of a distraction while you're driving my car, Sutton!"

Twenty-Eight
CASE

By the time I make it out to my car, Winnie's already in the driver's seat, banging her head to something very loud and with a whole lot of synthesizers. I toss my bag in the back seat and climb next to her.

"Whitesnake?" I guess. I don't know a ton of '80s music, but a decade with Walker taught me enough.

Winnie laughs. "Yep. Full disclosure, I'm not really well versed in music in general and definitely not '80s rock, so I went to my dad and asked him for a starting-off point and created a playlist of classics."

"You asked your dad?" I'm touched. Winnie rarely goes to her dad for anything.

"Yeah, well. I was in a pinch." She shrugs and passes me her phone. "I knew more than I thought, just not by name. It's not a total lost cause. I thought we could listen on our way to Austin, and by tonight, we'll be experts!"

I scroll through her playlist, impressed despite myself. This is several hours' worth of music. Walker would be super into it.

"And don't tell Kerry, but I made cupcakes for the occasion. Well, Garrett and I did. They won't be as good as whatever Kerry baked, but we had fun decorating."

Suddenly ravenous, I reach in the back seat for the plastic container and pop the top, immediately grabbing a chocolate-frosted one and stuffing my face with it. I don't hold back my moan. "Want one?" I ask after practically swallowing it whole.

"Um, no thank you." She shakes her head, her eyes full of laughter. "My dude, it's not even lunchtime."

"There aren't any rules on road trips. *Le temps n'est pas reel*," I declare.

"Time isn't real, huh?"

"I still can't believe we're doing this," I say.

"Believe it, man. I would've had T-shirts made, but I ran out of time. This is officially happening, and not to be weird on main, but I'm leaving the passenger-side back seat open for Walker. I know he's probably busy with his girlfriend, but I can't imagine he'd miss this weekend. He's the one who bought the tickets a year in advance, after all."

The way she says it, so matter-of-factly, sucks the air out of my lungs. In a good way.

"I used to see him all the time. After he died," I explain. "In my head, obviously, but to me, he was there."

Her eyes stay on the road, but her lips quirk in my direction, and I'm fortified enough to tell her the rest.

"I would call him *Ghost Walker*," I rush on. "And whenever shit went down, it was like he was right there."

"Not so weird on main, then. In that case, I should also tell you I left space in the middle in case his girlfriend came, too. Double date, you know?"

"No," I say. "Not so weird."

"So." She clears her throat, turning her full attention back to the highway in front of us. "Was this at the same time as the list stuff?"

I reach for another cupcake. "Yeah. You should have heard the way I reamed him out on top of that silo. Could have died climbing that thing."

"No kidding. And what about the friend thing? With me? Like, I know how we are now, obviously, and so it all worked out for the best, but I can't imagine what you must have thought when you first saw that."

"Actually, I spent the first month cussing at him because you were intimidating as fuck, and it was abundantly clear you hated me. I was in way over my head."

Winnie laughs freely, and I can't help but smile, despite my chagrin. "Excellent. That's exactly the vibe I was going for. In my defense, you didn't give the best first, second, or even third impression. And you were hooking up with any girl who batted her lashes at you back then, so I couldn't feel too special."

The cupcake turns to cement in my throat, and I choke, coughing until my sinuses run.

"Sorry, was that supposed to be a secret?"

I swallow, take a full breath, and swallow again. When I think it's safe to speak again, I croak, "No, not a secret. Not my proudest moments, uh . . ."

"Relax, Case. I'm not trying to put you on trial here. I felt like it might be the elephant in the room or whatever, and I've been meaning to bring it up. But saying, 'Hey, about that time you had sex with Christine . . .' felt awkward."

I relax at her tone. "I don't regret what happened, mostly. Walker died before . . . well. Anyway." I look to the back seat with an apologetic expression. *Sorry, man.* "It's not an excuse or anything. It's just for some reason I zeroed in on that. Like, it was this one thing I could take the reins on in my own life. I wasn't going down like that."

"A virgin?"

"Yeah. That said, I may have overcompensated."

She lifts a shoulder and tilts her head toward me, pragmatic as always. "Having sex is a natural human . . . thing."

"I know."

"I haven't had sex yet."

"Okay."

"Not that I don't want to. Opportunities haven't presented themselves."

The silence settles around us. Not quite uncomfortable, but there. My brain scrambles to latch onto the right words. I definitely want to have sex with Winnie. But I don't want her to feel pressured because I've already had sex. I don't expect it. I'm okay without it. I like how things are, and any way I can be with her is great.

"I guess, *oh my gosh*," she mutters, her face flaming pink and her fingers gripping the wheel so hard they turn white. "This is so embarrassing. Okay." She glances at me out of the corner of her eye. "I guess I'm trying to say I'm open to having sex. With you. I'm not *not* interested. Just inexperienced."

My blood rushes out of my head, and I shift in my seat. "I'm not experienced in being in a relationship. Just because I've had sex doesn't make me an expert, anyway. I guess what I'm saying is, when we're ready, we'll be equal partners. Like everything else, right?"

She exhales, relieved. "Right. Good. I like that."

"Me, too."

Winnie pulls into a gas station before she leans over and kisses me.

"What's that for?"

She smiles, taking off her seat belt. "Does there need to be a reason?"

—

After stopping to check into our hotel room, which turns into a detour for more kissing (some of which is on a very conveniently placed bed), we make it to the concert with minutes to spare. The venue is more crowded than I would have ever guessed, though we are the youngest people by at least a decade. Winnie forces me to buy two Whitesnake T-shirts we immediately put over our clothes. Apparently, of the hours and hours of songs we listened to this morning and afternoon, "Here I Go Again" is Winnie's new-old favorite song. She's also forced me to watch the music video twice. I'm not sure I understand how the lady dancing on the hoods of the cars fits with the lyrics, but I can appreciate the enthusiasm. I've already offered for Winnie to reenact on my Navigator whenever she wants.

Though I was raised on neon lights and loud crowds, this is another level. Screaming guitars, fried vocals, heavy bass you can feel in your bones. I have the time of my life. Winnie bangs her head and sings along to as many lyrics as she can, and I can't take my eyes off her. She's so light without responsibility weighing down her shoulders. The familiar piano chords of Journey's "Don't Stop Believin'" come on, and she screams. Straight up screams, jumping up and down.

That's when I start to lose it a little. Because she's so beautiful and fun, and I have this automatic thought like, *Walker would be wild for her* and *this entire night*, and I'm suddenly imagining how it would have been with the two of them, screaming along to Journey together and making fun of me for being boring and not knowing the lyrics. He'd have a matching T-shirt and would crash on the floor of our hotel room, happily cramping my style and—

And—he's not. He won't ever be here. For the rest of my life, I will want to show him things and experience things with him, and I can't.

I don't cry this time. For once, knowing all of this doesn't ruin my night. It hurts, but the pain doesn't suck me under the way it used to. Whether that is due to the passing of time or the girl singing her heart out next to me or something else, I don't know.

All I know is by the end of the song, I'm singing along to the chorus and losing myself in the crowd just like everyone else and I think for a second I can see my best friend there, on the periphery, fist in the air, hair flopping around, smile splitting across his face. I *feel* him next to us, and it's enough.

—

Winnie is quiet in the hotel elevator after the show.

"Tired?" I ask.

She nods, pressing against me. "Long day. Long drive. But mostly just feeling extra quiet. Everything was so loud at the venue."

"Did you have fun?"

"I did," she says, looking up at me. "You?"

I wrap my arm around her shoulders, pulling her in for an embrace and kissing the top of her head. "I did. Thanks for kidnapping me."

She snorts against my collarbone as the elevator dings on our floor.

We walk down the hall to our room, fingers tangled together, and Winnie pulls out the key card, opening the door. She leads me inside, closing the door before spinning us and pressing me up against the cold metal, capturing my mouth in a searing kiss.

I open my mouth immediately, inviting her taste, and a groan burns in the back of my throat as she bucks gently against me, covering me in her softness and stoking a fire in my blood. I force myself to step back, putting space between us.

"We don't have to do anything you don't want to."

"Okay," she pants, and I feel a flash of pride at the way her blush starts at her collarbone and rises to her cheeks.

"But for the record," I say before chickening out, "I want to do everything if and when *you* want to do everything."

She tilts her head, coy. "What if I want to do everything right now?"

My blood rushes south, my head spinning slightly.

"You do?" I cough, trying to cover for the high pitch to my voice. And try again. "You do?"

Her lips spread into a shy smile. "Uh-huh."

"Right now?" I clarify.

"Yes, please."

"You'll let me know if you change your mind. You can change your mind at any time and—"

She cuts me off with another long kiss, only pulling away after I've forgotten what I was even talking about in the first place.

"I won't change my mind," she tells me. "Unflinching, re-member?"

I take her hands in both of mine, walking us slowly back-ward toward the bed, kissing her over and over until my legs hit the edge of the mattress and she falls over on top of me. I decide right then and there I could spend the rest of my life like this and be happy about it. There's no place I'd rather be.

—

I wake up smothered in dark hair that smells like the best moment of my entire life, listening to my girlfriend snore. For a few minutes, I consider staying under the covers and watching her sleep, but that feels creepy, so instead, I roll out of bed and head for the shower. By the time I'm clean and dressed, Winnie's awake and propped against the headboard, sipping from a paper cup.

"Coffee?"

She winces. "And powdered creamer. Which should not be a real thing."

I cross over to her side of the bed and sit on the edge, reaching for her drink.

Before I steal a sip, I exhale and ask, "No regrets?"

She tilts her head, her smile reassuring. "None. You?"

"Of course not. I wanted to double-check because . . ."

This time, Winnie rolls her eyes and reaches to take the cup back. "That was my first time?"

I feel my face burn, and I clear my throat. "Yes. That."

She takes a lingering sip, thinking. She swallows slowly and puts her cup on the nightstand before reaching for my hand. "I was going to give you shit, but I realized I can't in this instance. Case, you were perfect. You were sweet and gentle. No regrets," she reiterates. "I'm glad it was you, and I can't wait to do it again."

I tug on the hand she's wrapped around mine and lean close to capture her lips. "Well, in that case . . ."

Twenty-Nine
WINNIE

The thing about falling in love with your friend is you get to kiss them whenever you want. If they're being sweet? Kiss them. If they look hot hauling hay bales? Kiss them. If they are being annoying and won't shut up about the statistical importance of something smart or other . . . kiss them to make them stop talking.

Kissing is literally always the answer.

Is Case perfect? No. Am I? Hell no. But *together*, we do pretty all right.

I meant what I said when I told him I would be mad if he didn't go to college. There are people who are destined to make the world a better place, and he's one of them. That's not to say he wouldn't be great in the PBR. I'm convinced he would be good at about anything he tried, but losing Walker changed him. Or maybe freed him. Not that he was trapped—that sounds bad—but he would have done anything for Walker. That stupid-ass list being case. in. point.

Now it's time to do something for himself.

If you told me six months ago I would feel that way about Case Michaels, I would have laughed in your face. But I didn't really know him. I only thought I did. I didn't know myself back then either. The Winnie of Before never in a million years thought she would race on the circuit, that she could make money doing it, that she could buy Mab with that money.

Present-Day Winnie owns a horse. A freaking horse.

Queen Mab belongs to me, totally. All of her parts, even her chompers.

Unreal.

Present-Day Winnie qualified for the Texas State Rodeo finals. As a rookie.

Present-Day Winnie has little girls lining up for her autograph. Girls who know not only her name but her horse's name. Girls who tell her they want to be like her when they grow up.

And Present-Day Winnie lost her virginity to a very kind, very handsome man who looks at her sometimes like she invented sunshine.

It hasn't been all rainbows and butterflies this summer. More like grit and blisters from working my ass off in the hot sun day in and day out, but it's exactly everything I was too afraid to dream up for myself.

That's the issue, though. Right *there*. Fear. This is exactly what I was afraid might happen. Things would work out and I would achieve my dreams, and now all of a sudden, I'm in it. I'm attached. I'm obsessed with this life. This morning, Garrett woke me up by jumping in my bed and yelling my name over and over. Apparently, a clip of me on Mab during our qualifying run last weekend was shown on some cable sports highlights show, and the national rodeo audience has gone buck wild trying to find out more about the rookies from outside

Amarillo. It's been turned into a Cinderella story; encouraging little poor girls everywhere they, *too*, can be champions.

Except I know the story of Cinderella. Every girl who grew up in a trailer knows that story—not the Disney version or the one with Hilary Duff texting on her ancient phone but the real version. The one where Cinderella has the fucking night of her life: the dress, the shoes, the boy, the magic, and then poof! Midnight comes and goes, and she goes back to her shitty servant job in her hovel of a home, because that's real life. This summer has been my magic ball, but with September comes midnight. Jesse and Garrett will be back in school or out of it, depending on my brother, and my dad will hide in his bedroom, only coming out to leave for work or eat the food I put on the table. Case will be off to school, and I'll be home, with a family to support and a horse all my own.

Case would say I'm being cynical. That things have changed this summer and I don't "have to carry everything on my shoulders." But isn't cynicism the armor of eldest daughters everywhere? It's kept me together this long. Why shed it now?

I've already qualified, but I'd registered and paid the fees for a second qualifier this weekend as a precaution, because I didn't want to put all my eggs in one basket when it came to state. So instead of sitting it out, I decide to go and invite my family. Today's competition is close enough to easily drive, so I asked my dad to bring Garrett and Jesse. Case is sitting in the crowd somewhere with them. He's not riding tonight, choosing to drop a few rodeos since he's no longer gunning for the PBR. He's told me his plans for Vegas and his promise to Walker to win the buckle for both of them. But he's ahead of the curve already with the wins in his pocket. As long as he does well at state, he'll qualify. He's accepted a place on the college rodeo team, though, which I think is great. Maybe doing it as an amateur will help him remember what he loved about it in the first place.

Anyway, I wanted my family to see me qualify, in case I never get the chance to do it again. I want Garrett to know I chased my dreams and found more of them along the way. I want Jesse to see what hard work can do for you. I want my dad to see me as something other than his housekeeper.

Armor, armor, armor.

Mab is in rare form and dances through the alley. She's flawless through the clover, and we pull some of our best times. At Camilla's encouragement, I've started working with a few other horses to back Mab up. She's plenty for local shows that are spread out and only two or three rounds, but we don't want to burn her out or cause her injury from overworking during the more extensive events. National events can have up to two rounds a night, ten days in a row.

But none of the horses have Mab's magic. They'll be close enough to be competitive, but I can tell she's gonna pitch the mother of all equine fits the first time she has to stay safe and cozy in her stall while I reach for the bridle of Risky Business or Pistol Annie.

Add the new horseflesh to the list of things I'm steadily ignoring as I prep for a career run I'm not convinced I'll be able to fulfill. Owning Mab means her chance for national glory lies solely with me. Can I in good conscience hold her back?

Ugh.

I press forward in my saddle, stroking Mab's neck while waiting to enter the arena for the victory lap. I eventually spot my family and Case near the fence line, behind the third barrel. Case is sandwiched between my siblings, waving another glittery handmade sign that says, MAB IS QUEEN OF OUR HEARTS.

Figures they'd be cheering on my horse. I snicker. "See that, Mab? You've got fans! You've practically reached pop star status."

Somehow, across the arena, I meet my father's eyes. He's staring at me, noticeably still amid a veritable sea of people buzzing with enthusiasm. I've never seen this look on his face before. He looks . . . thoughtful. Determined. There's a fire in his eyes that I can see from here. That I can *feel* from here.

I don't know what that means.

One of the rodeo organizers says, "All right, Winnie, you're up. We're ready for you! Take your lap!"

I spur Mab into a gallop. This is her favorite part. I think it has to do with all the cheering. My horse is kind of vain. I wave, beaming at my family and throwing a kiss their way. There are more signs than the one my sister made, some even with *my* name on them. It's nuts how fast news travels.

We complete our lap and slow to a walk, back through the alley and past a handful of other racers in various stages of brushing down their horses and removing tack. I get to the area designated for Mab, and I dismount before I realize we've been followed by a reporter with a camera. The flash shines brightly in my eyes and I flinch.

"Hi, Winnie. My name is Erica Jenkins, and I'm with *Horse Girl* magazine. I was hoping to ask you a few questions. Our readers are enormously invested in your story."

"Um . . ." I see Case and my family walking up. I meet Case's gaze, and he nods, pulling up short and saying something to my dad. "S-sure." I turn my full attention to the reporter. "Sorry. Yes."

She follows the direction of my gaze, but if she recognizes Case, she doesn't show it. "Winnie." She pauses. "Is it okay if I call you Winnie, or would you rather *Ms. Sutton*?"

"Winnie's great." Mab nuzzles the back of my head and snuffs in my hair. I wince at the familiar wetness. "And this is Queen Mab," I say. "Clearly, she's angling for the introduction."

The reporter laughs. "She's incredible. How long have you two been together?"

"About two and a half years. I work for CBM Ranch, and she was a rescue. She turned up one day and was a pain in the rear to everyone but me, for some reason. She picked me, and I picked her."

"Is it true this is your first season racing *ever*?"

I nod. "First for both of us. But I've been riding my entire life. I've always watched barrel racing and thought it was about as badass as you can get on horseback. When Mab showed up, I could tell she had a spark, and my boss gave her to me to see what she was made of. I was originally training her for someone else to ride, but . . . well, Mab is picky." I shrug. "Turns out, we were made for each other."

"I'll say! You two are all anyone's talking about. You've taken the barrel-racing circuit by storm this season. People are speculating you as front-runners in Vegas this winter. What do you think of that?"

She shoves the mic in my face, and the camera flashes, capturing my undoubtedly stunned expression.

"Oh, well . . ." I catch my dad's eyes again.

He's watching me intently, waiting for my response. And suddenly, it's obvious. That look on his face is realization. He finally gets it. I wish we could talk. I need to know what he's thinking. I blink and restart, focusing on the reporter and the mic outstretched in front of me.

"Every day I get to ride Mab and show her off is one I never thought I'd have. I can't say for sure about Vegas. It's hugely encouraging that people think we could make it that far, and I'm so grateful for all the support we've gotten. Everyone has been so welcoming. I feel incredibly blessed. We're gonna take it one day, one race, at a time and see where this journey takes us."

The reporter grins, no doubt finding me modest. And that's fine. I am modest, just not about what she thinks. The truth is, I know Mab and I could make it to Vegas. But I don't see how we will.

Thirty
WINNIE

'm feeling pretty wired after the event and the interview, so I send my family home with hugs and Mab home with Camilla and her giant F-150 to pull the trailer. Case offers to stay, no doubt picking up on my restlessness.

We end up walking the fair, like we did after the first rodeo, except this time we're hand in hand. The sun is beginning its descent, and the big Texas sky is more purple than the brilliant robin's-egg blue of this afternoon. We get some barbecue that we eat at a picnic table, drink tall fresh-squeezed lemonades, and avoid the noisy rides. In our ripped jeans, T-shirts, and ball caps, we could be any other kids at the fair. While I love my newfound rodeo reputation, this is nice, too. Simple and sweet. Case and I haven't had a ton of nights like this.

"There's some dancing under the pavilion," he says.

I consider his offer. I've never danced with anyone before—it might be kind of fun.

"Or," I say impishly, "we could find a place to do our own dancing."

His eyebrows raise under the brim of his cap. "You have my attention, despite the cheesy metaphor."

I laugh, shoving him sideways. "It's just that aside from stolen minutes in the tack room, which, to be clear, are always fun, we've barely had a moment to ourselves in weeks."

His too-attractive lips curl in a confident grin, setting off his dimples. "You saying you miss me, Sutton?"

I pull him closer, wrapping my arm snugly through his, tipping my head onto his firm shoulder, and taking a long, dragging hit of his dizzying-good smell. "Maybe."

"In that case"—he picks up his pace and leads us toward the exit—"I think I know a spot we could go. If you aren't opposed to nature."

I raise my pointer finger in the air. "Question: Will mosquitos be an issue?"

He shakes his head. "Not if we keep the windows up."

"Have I told you how much I love your stupid overpriced SUV with its ginormous back seat?"

"Convenient, right? You haven't waxed poetic before, but I'm up to the challenge of changing your mind."

"If it means I get to take my time kissing you, I'm already sold."

—

Case drops me off at home late, but not too late. We kiss in the drive and then again at the door before I shoo him away and tell him to text me when he's home safe. It's too tempting to run back to his car and beg him to take me with him wherever he goes until the end of time. I manage to collect myself and walk into my own house with some semblance of dignity.

Shockingly, my dad is awake in the living room, alone. He sees me and turns off the TV, getting to his feet. He looks me over, and I can feel my cheeks flaming at his scrutiny, but I refuse to back down. I'm a grown woman, and anyway, he's never paid attention before. Why start now?

"Hey, Dad. I wasn't expecting you to still be up. I would have called if I'd known you were waiting."

He shakes his head. "Nah. You're fine. I wanted to talk to you without the other two around." I glimpse the light still on under Jesse's door, but guess this is enough privacy for my dad's sake.

Please, God, don't let this be an afterthought of a sex talk.

"Oh, um, well, if this is about Case—" I start, and my dad straightens like a shot, turning red.

"Uh, no. Sorry." He coughs. "Not that kind of talk. Case is a good kid. I trust you two to . . . whatever it is you do. I don't want to know."

"Oh. Good," I say, sinking into a chair at the kitchen table with relief. "What did you want to talk about?"

He doesn't sit. "I had an interview this morning for a supervisory position at the plant. Day shift. They offered it to me on the spot. I start training in two weeks."

"What? Dad! That's incredible! I had no idea you were even looking! That's huge. Congrats!"

"Yeah, well. Thank you. That's what they said, too. It was nice to hear. That's not why I interviewed, though."

"It's not?"

My dad finally moves to the table, sitting stiffly. I'm tempted to offer him a glass of water, but I let him work it out. He's the one who called this meeting, after all.

"You're incredible, Win. The way you ride . . . it's . . . it doesn't even make sense, it's so good. Your grandmother, my mom, she rode like that. Did you know that?"

I shake my head. I know next to nothing about any of my

grandparents. My mom's parents were never in our lives, and my dad's parents both died when I was young.

"She grew up on a ranch, similar to the one you work at. She was a natural, and so are you." He hesitates, reaching for the saltshaker and wrapping his fingers around it. "Listen." He clears his throat and restarts. "Jesse came to me a few weeks back and gave me a bit of a talking-to."

"He what?"

My dad looks sheepish. "I deserved every word that came out of his mouth, of course. He told me how you threatened to file for guardianship if he didn't stay in school. He said you were flying through the rodeo ranks and people were talking about you making a national run and going pro . . . but you weren't going to do it because you needed to stay here and take care of us. Is that true?"

I'm dumbfounded and, for a solid minute, can't find my voice. I had no idea Jesse had put all of that together.

Finally, I say, "The guardianship part is true, but I swear I would have talked to you first. It was mostly a last-ditch effort to get Jesse in line. I was at my wit's end and—"

"Let me stop you there," my dad says, holding up a large hand between us. "That's where I went wrong. You were at your wit's end trying to get your brother to stay in school. To the point you were going to throw away your future to lock the kid down and force him to do the right thing."

"It was a gamble, sure, but—"

"I'm the dad," he cuts me off. I've never heard him use this tone before. At least not on me. It's as though he's scolding me. Which . . . what the fuck?

"I tried to ask you to help! I went to you, and you kept telling me boys were boys or whatever! Meanwhile, the school is calling *my* phone and telling me they were going to call the police for truancy. Police, Dad! Which, in case you have forgotten, also means CPS! You think the DCFS would waltz in here and be like, 'This is fine'? I couldn't even get you to talk to the school!"

"That doesn't mean you should throw away your future."

"You say that like I wasn't facing an impossible choice! How many times did I have to leave work early because you or Jesse didn't get Garrett? And let's not even talk about what happened when I left town for the first time *ever* and Garrett walked home alone. How many times did I have to pay late fees on our utility bills because you would forget to pay them that month? How many times have you made dinner or paid for Garrett's robotics competitions or Jesse's cell phone? You haven't!" I slap the table. "So while it's great for you to act like I'm the martyr, where would this family be without me?"

I'm panting now and feel pretty sure my raised voice has Jesse listening at the door, but I don't care. "Everyone acts like I chose this. Like I'm sitting here micromanaging your lives on purpose because I love being responsible so much. Well, fuck you. I know that's disrespectful, but I am who I am because *you* made me this way. You chose to make me like this by refusing to take care of shit. I begged you to do something for years, but eventually, it became easier to cut you out of the equation. I didn't have time to be the parent to you, too!"

My dad is silent for so long, I wonder if he's going to go to bed. Eventually, he speaks. "Be that as it may. It ends now. I accepted the promotion and will be working daytime hours. You don't need to be the parent anymore. You can go now."

I stagger back in my chair as if he'd slapped me across the face. Tears spring to my eyes. "I can *go now*?"

"Yes."

I laugh, but it's sardonic. "That's it. You're done with me? Ten years of taking care of everyone and everything, and now I can just go? You don't need me, I'm fired?"

"Winnie," he says irritably. "That's not what I meant."

"How did you mean it, then?"

"You're nineteen." He gestures to me. "You have a bright future ahead of you. It's time for you to chase it, and it's past time for me to take back this family."

"So that's it. 'You're nineteen, Winnie, get out. Thanks for your help.'"

He sighs. "I'm not saying you have to move out, but that's not a bad idea. It's time for you to think about yourself for a while."

"What about Jesse and Garrett? They need me, Garrett especially. I'm like her mom. I won't leave her like that."

My dad sighs heavily, exhaustion weighing down his words. "But you aren't her mom. It's not your job to fill that role. It's time for you to be the big sister. I'm not saying you can't be there for your siblings. They'll still want you around, but there must be boundaries."

I choke on a sputter. "Boundaries? Can you even *hear* yourself? I don't believe this. You, all of a sudden in the eleventh hour, lecturing me about healthy boundaries!"

"Look," my dad says more firmly. "I've given you a lot to think about. That's all I'm asking right now. You need to think about your career and your dreams and how we're holding you back from that. I suspect you already know what I'm saying is right."

"How can I possibly trust you to take care of them?"

He shakes his head, getting up. "Give me the time to prove it."

"You've had *ten years*."

He closes his mouth, rounding the table and patting me once on the back. "Good night, Winnie. You did real great out there tonight. I've never been prouder."

He walks to his bedroom, shutting the door and leaving me alone with my thoughts. I slowly turn off all the lights and lock the front door.

Fuck's sake, who's gonna close up the house every night if I'm not here?

I check my phone, seeing Case's made-it-home text, and I walk to my bedroom, shutting the door behind me. I get to my bed, and on my pillow is a note from Garrett.

You did so well tonight! I love you! Next stop, state!

Love, Garrett

I switch off the light, falling fully clothed into my bed, and cry.

Thirty-One
CASE

I wake up early Sunday morning because I'm used to it. I don't remember the last time I slept in, but it hasn't happened since the start of summer. I pull my phone off its wireless charger, noticing Winnie never texted back last night. She must have gone right to bed after I dropped her off.

I allow myself a few minutes of lying there, replaying the highlights from our night together until I'm startled out of bed by the sound of a car door slamming. I walk over to my open window and shove aside the curtain. Speaking of my gorgeous girlfriend, what the heck is she doing here at 7:00 a.m. on her day off?

I quickly throw on a clean shirt and a pair of dirty work jeans I'd flung over my desk chair and hop down the stairs, pulling on my socks. Sunday is Kerry's day off, too, so I grab a couple of apples off the counter and slip out the front door. The early-morning summer air is humid and comfortable, which will translate to insufferable in a few hours. Winnie's no longer at her car, but I can hear movement in the stables and head in that direction.

I make my way to the entrance, leaning against the door and placing the apples on a shelf. Winnie marches out of the tack room without noticing me. She looks kind of terrible. Objectively still good because she's Winnie, but her tangled hair is loose around her shoulders instead of braided and tucked away like usual. Her dark eyes are puffy and red-rimmed. She's making a sloppy attempt at saddling up her newest trainee, Pistol Annie, rushing through the steps. I gently clear my throat, and she jumps three feet clear into the air.

"Jesus, Case! You scared the shit out of me!"

"Hey," I say softly. One of the horses nickers. I move to turn on the giant fan because it's there and I'm here and I'm not sure what else to do with my hands. "Everything okay?"

She seemed okay when I dropped her off. More than, if I'm honest. But what if she's changed her mind or has some regrets about the things we've done? Of course I'd respect that, but the idea it could bring on this reaction feels like acid churning in my stomach.

I've never been happier. That she might not feel the same . . .

Doesn't matter right now. *She* matters.

Winnie sniffs loudly, working on a tiny buckle with trembling fingers. With a frustrated sob, she drops it to the floor and rushes toward me. I meet her in the middle of the aisle and catch her with an *oof*, wrapping her tightly within my arms. Silent sobs rack her tiny form and, fucking *alarmed*, I hold her even closer.

"Shhhhh," I say. "It's okay. You're okay. What's wrong? What can I do?"

She cries even harder.

I'm trying not to freak out, because she sounds like she's being torn apart. I mean, hell, her little sister was nearly gored by a longhorn and she was the one calming *me* down.

"Winnie, please. Did I do something? Are you hurt?"

She pulls back, swiping at her face with the sleeves of her sweatshirt.

"My dad got promoted," she says, looking down at her tear-stained sleeves. "He's taking a day shift."

I blink and swallow. "That's . . . good, right? Long overdue, even?"

She nods, taking a shaky breath and hiccupping. "He's telling me I can *leave* now. He's letting me go so I can race on the circuit."

I let that sink in for a beat before a grunt clears the back of my throat. *Christ.* I think I know where this is headed.

"Ten years, I've been holding them together. I finished school early and got a job the minute I could. I've practically *raised* Garrett, and he has the *fucking nerve* to tell me, 'I'm the dad. I'm the parent and you aren't. It's time for you to be the big sister and live your life.' He made it out like I've been some self-sacrificing martyr all these years!"

I cup her face, stroking her cheek with my fingertip. "On the one hand, you *do* deserve to be able to focus on your own career. You never should've had to be the parent."

"I know that!" she insists.

"But—" I step closer, looking deep into her eyes, still welling with tears. I wouldn't be surprised if this was an entire lifetime of tears pouring from them. Saved up from years and years of toughing it out for the sake of her family. "He never should have said it like that. He never should have made you feel that way. He should be thanking you on his knees and kissing the ground you walk on. He should be offering you the world on a platter. And above all else, he should have done this ten years ago."

Her head tips forward onto my collarbone, and she breaks into another round of silent sobs. I stroke her back over and over. I'm relieved she's not feeling regret over us, but I'm pissed her dad is such a complete idiot.

"What am I supposed to do? He's practically kicking me out."

"Move in with me?" I offer, only half joking. "Free muffins anytime you want?"

She sighs, wrapping her arms around me and squeezing once before stepping back. "You're moving away in like a month, college boy."

"True. I've heard dorm twin beds are even smaller than regular ones. If you have to, you can sleep directly on top of me. It's a sacrifice I'm willing to make."

She snickers, and I'm triumphant at the change.

"I could move into the Cook Shack," Winnie says, deep in thought.

The Cook Shack is anything but a shack. It's a modest, newly renovated two-bedroom cabin on the other side of the farthest pasture. Camilla and my dad talked about using it as an Airbnb, but it's sat empty because running an Airbnb requires someone to keep track of it. "Camilla brought it up months ago, but there was no way I could afford it at the time."

"You could probably work something out now."

"*If* I'm not paying for two kids, I could make it work."

"Would you be okay with that? I mean, it's a short drive home, but it's also space. And you'd be close to train and ride the horses whenever you want."

"I'd also have my own place right on the other side of that hill," she says suggestively, but sobers almost immediately and sighs. "I don't know. I've wanted my own space for a while. The chance to only think and worry about myself. But I don't know if I can turn it off—the worrying over Garrett, especially. What if she feels like I've abandoned her? Like our mom? I promised them I would never leave them like that." Her voice falters at the end.

"Then you have her over," I say. "She can come spend the night whenever you're in town. You can still do your movies or whatever. And I'll still be around, too. If you're gone, and I sincerely hope you are, because that means you're killing it on the circuit, and one of us is going to need to be the bread-winner at some point," I tease in a rush, and her eyes light up with a ghost of humor again. "I can come home that weekend if she needs. Or if Jesse needs. Or if you need. You're not alone, remember?"

Winnie brightens slightly. "Maybe I could get her one of those prepaid phones so she can reach me whenever she needs to while I'm on the road."

"There you go."

"And the sleepovers do sound fun."

"It will be different and the kids are so dependent, it might be a challenge for a while, but I don't think this is a bad move."

"Maybe not."

"The real question is, are you ready to chase the national buckles?"

Winnie shakes her head in wonder. "Honestly, I'm not sure. I thought I was, but I also thought there was no way I ever could, at least not for years."

"Fair." I lean back against a stall and smirk. "Know who is sure, though?"

"You?"

"Well, yeah," I agree easily. "Of course, but I meant the Queen. Mab was born ready."

Winnie straightens, sucking in a huge breath and releasing it slowly. "Guess I'd better start practicing, then, huh?"

"Maria's gonna lose her shit."

—

The news I'm no longer aiming for the PBR and am, in fact, leaving for college in a month to attend a nursing program goes over with my dad better than I'd anticipated.

"Texas Tech?" he asks me. His blue eyes crinkle under his hat. He's sitting on our wraparound porch at sunset, mostly still for once, swirling a large cube of ice in a glass of straight whiskey. He watches the ice continue to spin and clink the inside of his tumbler even after his hand stops moving. Eventually, his eyes meet mine. "They have a first-rate rodeo program there, if memory serves."

Of course he's gonna fixate on that. "They do. Already recruited me. I committed to ride bulls this fall since I'm still aiming for the NFR this winter. But I was thinking to maybe try bucking broncs in the future. Or maybe roping."

The corner of his mouth quirks in a knowing grin. "Switching to equine events, huh?"

I shrug a shoulder, all casual-like. "I wouldn't mind the challenge of something new."

"Boy, you could chase all the challenges in the world, but you ain't got a chance in hell of besting that girl of yours on horseback."

I snort, easing back into my chair and looking out over the ranch. Thank God for Winnie. At least *she's* a real cowboy he can be proud of.

"I'm not stupid. I just told you I got accepted into nursing school, didn't I? That's why I said bucking broncs or roping. Not racing. Winnie'd beat me up for trying."

Junior laughs low in his chest. "Did you see how fast your girlfriend whipped Pistol Annie into shape? *Shheet*. That girl's fearless."

I smile to myself. At least we can agree on that. "That she is."

"So." My dad clears his throat after a minute, swirling the cube again. "You want to be a *murse*. Sure you don't want to be a doctor? Or a surgeon or something?"

I swallow back a hundred different retorts, but I've planned for this. Let him get it out of his system. He can say whatever he wants. I know myself.

"Nope. I want to be a nurse. A pediatric nurse. You think you know what tough is. Not you, specifically," I clarify, though, *yeah, him*, "but you've never seen tough like a twelve-year-old kid starting his fifth round of chemo after remission. Or a five-year-old who's spent more time in hospitals than out, still finding a reason to smile every day. Or a seventeen-year-old who's been told they're going to die before they've had the chance at accomplishing any of their dreams."

"And you want to be around all of that? Relive what you went through with Walker over and over with each new kid?" Junior shakes his head. "Why the fuck would you want to do that?"

"Because I can," I say.

"We'll see," he says, tipping back his drink. I bristle at the skepticism in his dismissal, but then I see it. The slightest tremble in the hand holding his whiskey. A shake in his composure. And it hits me for the first time. *I think Junior is afraid of sick people.*

Because he came home one day to his young wife dead on

the ground of the ranch they shared, without even the chance to save her.

Holy shit. No wonder he kept Walker at a distance when things started to look bad.

Being a nurse, seeking a job where I would be surrounding myself with vulnerable kids day in and day out? That's his worst nightmare.

Junior doesn't think I'm too weak. Not really. Junior thinks I'm *too brave*.

He's wrong on like a thousand levels, and he'd never admit it, anyway, but *I* know I'm right. It makes so much sense.

For a moment, I let this revelation settle in my bones and try to think of something I could say or do to ease his mind. But everything I come up with would rattle the equilibrium. No matter what his reasons are, my dad isn't going to change any time soon. So I do the only thing that makes sense.

I settle back in my chair and change the subject.

"Did you see that write-up on Mab and Winnie in *Rodeo Times*?"

"The one that called our ranch 'paradise on earth'?"

I snort. "Clearly, they haven't been around these parts in January when everything is a muddy mess of clay and cow pies."

"I doubt you'll miss that when you're away at school."

"Maybe I'll come back to visit just to remind myself why I moved away."

"Kerry'd make you her muffins and you'd never leave again."

"True . . ."

Equilibrium restored.

———

One down, one to go. If I'm honest, I've been dreading this visit more than anything else. I've long suspected Brody has been using me as a stand-in for his little brother, and this is gonna sting.

I raise my hand and knock on the door of the Gibsons' home early Sunday morning. It's the first time I've knocked on this door in years, and it feels wrong. Like something from an alternate universe. Walker and I were encouraged to wander freely between our homes. We were family. I know his family still sees me as a second (third) son and they always will, but I don't think I can just walk in and invade their space the way I used to. Family, always; familiar, no longer.

Brody answers, and I'm a little relieved. I've seen Mr. and Mrs. Gibson a few times since the funeral, but I know I make them sad. I'd been hoping by coming on Sunday morning, they might be at church and I could save them the setback.

"Hey, did we have practice?"

"Nah, I was hoping to talk to you about something. Can I come in?"

Brody shuffles backward, opening the door wide and letting me in. I'm hit with a wave of nostalgia. It smells the same. The laundry is off the side of the foyer—Mrs. Gibson does a load every morning without fail. She used to say two teenage boys kept her up to her ears in sweaty socks.

I swallow hard, and Brody leads me to the kitchen. We pass the sitting room no one sits in, covered in years of school pictures and fresh flowers. I try not to get stuck on the reminders of Walker's young face through the years. I see a picture from our last rodeo, Walker and me sitting side by side on the fence in our full getup, arms flung around each other's shoulders. First- and second-place buckles like always.

Brody offers me coffee. I decline the caffeine, doubting they have enough oat milk creamer for this conversation.

"I've been accepted to Texas Tech. I leave in a month."

He blinks, putting his cup down on the counter. For a minute, he stares at the mug, but then his shoulders slip and he sighs, sitting down on a stool and gesturing for me to do the same. "How long have you known this?"

That's not the question I expected.

He shakes his head, continuing, "I'll tell you how long *I* knew. I knew that first ride that wasn't, when you nearly puked all over my boots."

"Shut the fuck up."

He cracks a half grin. "You weren't drunk."

"No," I confess. "I wasn't."

"I knew it, but I wasn't sure what the deal was, so I figured I'd let you work it out in your own time. Then you showed up more determined than ever, so I went along with it."

"I'm not him," I say in a strained almost-whisper.

Brody's eyes grow bright, but he doesn't crack. "No one could be. I'm sorry you thought you had to try for my sake."

I shake my head. "It wasn't like that. I thought I had to try for *my* sake and maybe for his. He left me this list—know what?" I choke on a laugh. "It doesn't really matter. The point is the PBR was *his* dream, and I wanted to make it happen for him. But I can't live my life for him, you know?"

Brody nods thoughtfully. "He wouldn't want that."

"No! He wouldn't. God, he would be so pissed at me if he knew I was still being such a bitch about the decision nearly a year after the fact."

He laughs and drinks from his cup. "So what are you thinking of doing?"

"Well, I've still got a scholarship to ride. And the NFR this winter. I owe Walker one last gold buckle. But after that? I'm thinking of maybe branching out into broncs and roping."

"You'd be killer at broncs. It's dangerous as fuck, but you've got a good head on your shoulders for that kind of thing."

"I like horses."

He smirks. "I'll bet you do."

"And I'm planning to go into pediatric nursing," I say, holding my breath. It only now occurs to me how much Brody's opinion on this means to me. More than my dad's, more than Winnie's, even. My big brother, coach, mentor: I want so much for him to understand.

Brody's inhale is sharp, and this time, his stoic eyes blink against tears.

"Fuck. That's . . ."

"Stupid?" I guess. "A female profession? Because it's not—"

Brody sets down his cup and rounds the counter, pulling me in for an embrace. "Shut up."

The hug is brief, and he clears his throat, returning to his coffee. "Bro. That's incredible. Are you sure? That shit is so hard. To watch kids fight for their lives—"

"I know. I'm sure."

"You'd be great. You *will* be great."

"Thanks."

Brody is still shaking off his emotions, and I almost crack a smile, but I don't, because it means too much.

"Well, hell, I guess this makes things easy. I was gonna tell you I'm joining the PBR, but I wasn't sure how you'd feel about competing against each other. Not that I was gonna let that stop me, but . . ."

"What? You are?"

He nods, scratching at the back of his neck, clearly proud. "I never shook the dream, and anyway, this place is suffocating. The memories, you know? It's great for Mom and Dad, and I know they need it, but I gotta get out of here. Chase some sunsets, break some records, whatever. Walker always gave me shit for quitting, and he was right. I don't regret it for one second, but it's time I get on with it."

"That's incredible. I'm so happy for you."

"Thanks." He laughs low. "This worked out."

"How long have *you* known?" I ask.

"Too long. We're both fucking idiots."

I shrug one shoulder. "We were sad idiots. There's a difference."

Brody nails me with a long look. "You're going to be a great nurse."

"You're just glad I'm not going to get in your way in the PBR. You know I'd kick your ass."

He flashes a grin. "Whatever you gotta tell yourself, Michaels."

—

The following Friday night, I'm under the lights, getting ready to jump in the chute. It's not the last time, but it feels like it. I've qualified for state, and from there, it's a hop, skip, and surely painful jump to Vegas this winter. I'm almost at the end. I've wondered how it felt for Walker, those last hours he was alive. Did it feel like the end? Did he know the timer was winding down on his last breaths? Or did it feel like falling asleep, only to wake up to a dream?

For me, Vegas feels like the inevitable conclusion. Even when I compete in rodeos in the future, it won't be like this. I'll be a part of something Walker never touched with his life.

But Ranch Rodeo was the competition I first met Walker, which feels all the more poetic. This is where it began. I'll do new things, accomplish new goals, make new friends and relationships, but I'll never replace Walker. This, tonight, is my memorial for him.

Since Brody is competing tonight, I take care of my own arrangements. Might as well get used to that. I pull my bull and give the management my music (while making a special request for Brody's turn). Then I warm up and drink my water. Honestly, I don't feel nervous. In fact, I'm buzzing with excitement. I'm not mourning tonight, I'm celebrating. Winnie's in the crowd, sitting somewhere alone. Her event's not until tomorrow afternoon, so she came with me, gave me a searing kiss for good luck, and then sauntered off to the stands. There're video crews here tonight, some cable sports shows hoping to catch early glimpses of favorites, and I know my girlfriend is on that list. Which is why she's wearing my old ball cap. Lying low so as not to be seen by anyone but me. I pick her out after a beat of looking, and she gives a piercing whistle before blowing a kiss and ducking her head again.

Brody goes first, and after easily hanging on for eight like the professional he is, he finds me and flips the middle-finger salute, laughing as he jumps the fence back to the waiting area. He's gonna kill me later for the AC/DC, maybe even try to say I was hoping to throw him and give myself the advantage, but we both know I wouldn't. The thing is, Walker was his brother first, and they're the ones who shared the dream, in the end.

Brody should be the one to inherit Walker's shitty intro song.

Two more riders go before my name is called, and when it is, the opening piano chords of "Don't Stop Believin'" pulse over the speakers. I see Winnie's head pop up. I doubt she sees my wink before I slip in my mouth guard, but later, she'll see it on the footage and laugh. I still think '80s rock is the worst, but I hate this song the least. And it makes me think of all the good things I have—the new, good memories I'm creating.

I straddle the bull, an oldie named Titanium, and reach for the clutch, wrapping my gloved fingers around it. The chute boss passes me my rope, and I work it tighter and tighter in my grip while the boss steadies me. Titanium is practically vibrating, and I have this uncontrollable urge to laugh. The lights, the sounds, the fifteen hundred pounds beneath me, the girl I love in the stands . . . it's a fucking gift.

Walker's laugh echoes in my head, shouting, *Giddyup!*

I nod at him in my mind, slapping my chest with my free hand. "Let's ride, brother."

And the chute opens on the rest of my life.

Thirty-Two

WINNIE

The August afternoon is blazing hot, and my brother releases a long-suffering breath, swiping his forehead.

"Tell me you'll have air-conditioning, at least."

I roll my eyes. "I'll probably install a window unit in the bedroom if I need it. But I get a good breeze up on the hill like this. It's not like I'll be inside much during the day."

"Even the trailer has air, Winnie," Garrett says. It's been two weeks since my dad gave me his "time to move on" speech, and as anticipated, my little sister has been a bit of a hard sell on the idea. Camilla and Case suggested bringing my siblings by to see the cabin firsthand so they could feel like they are active participants in the changes. It's clear Garrett especially needed this. I told her I wasn't moving in yet. I wanted to get her and Jesse's opinions first. Camilla has worked out such a deal on rent for me, though, I'm not sure I could afford anything else.

"I'm getting you on-site, Winnie. You're doing all of us a favor."

"But if I'm traveling . . ."

"Then we won't be any worse off than when no one lived here. Some is better than none. Besides, I've been talking to Junior about hiring some more help. With you touring and Case off to college, we'll need hands."

I pull out the key I got from Camilla and insert it into the lock.

"If I end up with this place," I say over my shoulder, "I'll give you both a spare key, just in case. Okay?"

Garrett's small face is pale but determined. She's working so hard to be grown-up about this whole thing, and her determination is enough to make me sob all over again. I won't do this if she's not okay. I refuse to abandon her, no matter what anyone else says. Yes, I know I'm not her mom. Yes, I realize I have to live my own life. Yes, I'm sure it says something about my own personal fucked-up psyche and abandonment issues.

I still won't do it to her.

Stepping into the dim space, I leave the door open wide behind me as my steps echo over the wood-planked floor. I hold my arms aloft, spinning around. "Come on in and tell me what you think. Snoop around. I want your opinions."

My brother and sister step in, pausing to automatically wipe their feet on the friendly mat at the door. Garrett's expression is reserved, but I can practically hear her brain cataloging the details. The large, bright windows, letting in sunshine and blessing us all with the view of the rolling fields of CBM Ranch. The clean lines of the whitewashed paneled walls brightening up the cozy space. The small kitchen, complete with a compact butcher-block island, cozy wood-burning stove for the winter months, and a tiny windowed nook framed by three rustic chairs. The inviting living area, complete with a small sofa and end table. There's a sweet-looking woven rug defining the space.

"The bedrooms and bath are through here." I lead them down a short hall to the back of the cottage. "I was thinking I could make this one a guest room, since I don't need an office space for the work I do. It would be a place for either of you, or maybe Jesse, and then Garrett can stay with me. If ever you wanted or needed . . ." I trail off.

Garrett slowly approaches the center of the room and takes it all in.

"There's even a closet, so I could get a few things for you to keep here. That way you wouldn't even have to pack. It could be like your second home."

Garrett turns to me with a sharp inhale, her heart in her eyes and her lips pressed tightly together. I cross the room to fold her in my arms, and she erupts into loud, racking sobs. Jesse meets my gaze over her tiny shuddering shoulders, a worried shadow darkening his features.

"Garre! It's okay. I don't—" I swallow hard. Suddenly, I find the words are sticking in my throat, making this more difficult to get out than I'd anticipated. I hoped she might give it some time. I restart. "I don't *have* to move. None of this is fixed. I promised I would never leave you and—"

She pulls back, her eyes wide. "No! You have to go!"

"But—" I look to Jesse, and he shakes his head, just as confused.

"Don't you like this place, Garrett?" he asks gently. "I think it looks perfect for Winnie. Feels like her in here, don't you think?"

Garrett nods quickly. "It does! This is perfect."

"Then?"

"I thought you wouldn't want us to visit. I thought you were moving on. But you have this room already picked out for us and this closet—" She slips into sobs again, and I stroke her soft hair.

"I *am* moving on, but that doesn't have to mean I'm leaving you guys behind. I won't be there when you come home every day after school, but I'm only a phone call away. Speaking of . . ." I reach into my bag. "I got something for you."

Case helped with this part, too. He thought maybe if Garrett had a way to reach me anytime, even when I'm on the road, that might give her some security.

I hold out a small prepaid phone. "I programmed my number, Case's number, Maria's number, Jesse's number, and Dad's number. You can reach me anytime, and no matter where I am, I will do my best to answer or call back as soon as I can."

Garrett holds the phone in her small hand, staring at it in wonder.

"It's not a smartphone," I warn her. "No internet. So don't be getting any ideas in that giant brain of yours. But it will allow you to reach any of us just in case."

"I can call Case?" she asks, her voice hushed.

Holding back my exasperated grin, I nod. "Anytime, apparently. Though he told me to tell you he prefers texting."

Her fingers are already rapidly typing across the keys, and I exchange looks with Jesse again, who snorts. "I see we've been replaced."

A moment later, all our pockets buzz. Garrett's started a family chat. Plus Case.

They're already chatting away. Her fingers are flying over the keys again, but she pauses at the doorway and looks up at me.

"This is my room when I come and stay?"

"Would you like that?"

"Yes. Can we still have sleepovers? When you're in town, I mean."

"Every weekend I'm around, if you want."

She throws her arms around me, squeezing tightly. "I want."

A moment later, she wanders off to the front porch, and Jesse lingers, clearly wanting to say something.

"I know you're probably too old for sleepovers, but you're welcome anytime. If you need a break or want to come for dinner or whatever."

"Cool," he says casually, but I can see the relief in his eyes. He might not show his feelings the same way as Garrett, but he feels it, too. He's grown up as quickly as I have in some ways, but mercifully, he's still a kid in others.

"I wanted to say I'm sorry."

I blink. "What on earth for?"

He smirks, self-deprecating. "Well, for lots of things, probably, but this time, it's for talking to Dad without telling you first."

I'd sort of forgotten he'd been the impetus for my dad taking the day shift job. I'd meant to ask him how it came about but then got preoccupied.

"You don't have to apologize for that."

"I'm not sorry I spoke up, but I'm sorry for how it hurt you. I—" He pauses, collecting himself. "I wanted Dad to take responsibility, and I wanted you to be able to compete. I knew—we *all* knew you wouldn't leave us, no matter how much you deserved the chance—"

I open my mouth to argue. Not that he's wrong, but I don't want him to think it's his fault.

"Shut your mouth, Winnie. I heard you when that reporter asked you about Vegas. It never occurred to you to leave us for the circuit. Garrett and I know that, despite her little freak-out a little bit ago. We know you aren't like Mom. You don't have to prove it anymore. No matter what happens with Dad and his new job, we know you love us more than anything else. And we love you, too."

He swallows against the emotion, but mine pours freely down my crumpled face. His face goes red in secondhand embarrassment, but to his credit, he doesn't make a snarky comment. "I heard what Dad said to you that night, and I'm sorry he made it sound like we didn't appreciate you. Or we didn't want you anymore. That's not it. I never meant for it to come out that way. I was trying to get him to step up for once."

I shake my head, swiping at my face. "I know. And you're right. I wouldn't have left if you guys didn't kick me out," I tease. "I needed the push. Maybe not quite the way Dad put it, but that's—" I take a deep, cleansing breath. "I think he was feeling defensive. Because he's a fucking idiot, but he does love us in his own way, and he was angry at himself for having to be shown the error of his ways by his kids. That's not your fault. I don't blame you for his tactlessness."

Jesse exhales in relief. "Good."

"Woof." I make a face. "This is more emotion than we Suttons need for a lifetime."

"You ain't kidding. You girls are flooding the place with your wailing."

"There it is," I say wryly. "I was waiting for it."

"So, if you make it to Vegas, can I come?"

"If you make honor roll and have perfect attendance, sure."

"There it is," he echoes. "I was waiting for it."

Ruffling his hair, I steer us out of the room. "Come on. I need to steal that phone out of Garrett's hands before she spills all my secrets to my boyfriend."

—

Later that night, I saddle up Mab and take her for a ride. I'd taken Jesse and Garrett out to dinner at the taco truck to celebrate signing a lease with Camilla and Mr. Michaels for the next year. They offered month to month, but Jesse pushed for the year commitment. "Give yourself a year, sis. It's gonna be rough for a bit."

I took his advice. He's a smart kid when his head's not up his ass. Garrett seems okay, distracted by the idea of decorating yet another bedroom in her favorite *aesthetic* and texting up a storm in our family chat (despite Jesse and me being right in front of her), but it will hit harder the first time she reaches for me and I'm in another state or even just across town.

We'll work it out in time, and maybe one day, we won't have to feel like every interaction we have between us is weighted with a lifetime of emotional baggage. Garrett is still pretty young. Maybe she'll grow up the most best-adjusted of all of us. There's hope for her yet.

I lead Mab through the pastures and out to the other side, past *my* cabin, and out into wide-open acreage where we can run. Once we're clear of the fences, I give her the reins, and she gives me the space I need to breathe. These last weeks have been some of the most intense of my life. Mostly in the best kind of way, but the ride's been wildly rocky with all the feelings and emotions and *tears* involved. I've been itching to escape. Between the training, the uptick in trail rides, and relationship navigation I've been doing, I haven't had as much time to take Mab out for *our* rides. I'm looking forward to making up for lost time now that I'll be living on-site. I can easily take her out for evening rides and give us both a chance to let our hair down, at least until the weather changes and the sun starts setting earlier.

Mab slows as we come to our favorite collection of trees, and I climb down, looping her rope on a low-lying limb close to the shore of a creek. Mab wastes no time in getting a drink from the steadily flowing water, and I follow her, slipping off my boots and socks and rolling up my jeans to my knees. I sit on the shore, dipping my feet and wincing at the chill. After a moment, the water feels refreshing rather than icy. I'm leaning forward to look for tadpoles when I hear the pounding of hooves behind me. I grin to myself. I knew he'd make it out here eventually.

Case loops Moses's reins near Mab's and comes to sit alongside me, removing his own boots and socks and dangling his feet in the current. He lets out a long sigh of relief and leans back on his hands, staring up at the leaves. We sit in companionable silence for a while, listening to the trilling of cicadas and the rushing of water, the way the breeze tosses the leaves around and sends them into rustling whispers.

I drop my head to his shoulder and let my eyes drift shut.

"You know," he says softly as if speaking aloud would ruin this serene moment. "If you wanted to get naked, you're already part of the way there—ow!" He cuts off, laughing at my faux outraged attack on this chest. He shrugs, his drawl lazy in the setting sun. "Just sayin'."

"You're shameless, Case Michaels."

"I'm smitten, is all."

I plant a small, chaste kiss on his full lips. "It's mutual."

His mouth chases mine, kissing and nibbling and tasting, before he settles back on his hands again, contentment on his face. It's a good look for him, this whole inner-peace thing. After finally opening up to his dad and Brody about his fall plans, he's been feeling more himself. Just in time, too, since he's leaving for Tech in two weeks.

"You get everything settled with Braids and Jesse?"

I snort. "As if you didn't already know. I'm gonna have to double-check the rules for that prepaid plan I put on Garrett's phone. You two are gonna blow through her data in no time."

Case shrugs. "I can't help it if we genius types have a lot in common."

"I'll remind you she's ten. I wouldn't brag about having a lot in common with a fourth grader."

"You're jealous because she wasn't asking you about condensed matter physics."

"You say *jealous*, I say *relieved*. I think I can safely speak for both myself and Jesse when I say *thank the Lord* someone else has entered the literal and metaphorical family chat."

"Well," Case says, looking a little pink. "I'm honored to have been invited to the family chat, even if you're kidding. You know the first time I came to your house and officially met Jesse, all I wanted was to get to know your siblings and be a part of you all. You guys are this solid little threesome, and I'm glad to be allowed in."

I reach for his face, turning it to mine, and gaze directly in his eyes. "I'm not kidding. I mean, I was teasing about the chat, but I don't think you realize how much it means to me you get it's never been just about me. I come as a package deal with those two. Half the time, I'm sure Garrett likes you more than me. I know Jesse does!"

He brushes that off. "That's because I don't have to yell at him about school."

"That and you're everything he wants to be one day. I can't blame him one bit."

"I'm gonna miss you when I leave in two weeks. We haven't had much time to talk about it, and I know long distance is hard, especially with your career and all."

I nod and pull my feet out of the water, crisscrossing them underneath me and turning toward him. A beat later, he does the same.

"I'm in if you are."

He releases his breath. "You're sure?"

"A hundred percent."

"It might suck."

"More than losing your best friend or raising your siblings?" I push.

The corner of his mouth quirks up. "Probably not that much."

"Know what I love about you . . ." I trail off meaningfully.

He stiffens before his lips spread in a full-blown smile. "No. What do you love about me?"

"You," I whisper, pressing closer to him. "I just love you." And then I kiss him.

He pulls back, putting space between us. "Hold on. I get to say it, too."

"You don't have to," I insist. "Wait till you mean it."

"I've meant it for months now. I love you, Winnie Sutton."

I make a face. "We're so gross. It's kind of embarrassing how in love we are."

He barks out a laugh, tugging me close and tipping us off-balance so he's on his back and I'm on top of him.

"Unflinching, remember? We'll handle anything that comes at us," he insists, his words a puff of air on my lips.

"Unflinching," I vow, sealing the deal with another long kiss.

Thirty-Three
EPILOGUE
New Year's Eve
CASE

I can't believe you talked us into this," Winnie mutters, sinking as far back from the ledge of the water tower platform as she can so only her boots are dangling.

I laugh, clutching the glass bottle of Dr Pepper in my fingers. "We should definitely have waited for summer. It's fucking cold out here."

"At least it's not my parents' corn silo this time," Pax drawls, taking a long draw of his soda while his arms loop through the metal railing.

"Eh. As amazing as that was, and truly, it was fantastic—"

Pax snorts. "You don't remember."

"I *mostly* remember," I correct him before continuing. "Anyway, there wasn't enough room for anyone else up there. One seater, max capacity. Did you know you could drown in one of those things? Fucking Walker."

"At least the silo had the benefit of a hot tub nearby," Pax points out.

Winnie lets out a small groan and drops her head back

against the metal with a dull thud. "A hot tub sounds nice and warm . . ."

"The silo also had police, fire trucks, and bullhorns." I reach for my girlfriend's hand, squeezing it and scooting closer to her side. "This is better."

"If you guys start making out, I'm climbing down."

Winnie rolls her eyes in the moonlight. "Settle yourself, Pax. I drove."

"My car," I add.

She lifts a shoulder, her breath puffing out into the crisp air between us. "What can I say? It's grown on me."

"Not to interrupt, but how long do we have to freeze our tits off?" comes Maria's muffled voice from the other side of Pax.

I let out an impatient sigh. "All right, fine. I thought we could all sit up here, enjoying the view—"

"View of what? It's practically pitch-black!" Pax complains.

"While celebrating the New Year—" I cut in, louder.

"We can celebrate in the hot tub," Maria whines. "I didn't know hot-tubbing was an option."

Winnie giggles next to me, cuddling even closer. "It was a nice idea."

"Yeah, yeah. Okay. How about this? A quick toast to Winnie Sutton, Wrangler NFR barrel-racing champion rookie and the best fucking cowboy I know . . ."

"Hear, hear!" Maria says, raising her bottle. "Until next year, that is!"

"Yehaw, girl!" Pax agrees.

Winnie's smiling is blinding even in the dark. "Thanks, guys."

"And to Maria Santos, who in her rookie professional season has collected not one, not two, but three gold buckles already and is considered a raging success . . ."

"Cheers to that!" Maria says, and we all clink bottles.

"And to Pax Richardson for completing his first semester at the University of Texas with a long-distance girlfriend . . ."

Pax shakes his head, laughing. "Thank God for sexting."

I clink my bottle to his and then raise it one last time. "And to Walker Gibson. I still miss you, brother."

Winnie wraps her arm around mine and holds up her bottle, clearing her throat. "One more, and then let's get our asses down and into that hot tub. To Case Michaels, who scored a straight four-point-oh his first semester of nursing school, can ride broncs *almost* as well as I can, and who, in his final time in the arena, won the gold buckle at the NFR bull-riding championship. Walker would be proud as hell of you, and so are we."

"Cheers!" Maria and Pax echo before carefully climbing to their feet.

Winnie doesn't move to get up. Instead, she whispers, "I love you."

"I love you, too."

"You know you're just as much a cowboy as I am. More, even."

I wave her off. "Only on scholarship."

She shakes her head. "Barrel racing doesn't make me a cowboy any more than being a nursing student doesn't make you one. If I'm a cowboy, it's because I've got grit and I've pulled myself up and out of the bullshit. By that definition, you're as much a cowboy as I am. Like it or not, Michaels," she drawls, rocking her shoulder into mine and kicking her feet out over the edge of the platform, "we're just a couple of kissing cowboys, you and I."

A low chuckle escapes from the back of my throat before I press myself forward and take her chin in between my finger and thumb. "Well, we ain't kissin' yet."

And then we are.

ACKNOWLEDGMENTS

I have it on good authority that every author has that one book—the one that nearly does them in, takes them down, shatters their heart into a thousand pieces.

This one did all three. I started writing this book in the fall of 2020. *Yeah.* You might remember what was happening at that time in the world. Well, in my corner of the world, everything was spiraling apart. A phone call from my in-laws telling us they couldn't come for my daughter's tenth birthday because they had Covid; my grandfather-in-law dying days later; Face-Timing my father-in-law in the hospital and immediately regretting it because he looked so unlike himself—so unwell—so scared; the hospital update phone calls on an unseasonably warm front porch; the way my mother-in-law screamed when she got his text that said "I'm fucked"; how we tried to take a family photo to send to him after that, showing him we'd take care of her; the haunted look on my husband's face the following morning when his family turned to him as the oldest to make the call to turn off the vent; the double funeral the day after Thanksgiving when my twelve-year-old son sobbed in my arms because he couldn't imagine a world without his best friend and grandpa.

And then it got worse. While my family grieved, we watched the rest of the world fight over whether the sickness that ripped apart our family was *even real*.

I say all of this because the story that I initially set out to write changed over the course of those months to reflect the reality I was living. In fact, I didn't even want to write this story anymore. My hurt was so overwhelming, I couldn't face writing it into existence for others to pick apart.

But I did it. Two people in particular made me face down my demons and finish this book. Vicki Lame and Vanessa Aguirre played the part of editors, authorities on all things Texas, and Sherpas through my swinging emotions. I'm endlessly grateful to the both of them for the way they challenged me, soothed me, and gave me their all from start to finish. This book would not exist without them.

Thank you to my entire Wednesday Books team. Kerri, Alexis, Kate, and Zoe, to name a few, for not only making my dreams come true with this book, but the three that came before. Thank you for believing my stories were worth telling. No matter where I go from here, I'll never forget where I got my start.

Thanks a bajillion to my agent Kate McKean for having my back and being my biggest cheerleader. Publishing can feel lonely, and it's an honor to have you in my corner.

Special thanks to my mom, Deborah Jenkins, who fell in love with Winnie and Mab in the very first paragraph and made sure I didn't embarrass myself when I talked about "eastern versus western style." I know it was only one summer, but you and Risky Business imprinted on my young heart and made me a horse girl forever. I have only ever wanted to do you both justice with this book.

Thank you for your crying selfies and cheering texts. In particular, Kelly Coon, Laura Namey, Lillian Clark, Karen McManus, and Kathleen Glasgow. Thank you to everyone who graciously offered a blurb. This is my final YA for now, and your words made me cry every single time.

Thank you to the NFR for getting me through a really fucking hard time. I hope I've done your sport justice. Any inaccuracies are all on me.

Thank you to my readers. I made you wait on this one. Publishing, man. But your enthusiasm for my "sad rodeo book" has never wavered. I wouldn't be here without you.

Finally, thank you Mike, Jones, and Al. I love you infinity times three.